THE
HIGHLANDER'S
UNEXPECTED
PROPOSAL

BROTHERS OF WOLF ISLE

THE HIGHLANDER'S UNEXPECTED PROPOSAL

BROTHERS OF WOLF ISLE

HEATHER McCOLLUM

Entangled Publishing, LLC
10940 S Parker Rd
Suite 327
Parker, CO 80134
rights@entangledpublishing.com

Scandalous is an imprint of Entangled Publishing, LLC.

Edited by Alethea Spiridon and Liz Pelletier
Cover design by Mayhem Cover Creations
Cover photography by Period Images
stokkete and letsgobowling/Deposit Photos

Manufactured in the United States of America

First Edition October 2020

SCANDALOUS

To Alethea, my wonderful editor!
Thank you for returning. I may not be the reason, but luck
was definitely with me (like Lark). Here is to many future
projects together!

Scots-Gaelic Words

Air do shocair – Slow down

Lasair – Flame (Adam's horse)

Mattucashlass – Short dagger

Mo chreach – My rage

Och, but – a mild exclamation of frustration

Sgian dubh – Black-handled knife

Stad – Stop

Ulva Isle – Wolf Island (Norse)

Samhain in the year of our Lord 1422

Wild and wicked, the gnarled crone spat before the large willow tree in the castle's bailey.

"A curse upon thee, Chief Wilyam Macquarie, and your land. For ripping my daughter, Elspeth's, heart in two after getting her with child and not wedding her, killing her as if ye wrapped the noose around her neck yourself... Until your clan ceases creating bastards, turning them out into the cruel world alone...until the day when your clan learns what love is, your land and all those upon it will be barren: Your crops and livestock will wither, illness will spread, and sorrow will prevail."

The witch clutched the dagger, stained with blood, and stabbed it into the tree. From that moment on, the tree bled, weeping for the Macquarie clan of Ulva.

Witnessed by
Chief Wilyam Macquarie
Randall Maclean
Dawy Macquarie
Flora Macquarie

Chapter One

1 May 1545
Glencoe North of Loch Lomand, Scotland

Adam Macquarie walked around the edge of the contest field to see if he could spot anyone that might cause trouble at the Beltane Festival he had chosen for his mission. Several men stood watching the caber toss. The large thrower grunted under the weight of the one-hundred-fifty-pound log as he lifted it toward the sky, flipping it to land close to the true-north position.

Adam dodged tents, laughing children, and several young lads who pointed to his sheathed sword, whispering guesses about how many men it had slain. The morning sun slanted down into the valley, sheltered from the Highland wind, and the shade of the small forest beckoned. It would grow hot, making him miss Wolf Isle off the west coast. He uncorked his leather flask and drank as he strode into the woods.

The soaring trees and saplings had already unfurled their spring leaves, and the canopy muted the cheers, music, and laughter below, bringing peace. He inhaled the cool zest of pine and took another drink before hiking a few more steps higher. A flash of blue on the ground caught his gaze.

A lady's shoe sat on top of the leaf litter below a thick, branched tree. He nudged it with his boot and glanced upward, spying the match balanced on a limb high above. The lass's other foot was bare, her toes curled to hold her in place. Blue skirts were rucked upward, twisted around her legs. Adam moved side to side to see past the leaves. Dark lashes framed wide eyes set in a heart-shaped face. Reddish hair hung to one side in a thick braid.

"Her father says he will not take her home, so she has to wed tonight." A man's voice broke the stillness of the wood. "She has no choice but to wed me."

"I have asked for her, too," came another man's reply. "Perhaps we could share her," he said with a bark of laughter, hitting the other man's arm.

"She will not wed either of us if we cannot find her," the first said.

"She could say no to us both."

"Roylin was half in the bag last night with whisky and said he'd sell her off tomorrow if she did not wed. With four other girls and no dowries, Lark must marry at this festival. Tonight."

"Bloody hell, five girls and not a single lad."

"Seems Roylin Montgomerie only makes lasses." The man spit.

Only lasses?

We need lasses on the isle if ye want to rebuild it. His father's old friend, Rabbie, uttered the reminder daily. The words burrowed through Adam's skull. As if he didn't already know his mission.

The two men stepped into the shade of the forest. "Oh, Lark," one called, extending the name like a song. "Where are ye, lass? Fergus and I have something to ask ye."

Adam bent to retrieve the lost slipper, sliding it into the drape of his plaid and stepping away from the tree. "Ho there," he called, making the men stop, their hands moving to their short swords. "Finding a bit of shade," Adam said with what he hoped was a smile. He didn't smile often, so it felt tight.

One fellow frowned, but the other raised a hand in greeting. "Have ye seen a lass with wavy red hair come through here?"

Adam looked off in another direction. "Nay, but I heard someone up that way. Twigs snapping, that sort of noise. Thought it was children hunting for berries."

"Thank ye…" the smiling man said, a question in his tone.

"Adam, Adam Macquarie." His sword hung casually by his side, easy to grab if they reacted poorly to his name.

"Macquarie? Not too many of ye around anymore. I am a Cameron, Giles Cameron."

The other man spit on the ground and didn't bother to introduce himself. They hiked off in the direction Adam had indicated. After a long minute, he leaned back against the tree. "Would ye like assistance?" he asked without looking up.

"Go away," she said, her words in a forceful whisper.

Adam pushed away from the tree. He would not press upon a reluctant lass, even one from a family that only produced females. His brother, Beck, would find a bride elsewhere.

"Blast," the woman whispered. Perhaps she was too stubborn to ask for help. Stubborn determination was something Adam knew well. It was what kept people alive, kept them moving forward when all seemed lost.

The leaves shook as the woman moved in the boughs

of the tree. Adam walked under the branch where bare toes reached down, flexing and pointing, as she felt around blindly. Her toes were tiny appendages, the nails neat and without dirt. The lass's skirts billowed out as she squatted. "God's teeth," she murmured.

Dodging the wildly circling kick, he reached up. "I will guide your foot to the branch," he said. Her toes flexed. Glancing up, he saw a pale face with large blue eyes tipped down toward him. A thick braid hung over one shoulder, and her lips looked soft and lush. A sprinkling of freckles sat along her high cheekbones and the bridge of her nose.

She blinked at him, her mouth closing into a tight line. "I need no help."

"Your cursing makes me think ye lie." Her toes dangled in the air an inch above the branch that she could not see due to the petticoats. She gasped as he caught her foot, tugging until the ball of it touched the branch, her perfectly formed little toes curling around to help her balance.

Holding tightly above her, she stretched while staring down at him. "Move back, and I can jump down," she said, narrowing her eyes.

She had the longest eyelashes, and some red curls had escaped her braid to slide forward along her smooth cheeks. "A leap from that high could break your ankle." He reached for her waist.

Shuffling sideways, she said, "I do not need any man to—" Her denial cut off as she lost her balance, falling forward, her hands grasping at the weak twigs with leaves, making the tree shudder. Adam caught her, his hands wrapping around her cinched waist to pull her toward him.

Her skirts caught on the branch, lifting them high as she descended. "Bloody hell." She slapped her petticoat off the fingerlike branches that seemed intent on exposing the secrets she kept beneath.

Her lush form slid down his, and he inhaled at the contact, as if the pressure of her plucked along every muscle in his body. She smelled of some type of flower and spice, making him suck in another breath as he held her form against him. She felt as soft as he was hard. For several heartbeats, they stared at one another, her face mere inches from his. *What does she taste like?*

Her eyes grew wide, making him wonder for a moment if he'd spoken aloud. "Put me down," she said, shoving against his chest.

Adam lowered her and stepped back as she righted the twisted blue gown around her trim waist, her full breasts pushing against the confines of her laced bodice. He could see why the two suitors were not taking rejection easily. Adam nodded in the direction the two swains had hurried. "They went that way. Ye should roll around in mud or go about with your hair soaked and straggly to keep them away."

Her lips opened as her brows raised, and he turned, traipsing away. The family only produced females, and the father was desperate to wed his daughter off. Halfway back to his camp, he realized that he still held her slipper. *Damn.* Pulling it from his sash, he frowned, knowing that he would give it to his brother, Beck, to return to her.

• • •

Lark Montgomerie wiped her arm against her brow without losing the rhythm of the dasher shooting up and down in the butter churn, her mind churning just as fast.

Ye will wed tonight. Lord, the sun was already starting to descend. Each second brought her closer to her being forced to take some irksome, lusty man as a husband.

Her stomach tightened on Roylin Montgomerie's words, making it twist so much she thought she might lose the little bit she'd eaten to break her fast. She glanced up into the woods behind the tent. Could she make it on foot to another town without being eaten by wolves or taken by wandering bandits? She was utterly ignorant on survival skills outside the home.

"Maybe being eaten by wolves would be better than marrying an arse," she murmured. But walking to safety would be impossible on foot, especially when missing a shoe.

Lark braced her feet on either side of the churn, frowning at her one bare foot, now speckled with dirt. Not only had the fierce, dark-haired Highlander held her against his hard body until she had flushed from her scalp to her toes, the blasted man had stolen her slipper. It didn't matter that he'd held her without any effort or that his gray eyes had studied her with real interest. Or that he had kept her from falling from the tree. He had held her against him, and she'd lost her mind for a moment. *Adam Macquarie.*

With renewed annoyance, Lark threw her muscle into her work, ignoring the ache forming in her shoulders. "Roll around in mud and soak my head?" Would that be enough to deter a man?

"Talking to yourself?" Anna asked as she brought up a bucket of spring water. Her pretty golden hair was tied up high, and she wore one of their mother's dresses that Lark had hemmed for her. She lifted out a wooden bowl and offered it to Lark. "With the way you are working that dasher, you have probably finished the butter."

"I lost a slipper," she said, taking the bowl. The cool water washed away the dryness in her mouth.

Anna planted hands on her hips. "How do you lose a slipper off your foot without noticing?"

"It dropped off when I was climbing a tree to escape Giles and Fergus, those foolhardy jackanapes. Then some bloody Highlander stole it."

"A mistake, one which I am now remedying." The deep voice cut through Lark's breath as she faced Anna's wide eyes.

It took all Lark's will not to smooth her hair and wipe the moisture from her brow before turning. But nothing could stop the blush from catching her cheeks on fire. Adam Macquarie seemed even larger standing between her family's two tents, but his size did not make her feel small. The wind blew, and for a moment, his presence seemed to block her worry, allowing her to breathe in fully. Broad shoulders led to bare, bronzed arms, arms that had held her without demanding anything from her. She noticed a scar along his jawline, near his ear. Had it been earned in battle? Dark hair caught in the breeze, moving haphazardly around a strong, smooth jaw, which had been covered with dark stubble before.

He stepped closer, and gray eyes stared intently into her own. "I have no need for a lady's slipper. I picked it up so those *jackanapes* did not find it, and I forgot I held it."

"You shaved," she said and nearly bit her tongue.

His empty hand rubbed his chin without releasing her gaze. "Aye." There was such depth to his gray eyes, like he'd seen the world but decided he'd rather look at her.

The man, who'd walked up with him, strode forward, taking the shoe from Adam's hand. "Shall I place it back where it belongs?" he asked, a full grin on his face. There was a resemblance between them, but he was fairer in coloring and smiled easily with practiced charm. He looked like a scoundrel.

"No," Lark said, snatching the shoe.

Anna came forward. "I am Annabella Montgomerie, and this is my older sister, Lark." She bobbed in greeting, as their mother had taught them when they were young girls trying to prove their worth. Lark had finally given up when she realized that nothing but hard work would prove her worth.

Lark worked her toes into the grass to get off as much dirt as she could. She slipped the shoe back onto her foot, wishing once again for boots.

"Beckett Macquarie," the man said, thumping his chest. "Although I go by Beck. And this is my older brother Adam, the chief of the Macquarie Clan."

"Chief?" Anna asked.

"Aye." Beck slapped a hand on his shoulder. "He is the eldest by a year and definitely the most serious. Perfect to be the new chief to our small clan on Ulva Isle off the west coast." He smiled at Anna and turned back to Lark. "And ye are the eldest Montgomerie," Beck said, tilting his head. "Will ye be at the Beltane fires tonight?"

"*I* will," Anna chimed in. "Lark does not like going, but our father will make her this year. She must choose a suitor and marry this very night."

"Holy Mother Mary," Lark whispered. Anna gave out unnecessary information as much as their father did when he was drinking.

Beck looked between the two of them. "Ye are not being married off tonight then?" he asked Anna.

She giggled. "No," Anna said. "Only Lark."

Beck shifted closer to her sister. "We happen to be looking for brides," he said.

"Oh," Anna said, the word coming out more like a gasp.

"We are a small clan that needs to grow," he added quickly.

Lark glanced at Adam. Where his brother was all smiles and teasing good looks, the leader of their clan was fierce and serious with that scar and lowered brows. As if he would be more comfortable slashing foes on a battlefield than discussing brides.

Anna clasped her hands before her and nodded her way. "Lark's the eldest, well past time to wed, so Da is focused on marrying her off at this festival."

"Anna," Lark snapped.

"Although," Anna continued, "that has been rather daunting."

Lark kicked Anna through the long folds of her dress, making her sister frown.

"'Tis true," Anna said. "You do not like anyone."

"I certainly do not like *you* right now," Lark said and busied herself by looking inside the churn at the clumps of butter in the clear liquid.

"Ye do not wish to marry?" Adam asked, his deep voice teasing a shiver through her. It beckoned her like the waves she had seen crashing on the shore during their journey there. Powerful and rugged yet bound by the reality of the rocks surrounding them.

She could refuse the whole institution of marriage, but the thought of staying in Roylin Montgomerie's house made her stomach twist just as hard as considering Giles and Fergus. She slid her gaze away from the trees, where the sun had already started its decline, to Adam's intense eyes. "Not when I am forced to choose a young idiot who would rather chase after me than attend more serious endeavors."

"Such as?" Adam asked.

She tipped her head, studying him. "I prefer a man interested in securing a home for a family, debating the poor state of the government with English troops invading our country to steal away our child queen, planning crops and purchasing livestock to enhance his family's chances of surviving the winter." What type of man was Adam Macquarie? He'd helped hide her in the tree and returned her slipper. *We are looking for brides.* Was Adam part of the "we" his brother had mentioned?

Lark realized her hands had found their way to her hips, and she slid them down into the folds of her skirt. Her mother had often stood with hands on her wide hips, frowning. After the shock of her dying in illness two years ago, her sisters began to tease Lark that she had become her. Heat rose in her cheeks, with her stomach pitching, as she remembered her father's slurred words about the resemblance.

Beck raised his eyebrows high. "Those are indeed serious endeavors." He closed his mouth as if not sure what else to say.

"My sister likes to ponder important topics, which are rather dull," Anna said.

"Survival is not dull," Lark countered. Survival had been her aim ever since her mother died. But could survival in a hellish life be better than death?

"So ye wish for a serious husband," Adam said, pulling her thoughts back from the macabre.

"That is not mandatory." Lord, she must find a husband today.

She felt the brawny Highlander's gaze on her. "What is mandatory?"

Lark's lips pressed closed as she thought about her mother's flushed face when her father didn't come home until morning. She looked away from the lumps of butter and met Adam's stare. "Trust."

"So…" Beck drew out. "I could be a slovenly drunk most of the time, but as long as I tell ye the truth that I am going to be drunk all the time, ye would consider marrying me?"

Lark cut her eyes to Beck. "No." The word came out like a slap.

"Although, I do not drink…much," Beck added quickly.

Her sister covered her mouth to muffle a laugh and lowered it. "See, not easy finding her a husband."

"Not easy finding a sober, serious man in this country," Lark countered. "And a drunk is not trustworthy," she said with a frown at Beck. She picked a thistle thorn out of the heel of her slipper. "I best get the butter inside." She glanced back at Adam, the breeze playing with the curls around her cheeks. "Thank you for returning my slipper."

He bowed his head, and she turned away while his brother spouted a promise to meet up with them later at the bonfires.

• • •

"The elder sister looks like she'd rather beat me with that butter dasher than marry me," Beck said, frowning at Adam. For the last hour, his younger brother had been coming up with every excuse not to ask for Lark Montgomerie's hand. Adam agreed with all of them.

"Does not matter," Rabbie, their father's old friend, said as they walked away from their campfire. "Make her father an offer." He scratched his bushy gray beard and squinted hard at Beck as if he could force him to do what he said.

"She is bloody serious and frowny. She is bonnie, but she will nag me every time I sip whisky." He shook his head, his humor gone. "She is likely to be a shrew and might even stab me if I so much as look at another lass."

"Ye will heal," Rabbie said.

"Now the younger lass, Anna, seems much more willing," Beck said and grinned slightly. "Reminds me of my sweet Matilda at last year's Beltane."

"Her name was Millie," Adam said, his voice dry.

Rabbie coughed into his fist. "'Tis all fun until there's a lynching or a bastard born."

"And now we cannot go back to Beltane on Skye," Adam said with a pointed look at his wild brother.

"Too many MacLeods on Skye anyway," Beck muttered. He shook his head. "Anna says her older sister must wed first. Ye should wed her, Adam. I will take sweet Anna."

Adam snorted, but the idea of Beck wedding Anna

instead of Lark lessened the tightness in his chest.

"Does that mean aye or nay?" Rabbie asked, fingering the sack he continued to carry around as if he might throw it over some stray girl to carry her back home.

"I have no time for a wife." But he also didn't want Beck marrying the beautiful red-haired woman. *She does not want to marry anyone.* Lark had chosen to hide in a tree rather than accept a proposal.

"If ye will not ask for Lark, then ask her father for Anna," Adam said. "He has five daughters and no wife from what I have heard. He would likely appreciate one less mouth to feed."

Rabbie walked even with him. "Ye will need to marry, too, for the good of the clan."

"The good of the clan needs me focused on building it back from the ashes. For now, I will leave the daughter making to the rest of my brothers." Adam shifted the weight of his father's sword on his shoulder, its weight reminding him of the huge responsibilities he bore. *Do everything and anything to bring our clan back.* His father's words were never far from Adam's mind.

The three strode through the temporary village of tents toward two smoking Beltane bonfires at the far end. A fiddle broke through the murmur of excited festivalgoers, adding to the lively tune. Boys with switches spurred cattle and sheep between the two fires to bless them. Adam stopped at the far end with Beck and Rabbie and scanned those gathered, but Lark wasn't there.

"Go talk to those lasses over there," Rabbie said to Beck, pointing to a group whispering together. "See if ye can find one who can birth lasses and ask her to wed."

"That is a difficult trait to spot, don't ye think," Beck said, tipping his head. "Pardon me, lass. Your hips look wide enough to pass bairns, but do ye happen to know if they will be wee lasses, not lads?" Rabbie snorted, and Beck continued to walk with them.

At the end of the song, a middle-aged man with a full dark beard strode up between the fires to stop before the crowd of men, women, and children. He raised his clenched hands high and tipped his face to the darkening sky, bringing a rapid hush amongst the people.

"We ask for blessings this Beltane." The man's voice filled the space, his arms open as if addressing the sky. "Blessings for our animals, blessings for our children, and blessings for our Beltane brides."

Adam's gaze snapped to a line of lasses who walked out from a tent as if they'd been waiting for the word to set them moving. He counted them as they emerged. One, two...they smiled brightly. Three, four, five...looked straight ahead but still smiled. The sixth one made his gut clench. Lark Montgomerie had not escaped her father's order to wed. She was dressed in her blue dress, half her glorious hair bound up in ribbons while the rest fell down her back in waves. Her beautiful features were dull with acceptance as if she walked to a scaffold.

Adam inhaled fully through his nose. "Ready the horses," he said low to Beck.

"They are always ready," Beck answered. "Looks like Lark Montgomerie chose one of her suitors."

The line of brides stopped before the fires where a tall man in the brown robes of a priest walked up next to the bearded man. Adam studied Lark's heart-shaped face, his muscles flooding with restless energy. *Bloody hell.* Worry sat in the roundness of her eyes. Was she afraid? The thought tossed like a rotten turnip in his gut. "Ye have that sack?" Adam asked Rabbie.

"Aye. Ye plan to use it?"

Beck's eyes widened. "Adam? Are we not going to be

welcome back to Glencoe Beltane next year? Because I have a desire to see Anna Montgomerie again."

The women lined up between the fires, and the bearded man beckoned the tall priest. The clergyman's hair was cropped, and the skin of his forehead and nose was dark as if he spent hours in the sun. His chin was pale, showing he'd recently sheered a full beard. He clutched a Bible, while his sharp gaze scanned the crowd, stopping on Adam. Adam tried to relax the tension in his face. His brothers said he wore his anger as if he could strike people down with a glance.

Rabbie handed Adam the sack while Beck cursed under his breath and grabbed the back of his neck. "Damn Adam," Beck said. "I was having a bloody good time here."

"Don't ye be fathering any bastards," Rabbie said. "It will be the end of Clan Macquarie."

"I know," Beck said, his voice low with frustration. "Da told us every day from the time we first noticed that lasses smelled better than us. *Spill your seed outside a lass*," Beck mumbled their father's repeated saying. "We should have put it on his grave marker."

"And a bairn made on Beltane shall prosper and always find luck," the bearded man pronounced, which made the cleric's mouth turn up in a lecherous grin.

Lark's two suitors argued good-naturedly, Giles Cameron punching the other in the arm as he adjusted his cod through his kilt. Had Lark picked him? It didn't matter. The woman had hidden away from both of those fools, risking her neck climbing into a tree. She sure as Hell didn't want to marry either one of them.

"Get the horses," Adam said.

"Shite," Beck murmured and jogged away while Rabbie chuckled.

The first lass stepped before the priest with her father. The old man handed her off to a young man, who smiled like the whole bloody world was his. Within minutes, the two were wed, and bride number two stood before the cleric. Even the anxious lasses followed their father's orders. Lark moved up in line, her eyes cast straight ahead.

Beck ran up. "They are loosely tethered by the tree line. Damn, she does *not* look happy."

Lark Montgomerie's mouth squeezed tight, her eyes belligerent. She held her hands clasped before her, and Adam wouldn't be surprised if her nails dug so far into the backs of her hands as to bloody the skin.

"Lark Montgomerie," the bearded man intoned. "Ye must choose from your suitors."

She hadn't chosen yet. Adam released his breath.

Stopping before the cleric, the bearded man came to stand by her side. Was he her father?

"Ye will choose now," he said, loud enough for everyone to hear. The two swains stepped closer, as did Adam, the bag in his hands. He'd be damned if he would watch her be forced to marry. He'd steal her away and release her wherever she wished.

Adam stepped closer, making Giles and the other man frown his way. Lark followed their gazes. Her lips parted as if she was surprised to see him. Without thought, he took several more steps toward to her, his hands clutching the sack.

"Who will it be?" the cleric asked again, his accent odd as if he'd traveled far to do his preaching. He leaned in toward her until she likely smelled his breath. "Unless ye wish to take holy vows?" He laid a hand on her shoulder. "Ye may escape a union by going with me tonight." His appreciative gaze made Adam's hand tighten into a fist.

Lark Montgomerie stood tall, and the mutinous apathy faded from her face as she extended her finger. Everyone turned to follow her gesture, the entire crowd looking toward...him. Her voice came clear and loud. "I choose

Adam Macquarie."

Lark held her breath as she stared at the giant Highlander. With his deep frown, broad shoulders, and the lethal sword at his side, he looked able to slice through Hell and carry her away.

"I choose Adam Macquarie," she repeated. *If he had no interest, he wouldn't have stepped forward.* Her face warmed in the continued silence. Adam took a step forward, making her able to draw in breath.

"I am marrying her," Fergus MacLeod yelled, barreling his way through the watching crowd.

Giles Cameron was half a step behind Fergus. "Or me. I asked for her hand first."

Roylin made a noise in the back of his throat, his eyes narrowing on Adam. "Ye want to wed Lark?" She dropped her gaze to the ground at his rough tone, pushing the ache of his neglect down into a deep well within her.

Giles and Fergus stood breathing like a pair of ornery oxen. She couldn't imagine herself living with one of them or, nightmare of nightmares, lying naked with one or both of them while they pawed her. A wave of nausea made her turn back to look at Adam. It was him or wolves.

"He is looking for a bride," she said, trying to ignore all the watching eyes and whispers broken only by the crackle of the flames. She would be talked about for years after this. The townspeople already had enough to gossip about with Roylin's drunken spouting off about his sins. But life on Adam's isle would be private. No one there would know her at all. None of her new neighbors would have lifted Roylin out of a ditch or complained that he'd fouled their doorstep or would come by to warn her that he'd talked endlessly about her looking like her mother.

"I would speak to Lark alone," Adam said, his warm hand wrapping around her clutched fist. It was solid but not rough.

"Ye are not taking her anywhere," Fergus MacLeod said, pulling his sword.

Adam's brother and an older man appeared, their swords drawn and their faces just as lethal as the glinting blades. Adam looked to Roylin. "Unless ye wish for your Beltane Festival and all these other weddings to be tainted with the spilling of human blood, I suggest ye let me talk to Lark alone."

Her father waved his hand at Adam. "Take her. Giles and Fergus, stand back."

Lark walked off with him, the two of them tethered with his grasp. He stopped near three saddled horses and dropped her hand to turn to her. "Lass," he said, searching her face, "I am a stranger to ye."

"You said you need a wife. Well, your brother did." She stared up into his darkly handsome face. His closed expression told her nothing of his thoughts. She inhaled. "And I am in need of an escape, one that is legal and binding."

Adam grasped the back of his neck like he might have a pain there. "Ye need to know where I live was ill-used and needs hard work to make it fresh and thriving again."

"I was raised on hard work." Lord knew she was a servant more than a daughter all these years, even with her mother's protection.

"The isle has few people on it," he said, glancing past her.

She looked over her shoulder where Adam's brother was having some heated words with Giles and Cameron. Time was moving quickly, and those two idiots might decide they would rather start a war than give up their prize.

"Privacy would be a pleasure," she said, looking back to

him.

"And I have brothers who—"

"I am used to large families." She took a step closer, desperation making her bold. Her hands curled into his tunic as she looked up at him. She watched the lines of his face and the tilt of his lips. "Will you beat me?" she asked.

He blinked, frowning deeper. "Never."

"Do you get drunk most nights?"

"Nay."

She paused, searching his face for hesitation or lies, but she saw none. "Are you an honorable man?"

"I try to be."

He didn't sound like a liar, someone who would boast about their integrity.

"And you need a wife?"

He paused, watching her closely, and then glanced over toward his brother. "Aye."

Lark yanked on his tunic, making him look back at her. "Then marry me, Adam Macquarie, and get me the hell out of here."

Chapter Two

"Until death do us part." Adam repeated the vow Lark had recited. He did not sound joyful, but she did not need joy.

She needed to be free, and Adam was certainly better than either Giles or Fergus. At least she hoped so.

"You may kiss your bride," the priest said, although the grin he wore made him look like he did not take his celibacy oath seriously.

Lark frowned at him, using the judgmental stare that made her sisters behave properly. She turned her eyes to the Highland chief she had moments ago pledged to be with before God and a hundred witnesses. Adam Macquarie wore a serious look as he stepped closer to her, his large body stiff and his gaze taking in the people around them as if he expected an attack. From who? Giles and Fergus? They'd be fools. Just looking at the thickness of her new husband's arms, the strength evident in his stance, made Lark's knees feel slightly weak.

She took a full breath and startled as his hand touched her back. Lord, her heart felt like it might burst from her chest, and she pressed a hand against it. Wouldn't that make the Beltane Festival even more memorable? *Beltane bride's heart flies from her chest to fall on the ground before her as she dies in her groom's brawny arms.* Bards would sing about it for generations.

Adam's large hand rose, and Lark made herself remain still as it came closer to her face. Even her breath stilled. The back of Adam's finger slid across her cheek to brush a strand of her hair, tucking it behind her ear. The touch was soft despite the roughness of his skin, his gentleness capturing her shallow breath. He leaned forward, and his hand moved behind her head, keeping it there as his lips pressed against hers. The kiss was warm and soft, completely opposite of the man himself. Her eyes closed as the kiss deepened. Heat and sensation washed through Lark, keeping her heart racing. Without an anchor, the world tilted, and she clung to him so she wouldn't fall. The kiss ended quickly, but her new husband didn't move away.

"Sign the book, Macquarie," Roylin said. "Lark signed it earlier in our tent."

She took a deep breath as Adam pulled back, watching her as if making sure she wouldn't fall into a heap. She nodded, dropping her hands, and he turned to her father. Without Adam against her, the rush of the twilight breeze made her shiver.

Anna and her other three sisters ran up to Lark, tears in their eyes. Taking a deep breath to fully wake herself from whatever spell Adam Macquarie had weaved with his simple touch, Lark met her sisters' gazes. "Be good," she said to Agnes, Jonet, and little Katherine. "Listen to Anna better than you listen to me." She blinked back tears and grinned as they all promised, and each kissed her cheek. Anna tugged Lark toward the warmth of the fire as the little ones clung to her hands and skirts, bidding their farewells. "Will you tell him your secret?" Anna whispered at her ear.

Lark's chest squeezed around her heart, making her breath stutter. "There is no reason. I am going where no one will know me or my past."

Anna nodded. "'Tis best." She wrapped her arms around Lark's neck. "Promise me you will be well with him."

Hugging back, Lark's gaze cut over Anna's shoulder through the shadows that grew as the sun sank below the tree line. Her husband stood taller than any of the men around her father. She watched him shake Roylin's hand as if watching someone else's bizarre life.

"God willing," Lark said and slowly rubbed her lips together, remembering the feel of him pressed there, the heat that had leaped within her. She raised her hand to her cheek where he had touched her so softly despite the harshness of the night and the anger, surprise, and whispers around them. It was as if the kiss had branded her.

She took in a long breath to straighten her spine. *What have I gotten myself into?* Adam was no boy, and his kiss had ignited something within Lark, something new and molten. And she'd pledged her life to him. But what type of life would that be? He had brothers, and they would surely visit. But there would be no ribbons to tie for her sisters, no hair to comb and weave. No petticoats to press and waspish tongues to curb. And more importantly, no shadows to avoid.

This is the right choice.

Anna pressed a white handkerchief, which had been their mother's, into Lark's hand. "For your tears if it ends up being horrible."

Lark narrowed her eyes. "What a lovely sentiment."

The look on Anna's face showed she truly worried, and she threw herself back into Lark's arms, the two of them clinging. Despite her flighty ramblings, Anna was Lark's best friend. "I will miss your delicious tarts," Lark said close to her ear and heard Anna sniff, which made tears gather in her own eyes.

Lark pulled back, a forced smile on her lips. "No wiping your nose in my hair, sister." She kissed Anna's cheek. Each of her little sisters pressed small bunches of heather, marigold, and purple milkwort flowers into Lark's hand and ran off.

"Once I am settled and the littles are grown some," Lark said to Anna, "I will send for you. Perhaps you can start that bakery you have always wanted. Adam is the clan chief, so surely we can find a vacant cottage for you."

"Where will you be? How will I get there?"

Lark's stomach tightened. Where was Ulva Isle? She squeezed her sister's hand. "I will have answers once I discover them, and I will write to you." Their mother had taught them how to read and write despite their father's irritation about educating women.

Lark smiled and hoped it reached her eyes. "It will be a year or two before Agnes will be old enough to run the house. Or…" Her smile faded. "Bring them with you if things get bad. We can find a place for all of you on the Macquaries' isle."

Anna nodded, her words coming in a whisper. "He does not bother any of us like you."

"I know, but come if that changes," Lark whispered at Anna's ear as she hugged her tight one more time.

"We ride now."

Lark jumped at Adam's voice beside her. "Tonight?"

His hard face was outlined by shadows and shards of firelight. He gazed across the fires where Giles and Fergus spoke to a group of men.

"'Twould be bad luck if I must kill a man or two on our wedding night," he said.

"I suppose it would." Lark wrung her hands, turning the band of iron Adam had produced from his satchel.

Apparently, he had truly been looking for a bride. Would he have asked someone else if she hadn't chosen him before the crowd? An ache started in the back of her head.

"Best to get moving," her father said, his voice booming. Roylin Montgomerie was not a man for sentiments. His only two emotions were gruff and foolish with liquor. Her mother had been the only one who could gentle him, and now that she was gone, he rarely even smiled.

"Yes, Father," she said. He came up, meeting her gaze. At least his eyes weren't floating around. He was sober, so he would remember her leaving.

"Be a good wife, like your mother. Bless her soul." He gave one more nod and traipsed back to the fires as her sisters ran forward with even more picked wildflowers to press into her hands.

She exhaled the breath she'd been holding and watched him walk away with a tightness in her throat. Looking down, she gathered the flowers and hugged her little sisters once more. "Love you all," she said and turned to put one foot in front of the other. Anna looped her arm through hers as they walked toward the waiting horses.

Lark squeezed her. "Make sure the girls get fed and Father doesn't ride when he's into his cups. Come to Ulva Isle if anything terrible happens."

"Love you, Lark," Anna said, stepping back, her eyes round.

Lark turned to see Adam watching them, waiting for her to come. "Love you, Anna. Take care of them. Promise."

Anna nodded, and Lark left her to walk through the tall grasses that were already growing damp with the night air. The fires crackled behind her, and the wind blew the trees that encircled the valley. The pipes started up again as she looked back to see Anna and her other three sisters waving, silhouetted by the firelight.

And like that, she no longer belonged to the Montgomeries.

"Ye will ride with me," Adam said, which was good since she did not even own a horse to bring as a dowry. He clasped her waist, and the warmth from his hands penetrated the cloth, making her realize how cold it was without the heat of the fires. She never would have survived by herself on foot.

Adam lifted her onto a large dark horse who shifted and sniffed at the breeze. With hardly an effort, Adam swung up behind her, settling her between his spread thighs. Holy Mary, he was large. If he wanted to, his whole body could swallow her until there was nothing left. She fought the slight tremble in her flower-clutching hands by taking deep breaths, inhaling the faint smell of clean man, leather, and horse. He shook out the length of wool that covered his chest, throwing it over to tuck around her body without touching her as a husband might. Perhaps he truly was honorable.

They rode, breaking quickly into a canter that pushed her farther between his spread legs. Adam led the way, skirting the tents to the far end where the path rose out of the Glencoe basin. The incline pushed her back even more, and she leaned into him, her heart beating wildly as his body heat penetrated her, bringing a flush to her face that the shadows hid. The moon rose high into the starry sky, the wind, still tinged by the bite of winter, blowing against her cheeks.

"*Air do shocair*, Lasair," Adam said in the burbled notes of Gaelic, pulling back on the reins, and the horse broke from its run into a walk. His brother pulled up beside him.

"We will ride into the forest some ways before stopping," Adam said.

Lark shifted under the wool sash, watching Beck ride ahead.

"Sleep. I will not let ye fall," Adam said. How could she with his strong arms around her?

She shut her eyes for several long minutes, but her mind whirled over the events of the day leading up to her new predicament. "I am sorry," she whispered.

She felt Adam's chin brush her hair as if he looked down on her head, and her heart thumped harder. "What sins have ye committed?" he asked.

Too many. She pulled out a hand from the woolen cloth and scratched an itch along her nose. "Would you have picked another woman at the festival if I had not chosen you before everyone?" she asked, keeping her breathing even.

Adam didn't say anything for a moment, making her chest squeeze. Beck looked back over his shoulder. "He was going to throw ye into a sack and snatch ye away." He chuckled.

She tipped her chin up to see Adam, the top of her head sliding along his chest. "A sack?" She remembered he had something in his hands when he'd walked up. "I doubt I would have fit." Adam stared at Beck's back, a frown in place, and she leveled her gaze outward again.

"It would not have had to cover all of ye," the older man added as he rode up next to her. "Probably only down to your waist," he said, sizing her up. "I am Rabbie MacDougall, advisor to the Macquarie clan."

She gave him a small nod and looked back up at Adam's solemn face. Would he really have snatched her away? After a long pause, his gaze dropped to her eyes before looking back out at the night. "Ye did not want to wed one of them. If I had taken ye before they forced ye to wed, I could have ridden ye to safety and helped ye find a different path than marrying."

It was the maddest plan she'd ever heard. That he'd been willing to go to war to help her... It was also the kindest thing anyone had almost done for her. She smiled softly, feeling herself relax, and turned front again. *He is honorable.* "Thank you." He did not answer.

"How far is your home?" she asked.

"It will take two days," Adam said. "Perhaps three if the sea is rough."

"Rough?" Panic teased her stomach. "Do you live far across the sea?"

"Not too far," he answered. He leaned in, his warm breath on her exposed ear. "I will not let ye drown."

"How about vomit? Will you let me vomit?" she asked, her voice riding up in pitch. She'd heard how long voyages could bring on nausea.

"If you do, I will hold ye over the side."

"Very gallant," she whispered and felt the rumble of laughter deep within Adam's chest. But when she turned to look up into his face, illuminated by the rising moon, she only saw the stern, haunted face of a determined warrior.

• • •

Adam leaned against the rocky outcropping, waiting for Lark to return from washing at the stream where they had camped. It was just past dawn, and Rabbie walked slowly toward a bucket of water.

"Your brittle bones snapping is almost as loud as your snoring," Beck muttered, keeping an arm thrown over his eyes. He was an ornery arse in the mornings.

Lark stepped back around the boulder, combing fingers through the snarls of her long hair. It fell in coppery waves down to her cinched waist. He knew it was silky and fragrant from holding her before him on the journey the night before.

"Are they rising?" she asked.

"Nay," Beck called.

"Aye," Rabbie said at the same time.

"We will ride soon," Adam said. She had finally relaxed into him while they rode, her softness seeming to fit against him perfectly. Aye, he was more than ready to hold her against him again.

Beck cursed and rolled onto his stomach where his kilt came dangerously close to rising past the underside of his arse. Adam walked over and used his boot to push the wool length down, earning him a one-eyed glare from his brother.

Lark pulled the tarp from the thick tree limb that he'd set up for her to sleep under last eve. With her stiffness when they'd dismounted, it was best he slept apart despite Rabbie calling it their wedding night.

Lark maneuvered around their horses' saddles to Rabbie. "Do your joints pain you?"

"Only in the morn, and night, and when..." He tapered off and pushed his lips out. "Aye."

"I have some paste I made from willow bark that could help."

The old man eyed her suspiciously. "Ye a healer or a witch?"

Lark stared at him for a moment. "Neither..." she said slowly. "Although I made cures for my sisters. I would like to help my new clan in that way." Lark retrieved one of her bags and began rooting around in it. "Is there an herb garden where we are going?"

Beck snorted. "Aye, but ye would need to work miracles to get anything from it."

"What he means to say," Rabbie said quickly, "is that it needs some tending, but aye, I am certain ye can get it up and growing again."

Lark didn't seem concerned as she brought over a clay pot to Rabbie. She had no idea where she was going to live. Adam had tried to warn her about his isle, but there hadn't been time to make her truly understand. Was her life before so difficult that she thought it could not be worse?

"Rub this on your knees and anywhere else that pops and

aches," she said.

"Ye do not mind hard work," Adam said.

Lark shrugged. "I have been working hard my whole life. 'Tis what one does, I suppose. Although, it will be nice not to have to take care of a brood of five now."

Beck choked on an inhale and coughed into his fist where he sat on a half-rotted log. She glanced his way, her brows lowering in concern, but Beck waved it away. "Choking on air," he managed to mumble between coughs. "It is too thick at dawn."

"Ye mean your sisters?" Adam asked, crossing his arms over his chest.

"Yes. Four sisters and a father who needed as much tending as an unbreeched lad. I love my sisters, but they need a lot of tending. So, yes, you have rescued me from drudgery taking care of a large family. I am looking forward to…" Her words trailed off. "Well, starting a smaller family."

"Well, now—" Beck began, but Rabbie interrupted.

"Aye, 'tis a good thing ye wed our chief then," Rabbie said, cutting a sharp look at Beck and then at Adam.

"I would not mind having a large family of my own," she added quickly, glancing toward Adam. "Slowly perhaps. I like people in general, which is why I learned healing from my mother. Living out in the country hasn't given me a chance to practice much." She smiled broadly. "Joining your clan will give me ample opportunity to help lots of people in your town."

"Town?" Beck asked.

"Aye," Rabbie said over top of him and handed the clay jar back to her. "Thank ye."

Lark's bonnie face was open with happiness, and her blue eyes seemed to sparkle. "I saw some sorrel over there. If the herb garden is not well tended, I should cut some. It might keep a few days." She hurried past Adam, and all three of them watched her go.

Rabbie flapped his hand to bring Adam over to him as he hobbled quickly to Beck.

Beck looked up from the stump. "Ye did not tell her what the isle was like? Or Gylin Castle?"

"There was not enough time."

"Ye could tell her now," Beck said.

"Bloody hell no," Rabbie said, his eyes wide enough to make them look like they could fall out of his weathered face. "She does not need to know where we live until we get her on the isle."

"She is not a prisoner," Beck said. "She is a wife."

"Same difference if she is not happy about it. Her oath is the lock." Rabbie made a twisting motion with his hand. "Ye should make that marriage complete before we get there and she demands an annulment." He nodded quickly. "Beck and I will give ye all the privacy ye need."

Beck's mouth dropped open.

Adam frowned. "I am not going to tup my bride in the dirt."

"There is a lot ye can do standing up," Rabbie said. "Make it a game of All Hid and find her. Some lasses like the sport of being chased. Catch her and consummate the union."

"What kind of women are ye tupping?" Beck asked Rabbie, his grin returning. "The widow Gunn does not seem like the type of woman who would let ye run her down in the woods."

"A wonderful idea," Lark said, making all three men pivot toward her. She walked into the clearing; a bunch of plants caught in her hand.

Beck stood. "What is a wonderful idea?" he asked, his voice a bit choked, and he looked at Adam.

She paused, eyeing them. "If the sorrel wilts on the journey," she said, slowly, "I will make it into a tincture. It is full of health."

They stared at her for a long minute while the knot in Adam's stomach tightened.

"For the people in town," she said, her brows lowering in question.

The lass thought she was going to a busy town, a place where the two of them would live alone until they started having their own children. All common, logical ideas considering the little information she'd been given.

All very opposite of his reality.

• • •

Lark stared at the draped woolen blanket where Adam was anchoring down the corners. He straightened, dusting his hands. They were large hands, ones she had been watching all day as she rode before him on his horse.

Adam hadn't talked much; none of them had. Even his joking brother had seemed pensive as they crossed the miles toward their home. Any of her questions were answered in the simplest of terms, and mostly by Rabbie.

She was already on edge. Worry about Anna taking care of her younger sisters made her tense, as well as not knowing exactly what she had gotten herself into by wedding Adam. The added quiet of the men was unnerving. The only thing that had kept her calm was watching the gentle yet strong way Adam held the horse's reins. But now her heart quickened with the awkwardness of the sleeping arrangements.

"Will you be sleeping near the fire tonight?" Lark asked. She glanced over where they had picked apart a roasted rabbit that Beck had caught and a pheasant that Adam had flushed out of the bushes. Rabbie had insisted that the one tent be set up over a thick branch quite away from the fire, remarking that he didn't want to keep her awake with his snoring.

The breeze blew through the trees, making them sway. Was a storm moving in? "I could stay here with ye," he said, "if ye are worried about animals or…" He dropped his hands along the narrowness of his hips wrapped in the kilt.

Lark let out her breath, her hands going to her face. "Good Lord," she whispered at the stilted conversation.

"I will sleep at the fire, then," Adam said and began to step past her.

Her hand caught his upper arm, his muscles thick there. "Wait." He turned her way, and she met his gaze. "You are my husband, Adam," she said, making her voice sound stronger than she felt. "You can share my tent." She shook her head. "Nothing about this marriage has been usual. We hardly know one another. I did not bring a dowry. I know nothing about the Macquarie clan, and yet I am about to be the lady of it." She slid her hand off his arm. "Perhaps we wouldn't feel so odd if we…got to know each other better."

His eyebrows rose in question.

"I mean," she said quickly, "we can at least share the tent to sleep."

"Sleep. Aye," he said, nodding. "I will let ye get comfortable and join ye in a bit."

When he turned, she let her breath out in a silent ribbon. "Good Lord indeed," she whispered when he reached the fire where Rabbie stood up to talk to him.

He was her husband, and she couldn't get their brief wedding kiss out of her mind. She'd blame her immediate heart-fluttering reaction on the fact that she was a maiden. Her only information about what occurred in the marriage bed had come from Anna, who had the misfortune of witnessing a tryst between a groom and his mistress outside a country ball. Lots of panting and moaning between kisses in the stables had kept Anna whispering to Lark for an hour as she fanned herself.

"Damn," she whispered. She hadn't even seen a man's jack before. She hated being ignorant. Whatever happened between her and Adam tonight, she would keep careful attention like she did learning any new subject. It was a natural act, more commonplace than dancing. Aye, she would pay attention to the movements as she did when learning a new reel before a country dance.

She washed with the water Adam had hauled up from a stream, rubbing mint on her teeth, and combed through her long hair. She left it down instead of re-plaiting it, because Anna said that most men liked a lass's hair down.

Lark loosened her stays, sliding them off with her petticoat, sleeves, and gartered stockings, to leave her only in her long, white smock. Heart thumping, Lark laid back on the blankets, arms stiff at her sides, and waited.

Her mind settled on their wedding kiss, the heat that had flooded through her, and his gentle touch on her cheek. His strong arms had encircled her all day as they rode, powerful, protective arms. She'd never felt so safe before. Was it too soon to trust a man she'd only met two days ago? *Yes.* She wanted trust more than anything, the elusive feeling she'd never known but had seen in loving couples in her town. Even if it was too soon, she was certain trust could grow between them. She felt her body relax as she remembered the feel of Adam holding her.

A branch snapped, and she sucked in a quick breath. "Lark?" Adam said.

"Yes?" she said, her heart thumping.

"Can I come in?"

A mix of worry and want made her legs shift, and she sat up in the dark, swallowing past her ridiculous concerns. For trust to grow between them, she must open up to Adam, let him touch her. He was her husband. She drew a full inhale. "Yes."

Chapter Three

Go plant a wee lass in her womb.

Rabbie's harsh whispers, when he'd walked out to the fire, weighed on Adam's shoulders as much as his responsibility to raise his clan from the ashes. *She's not fighting ye off. Go do your duty, man.*

Rabbie could certainly take the fire out of tupping. Beck had come to Adam's defense, but hearing his brother extolling Adam's prowess with women hadn't helped him relax. *Sard it.* He'd been bedding lasses since he was seventeen, but this was different. Lark was a virgin, and she was his wife, a wife who might leave him when she found out where she would be living.

Darkness from the cloudy night made seeing Lark nearly impossible, but he could tell that she wore her long white smock where she sat on the blanket. He'd already pulled off his tunic, hanging it outside on a branch, but had kept his kilt wrapped around his hips. "'Tis hard to see," he said.

"I am right here." She thumped the ground next to her. "There is room for you." Her voice was a rushed whisper.

Was she nervous? Adam knelt onto the blanket. "Lark."

"Yes?"

"I will not touch ye if ye do not want to be touched."

"Oh." He watched her pull her legs up to cross under her. "I am fairly sure I already knew that."

"Good," he said, sitting down on the blanket. An awkward silence made the pinch in the back of his neck even tighter.

"Sleeping next to a man," she started, her voice seeming loud in the silence, and she lowered it, "is something I have never done. My maidenhood is the only dowry I bring then. I am sorry about that."

"Your father gave me a barrel of fine Montgomerie whisky," he said. "'Tis tied to the back of Rabbie's horse."

"I suppose I bring *spirit* to the marriage, then," she said, but the jest fell flat with the nervousness in her voice. She sighed. "Maybe I should have a gulp of that fine Montgomerie whisky."

Och. "Lark, do ye know what happens between a man and woman? In the marriage bed?"

"I have been told…how things work." Her toes brushed his leg, and he could feel that they were bare. He remembered their perfection as she clung to the branch to hide from the two arses hunting her.

Adam grasped the back of his neck. "There is a whole range of things that can happen…" He stopped, looking closer at her. "Good things that do not have to lead to full on tupping."

"Then you need to tell me about these things, because I despise being ignorant." Her words came out in a rush like she'd been holding her breath. "You will realize that fact once you get to know me. If I do not know how to fix an illness or bake a certain bread or throw a *sgian dubh* to hit its mark, I go out and learn it."

"Ye throw *sgian dubhs*?"

"Yes. Quite accurately."   ·

"Are ye armed now?" he asked. "'Tis something a bridegroom should know."

A small laugh came from her, and he felt the tension across his shoulders lessen. "No. Since you did not try to paw my breasts or ruck up my skirts while riding here, I left it in the satchel tied to your saddle." Her voice lowered, and he could tell her smile had faded. "Although, I suppose since you are my husband, you are allowed to do such things, and I am not allowed to gut you."

Adam leaned forward in the darkness until he was on level with her face. It was pale in the darkness, her eyes wide, and her hair down around her shoulders like a shawl that he knew was red and gold. "I do not know what type of husbands ye have met before, and I have never been one, but pawing and rucking are not something I would do unless ye ask, wife or not."

She watched him for several heartbeats. Her mouth opened, and she whispered, "Ask with words or with…a kiss or a touch?"

The timid encouragement that tinged her tone shot heat through him, making him harden immediately. His jack was ignoring his intent to remain a gentleman despite Rabbie's insistence that Adam climb upon his bride like a randy stallion.

He exhaled. "Lark, lass, ye could write it out in the dirt or whisper it in my ear or even sing it at the top of your voice."

"Rabbie might take exception to my loud singing about tupping," she said, the smile back in her tone.

"Highly doubtful," Adam murmured. He lowered to his side, straightening his legs, his boots still on as he faced her in the dark. She imitated him by lying on her side so that they faced one another. He was close enough to her that he could smell flowers coming from her unbraided hair.

Her toes were a distraction where they curled, slightly brushing his shin. "So ye have no personal experience with men?" he asked.

"A kiss or two, nothing like...our wedding kiss. The others were...unpleasant, stolen, wet things." She swallowed. "Or unwanted."

Had her suitors caught her before? The thought made his fist clench. "Like I said, I will only kiss ye if ye want, Lark."

"It is my decision alone?" she asked, leaning forward slightly. "Even if you do not want me to touch you?"

A grin crept onto his face. He leaned in toward her the same amount. "Lark, lass, ye have my permission to touch me whenever ye wish."

She narrowed the separation to inches. "Even when I have been rolling in mud or dancing in the rain?"

"Do ye dance in the rain often?"

"No, only when it is raining," she answered.

He snorted. "Aye, even then."

The shadows were thick, shrouding them, making it easier to talk freely. Maybe he should give her more information about Ulva Isle and the condition of Gylin Castle and Ormaig Village behind it.

Before he could utter a word, she crossed the shadowed gap. His words deserted him as her hand slid up to cup the side of his face, and she pressed her lips to his. Instead of the tentative touch of their wedding kiss, Lark immediately melted into him, tilting her face and sliding closer. Her soft body molded against the muscles of his chest and torso, her leg hitching up to slide over his hip. She tasted of mint, and the hesitant touch of her tongue cracked like a hammered chisel through his restraint.

Lark's hand slid up his chest, her palm skimming along as if exploring. "Your skin is so warm," she murmured and stroked up over the expanse to his shoulder. Lush breasts pressed against him as if they were begging for attention, and her leg hooked up higher onto his hip, bringing the juncture of her legs closer to his aching jack.

He caressed a trail up the linen of her smock to cup her breast through it, and he felt her nipple harden. She made a soft mewing sound as he lifted and squeezed it, his fingers rolling her sensitive flesh. She rocked into him, her pelvis rubbing, and the rest of his restraint shattered.

Adam's fingers tangled into her silky hair as he pushed her onto her back. Their kiss became wild, slanting and breathy, as his fingers edged up her smock. He moved slowly, seeing if she would stiffen or pull away, but she only pressed further into him.

Skin soft and smooth spanned across her hip as he stroked upward along her thigh and the bared curve of her waist. She moaned against his mouth, kissing him and arching her back. Her breast was soft and heavy in his hand. "Lord, lass," he murmured. "Ye are made of curves and softness everywhere." He moved to the second breast, loving it like the first.

Lark stroked a hand down his chest in the small crevice separating their bodies. "And you are hard everywhere," she whispered as her hand pressed flat against his rigid jack through his kilt. She slid along it as if testing the length and thickness.

Her bare feet stroked up his shins, and her fingers began to pull up the length of his kilt. If she went much further, he might be taking Lark there in the dirt with Rabbie and Beck not too far off. The silence around them was no cover to the moaning he wanted to tease out of her.

"Lass," he said against her mouth but then lost himself again as she maneuvered one of her feet under his kilt to rest on his naked arse. Kissing Lark was like submerging into warm water where all thoughts dissolved except her. Without the gawking people at the festival, alone here in the tent, Adam felt as if he could drown in her sweetness and little noises.

His hand slid from her breast, stroking a path between them to her stomach and lower, brushing against her mound at the juncture of her legs. "I ache," she whispered, pressing upward into his hand.

He touched her heat, sinking his finger into the proof of her pleasure. She moaned into his mouth as he caught the sound with a heated kiss.

"Where is she?" The rough voice, coming from the clearing, jarred Adam, dousing him in ice. He jerked his hand from Lark's willing body, breaking their kiss.

"Where is who?" Beck asked, loudly for Adam to hear.

Adam slid his mouth to Lark's ear. "Stay still and silent."

Lark's hitched foot slipped back to the blanket beneath them. She lay flat, her breath coming fast but quiet, and she stared upward at him. He shifted, pressing backward onto the balls of his feet, and unsheathed one of his daggers. Without a word, he found Lark's hand in the dark and wrapped her fingers around the handle.

"The lass ye left with."

"The one who chose Adam Macquarie to wed."

Rabbie's voice rose a bit too loud in a poor attempt to sound natural. "They went on without us to be left alone for their wedding night. Probably a few hours ahead."

"What do ye want with her?" Beck asked.

"I could think of a thing or two," one bastard said with a dark laugh.

"The captain wants her, you idiot. Him first, as usual."

Rage swelled inside Adam as they talked casually about abduction and rape. The bastards would die today, probably saving countless lasses like Lark. And who the bloody hell was their captain? He'd seen no English reds in Glencoe, and these men did not have English accents either. Mercenaries?

Lark sat in the dark in her white smock, and he gestured for her to stay. She held the *sgian dubh* before her, her mouth set in determination even though her eyes were wide.

Adam crept out the back and circled the edge of the camp. There were four bloody bandits, three with swords and one with a matchlock pistol aimed at Beck. The men were dressed in mismatched trousers and shirts and grinned as if they had the advantage. But being hungry to rebuild the strength of the Macquarie clan, made daily training in combat mandatory. Even Rabbie could topple a head from a set of shoulders.

But it was the gun trained on Beck that made Adam hesitate to charge into the clearing. He slid a double-edged *mattucashlass* from his boot. He raised his arm, but motion on the other side of the clearing made him pause. *Blast and damnit!* Lark was sneaking up behind them, nearly naked in her white smock. She clutched the *sgian dubh* he'd left her over her shoulder as if poised to throw while her other hand held the length of white linen so she wouldn't trip. *Mo chreach!*

If they heard her, they could shoot her before realizing she was the prize they sought. Would he shoot if Adam hit his head or chest? Damn, Adam needed him to drop his gun. Stepping out of the bushes with a powerful thrust, Adam sent his blade sailing. It struck the man's upper arm. Yelping, he dropped the gun, but one of the other men leaped over to yank it off the ground, turning toward Adam.

Before Adam could roll out of the path, the man yelled, falling forward, face into the dirt to show a *sgian dubh* embedded in the back of his skull. Lark stood, her arm extended with her follow-through. Without hesitation, Beck and Rabbie lunged at the men before them while the one he'd hit first leaped for Lark. She stood without her blade, eyes widening as the man ran forward, his meaty hands grabbing her.

Adam surged forward, his sword coming out as his boots ate up the space across the clearing. The man caught Lark's arm to pull her into him with his one good arm in an attempt to use her as a shield. But the lass had other plans and used the heel of her palm to jam against the hilt of the knife protruding from his arm.

"Foking wench," the man yelled as the knife cut further into his muscle.

"Let go! Let go!" she screamed, twisting like a caught fish. Her knee jerked up several times, until she made contact with the bastard's ballocks. She jumped back as he collapsed to his knees, a groan coming out with another curse.

Adam caught her arm, and she spun as if ready to strike. "Lark!" he said. She blinked and nodded quickly, like a bird tapping a tree, as she breathed in hard gusts. She shook all over.

Rabbie dispatched the bastard before him. Beck yanked his bloodied sword from the fourth man and ran over to them.

"We will keep him alive," Adam said, crouching before the man who was curled into a tight ball, clutching his ballocks, as his arm bled. "Who the hell sent ye? Captain who?"

He didn't answer.

"We will let the lass at ye again," Beck said. "If ye do not start talking."

"Bastard might not be able to with her shoving his ballocks up into his stomach," Rabbie said, bending to look into the pained face.

"'Tis what he deserves for grabbing me and trying to kill you all," Lark said, her arms crossed, fingers curling into the fabric of her smock.

"Do ye know a captain?" Adam asked, but she shook her

head. "What type of captain leads ye?" he asked the man.

In response, the man turned his face to the dirt and vomited.

"Pretty powerful kick there, lass," Beck said, his voice a mix of impressed amazement and trepidation.

"Aye," Rabbie said as he walked over to the man that had grabbed up the fallen musket. The *sgian dubh* that Adam had given Lark was embedded in the back of the bandit's skull, killing him before he got a shot off. "Mighty fine aim, too," he said and yanked the knife out.

Lark hurried over to him, staring down as he wiped the blood off the blade with the edge of the man's shirt. She stared down, clasping her smock in tight fists. "Are his eyes open?"

Rabbie turned him over. "Seems to be."

"Should we close them?" she asked, looking up at him. She blinked, her lips tightening in a frown. "Or will leaving them open let the birds peck them out?"

"Peck them?" Rabbie asked.

She stood straight. "He deserves the worst. Was going to take me to his captain where he'd be *having me first*," she said, repeating the man's threat.

She narrowed her eyes, her face flushing with hot anger. "Why is it that wicked men always want to steal away women to rape and enslave us?" She threw her arms out. "Men they just kill off. I would rather be killed, but women must endure vile cruelty and terror before eventual death."

She strode over to the man she'd kicked. He'd stopped vomiting but still clutched himself on the ground. "Tell me! Who the hell is this captain of yours?"

He spit toward her but didn't say anything. Instead of leaping back, Lark spit back at him, hitting him in the face. "You tell this captain of yours he better stay well away from me or else he'll be vomiting in a ball in the dirt, too, or stabbed through the brain."

"Foking doxy," he ground out, his face pinched with hatred. "We will each take a turn f—"

Adam didn't let him finish but grabbed him by the throat, lifting him straight up, fury adding to his strength. "Ye finish that sentence and I'll be slicing ye slowly from your ballocks up to your throat so ye can watch your entrails roll out."

"Tell him who your captain is or he will do it," Rabbie said next to him.

Adam loosened his grip slightly so the bastard could swallow but leaned forward, a snarl on his face to match the threat in his eyes. "Look at the lady and ye'll be writhing back on the ground."

The man pulled back his lips. "Captain Jandeau always wins the prize he seeks."

Lark stood off to the side. "Well, if he tries to seek me, I will..." She seemed to be struggling with thinking up something vile. "I will have him tied up and find someone to defile him, strip him down, and...and do dastardly things to him before he is killed." They all stared at her, Rabbie's mouth hanging open and Beck's eyes wide. She nodded, her frown fierce. "See how he likes it."

Adam shoved him at Beck and stepped over to pull Lark to him. She trembled like a brittle limb in a storm. A need to protect her flooded him, and he turned her away from the sight of the dead men. He looked over her head toward Beck and Rabbie. "Tie him to a tree," he said. "We ride tonight."

• • •

Lark racked her brain.

She didn't know any captains except for the few Roylin had paraded her before in Edinburgh when he'd brought her on one trip, none of which were a Captain Jandeau. "Jandeau," she murmured where she rode, her back pushed against Adam's chest. "The name sounds French."

"He may have lied about the name," Adam answered.

"His accent sounded foreign. Perhaps he is a sea captain."

They had ridden all night, stopping at dawn to rest the horses while the men took turns guarding the camp. Even though they didn't work her into the rotation, she'd stood guard, because Rabbie fell asleep on his shift. But no more scoundrels came upon them, and they had ridden on their way to the coast, boarding a ferry over to the Isle of Mull.

Lark stifled a groan at the ache in her back as she twisted in the saddle to see the bustling harbor where they had led the horses onto the island. "So this is not Ulva Isle or Wolf Isle? They are the same, correct?"

"Nay and aye," Adam answered.

Since their kiss in the tent... Actually, it was well past a kiss, bordering on ravishment. After that, Adam hadn't said but a handful of words to her, his frown increasing the closer they rode to his home. Was he disappointed they'd been interrupted? She certainly was, although having a wedding night in a tent on the hard ground was not what she'd imagined in her foolish girlhood dreams. Adam was not the smiling, flower-giving swain she had imagined, either. No, he was much more...everything. Larger, more serious, and as rugged as the Highland landscape. The only softness she'd detected in him were his lips and the gentleness of his touch when he brushed her hair back from her cheek. Lord, how that set her heart flying. And now she was his wife and would likely share his bed that night. The thought brought a blush to her cheeks and an ache melting down to the crux of her legs.

Lark shifted in her seat and tried to divert her carnal musings. She stared up at the castle on the water's edge, the sprawling village winding out from it. People bustled about, their day drawing to a close. A lady with a cart of tarts for sale wrapped them in linen to save. A lad with a lamb about his shoulders hurried to keep up with his father. Warriors training in the meadow drank from bladders as they walked toward the castle.

Mull Isle was civilized and bustling. A lady churned butter outside her doorway as she laughed with an older child who held a babe for her mother. Several elderly men sat on a bench talking with large arm gestures. A small group of children ran together as they chased a dog who had a woven reed hat clasped in its teeth. And none of them knew her shame. Not one, not even Adam. She could forget about her past and move forward. She breathed in the salt air, a relaxed smile settling on her mouth.

"Adam Macquarie," one man called, stepping from a thatch-roofed cottage. He had light brown hair and an easy smile. "Good to see ye. Not dead yet, then?" He laughed, his eyes assessing.

"Macquaries are made of tougher stuff," Beck called out, a large grin in place. "We will see ye at Julia's wedding next week."

"I did not expect ye back so soon. Did ye get run off from Glencoe Beltane like Skye last year?"

Her smile faltered somewhat. Had they been hunting brides then, too?

"Adam found a wife," Beck said, and the man's gaze fastened onto her.

Lark smiled. "I am Lark Montgomerie. I am part of the Macquaries now."

"Wife?" the man said, glancing at Adam.

"Lark, this is Liam Maclean," Adam said from behind her. The deepness of his voice sent a calming warmth through her. If he talked more, she would be less nervous.

"Cousin to Tor Maclean, the laird of the Macleans of Aros Castle and Mull," Liam added and gestured to the castle at his back.

Lark nodded in greeting.

He kept his gaze on her as he spoke to Adam. "I will let Tor know ye've returned."

"Thank ye," Adam said. "We have no time to pay our respects."

Liam waved off the comment, surprise still bright in the pinch of his brows. "And I will say a prayer for ye," he said to Lark. With a final bob of his head, he walked briskly off toward the castle.

Lark frowned. Pray for her? Was she in need of divine help?

The hooves of Adam's horse clipped on the rocks laid out in the cobblestone road. Thunder rumbled far in the distance. They passed the dark window of a milliner's shop, headed toward the dock.

"We are not staying here for the night?" Lark asked. "An inn perhaps with dinner, a bath, and a bed?" Lord, how she wanted a bath. "And I will need to purchase a few things, unless your village has an apothecary and milliner. My mother left me some coin to use once I wed."

"We will stop to eat at the tavern," Adam said. "Ye can make a list for Beck of the things ye need, and we will go on to Ulva this eve. Beck can return tomorrow."

Disappointment added to the slight nausea that still plagued her from the first crossing. "Will the trip across to Ulva Isle be as far as the one across to Mull?"

"Nay, lass," Rabbie said. "Ye can practically spit on Ulva from the back side of Mull. A quick float across and then we be home."

Lark relaxed in the saddle, leaning against Adam. The hardness of his chest had grown familiar, and his warmth seeped through the cloth of her bodice. Of course, he would want to sleep in his own bed after days of travel. And she would share it. Giddy heat spread through her limbs with her quickened heartbeat.

"Well, then, let us eat and float our way across. I will enjoy a warm bath and clean sheets in my own dwelling." She would be lady of her own house at last. One without fear or shame or penance.

She caught an uneasy glance passing between Beck and Adam. Pray for her? No matter. Like the Macquaries, she was made of tougher stuff. If there wasn't a bath in the castle, she would find one.

Chapter Four

"Welcome to Wolf Isle," Adam said.

Lark inhaled, and the tang of saltwater warred with the fresh pine scent of the trees above the rocky beach. It was sweet and fresh and wild. *My new home.*

Sharp pebbles poked through her slippers, bruising the arches of her feet as she walked up the slip of beach to the bluff while Beck and Rabbie led the horses from the barge they had poled across. "So Ulva means Wolf?" she asked, her voice loud in the lull of wind.

"Aye," Adam said. "In the ancient language of the Norsemen who found it."

Where the docks of Mull bustled with people, Ulva's dock was vacant. "Do wolves live here?" She looked toward the span of trees that loomed in the dark ahead. The twisted pines bent and creaked in the wind of an incoming storm.

"Not for generations," Adam said.

A chill blew in to slide up her spine. She felt a gaze on her, as if the trees watched her intrude upon their isle. "You said you have brothers? Do they live close?" she asked, looking away from the dark forest.

"Quite close," Beck said. "Our isle is only fifteen square miles."

"But the mountains in the middle rise up tall and are bonnie for sheep," Rabbie said. "There are a number of lochs with fish in them and clear, clean spring water."

They trudged toward a path that led into the forest, the horses behind them. "How far away is your home?" she asked, tipping her face up to look at the nearly full moon. Clouds raced fast, covering it.

"A bit up the coastline," Adam said.

Beck came up beside them. "Castle Gylin overlooks the strait we just crossed." He pointed up the strand.

A large mass perched farther up, looking like a mythical dragon staring out toward Mull. As thick clouds rushed to cover the moon, it became a dark shadow. "There are no torches lighting it," she said, squinting.

"The Macquarie brothers do not need to waste candles and oil when they don't know we are returning tonight," Rabbie said.

"Of course." She wrapped her shawl closer about her neck. Lark startled, jumping forward, when Adam touched her lower back. "Sorry," she murmured.

Adam's boots crunched, and the wind tugged her hair as he led her through the narrow copse of trees. "Is there a chapel?" she asked.

"Not one that is fit for use," Rabbie said, he and Beck leading the horses behind them.

"A school for the children? I can teach them how to read and write if there is need for a teacher. I know how." She would be an asset to the village. Perhaps teaching would give her a way to get the local people to trust her enough to take her cures, too.

"No school," Beck said, his voice without humor.

Exhaustion was making Lark twitchy and given to wild worries. Of course, the darkness and storm blowing in did not help ease her anxiousness. "I can always hold school in a vacant cottage. Are there any about?"

Rabbie marched up next to them and yanked at his fuzzy beard. "A good number of vacant cottages, lass. Ye can do with them as ye like."

"We can make one into a church and another into a school," she said. They would need to find a priest to visit, one from Mull perhaps. Hopefully, he was nothing like Father Lowder at the Beltane Festival, his judgmental gaze following her around. If she was going to confess to a priest, he must be someone with a kind heart.

Adam led them across the narrow moor of tall grasses and easily found a path that led toward the castle. Lark turned her head this way and that, but she couldn't see anything in the darkness. They broke through another narrow copse of trees onto a cliff above the strait. The moon was a hazy glow behind the clouds as thunder rumbled closer. Thank the Lord they weren't still on the barge tossing on the angry sea. The wind whipped against her, making her clutch the shawl even tighter. The outline of Gylin Castle sat on the highest point ahead of them.

"Where is the village?" she asked.

"Ormaig sits behind the castle," Adam said near her ear, the words battling against the rushing sound of the newly unfurled leaves above.

"I smell no hearth fires blowing this way," she said, twisting to meet Adam's gaze. "Where is everyone?" she asked.

"Most likely up at the castle," Beck said.

"The wind is blowing the other way," Rabbie said on top of him.

Their quick answers sent another trickle of apprehension

through Lark. She didn't bother to hide the questions on her face as she studied Adam.

"Let us get out of the storm," he said. "And I will explain everything."

Explain everything? What was there to explain? She knew the castle and town needed work to right it. She would use the skills that her mother taught her to benefit her new clan, and she would be trusted and renowned for her compassion and wisdom. She would create a place of safety and comfort for her family and herself. Her heart squeezed in warning, holding tightly to her hopes as if the gusts of wind might snatch them away.

As they approached the closed portcullis, Adam released her hand to cup both of his around his mouth. "Macquaries return," he yelled out, making her jump.

"*Mo chreach*," she murmured.

Lark looked past the fortress to the dark outline of the tops of cottages beyond, but she saw no glow of hearth fires. Was everyone already abed?

"Ho there," someone called from the watchtower. "I was about to go inside." A dark figure leaned over the low wall. "Bloody hell, ye brought back a woman."

"She is a bride," Adam said.

"And she is standing next to ye, Adam?"

"She is *my* bride," he said.

"By the devil," the man called and disappeared inside to crank the gears to raise the pointy-toothed portcullis. At least it looked solid enough to keep any possible wolves out. "I thought the plan was to bring a bride back for Beck." His words came out with a grunt as he worked.

Unable to stop herself, Lark turned narrowed eyes up at Adam. "Plan?"

"We mentioned we were looking for brides," Beck said, leading his and Adam's horses forward. "A man must make plans if he is to create a family."

"A family in the eyes of God. No bastards here," Rabbie added.

Lark's face snapped toward the old man who led his horse behind him. But Adam's hand clasped hers, tugging her along. She faced front as he led her toward the rising bars, dodging one of the points in his haste to enter. The bailey was a circle of packed dirt and was completely dark like the rest of what she'd seen of Ulva Isle.

The silhouette of a tree stood in the middle, its twisted trunk seeming to cling to the rocky ground like a talon. Lightning splintered across the sky, revealing bare tendrils of branches tossing like whips. A willow tree. Thunder rumbled like the angry voice of God, making Lark's shoulders rise higher as she stared at the leafless, snapping limbs. "Is that tree dead?" she asked.

"We have hopes it will come back." Adam took the lead rope that was hooked to his horse's bridle. Fat drops of rain began to pelt them. "We need to shelter the horses," Adam said.

Lark raised her skirts, glancing once more over her shoulder at the willow, and followed the three men to a set of stables along the side of the castle. The smell of freshly hewn wood mixed with the sweet tang of the incoming rain. She heard more animals shifting in the dark stalls.

"Can you even see what you are doing?" she asked, looking around for a torch that could be lit.

"Aye," Beck said. "We could untack and tack up our mounts blind. But the lightning helps."

Crack! Thunder split the sound of the wind and rain with a close lightning strike. Lark pressed against a stall where a horse neighed. Its large head moved over the door, brushing against her hair. Lark shot forward, away from its mouth that had been ready to lip at her hair. She knew nothing of horses. ·

Surely, if the creature were a biter, Adam would have warned her. She swallowed hard. Wouldn't he?

The tapping of rain increased on the roof. "At least it's dry in here," Beck said. "Let's hope the castle is, too."

Every word out of their mouths made Lark's stomach tighten more. Pray for her? No fires? Why would it not be dry inside a stone fortification? Questions mounded up so high within her that she began to feel buried under their weight. Questions to which Adam had the answers, answers he kept silent about over the last two days of travel.

Lark gasped softly as a man appeared in the open entry, lightning illuminating him like an unholy presence, but she realized it was the guard from the gate tower. "'Tis blasted wet out." He walked up to Lark, but in the dark, it was hard to see much more than that he was as tall as Adam and Beck. A flash of lightning showed a lopsided grin set under a straight nose and surrounded by a close-cropped beard. "I am Callum, Adam's brother."

"Greetings," she managed to say. "I am Lark."

"Like the bird?"

"Yes."

Callum came closer to her in the dark to run a hand down the nose of the horse that had nearly eaten her hair. Lark took an involuntary step into Adam's side. Four large men, surrounded by lightning and snorting horses, soaked through with darkness… Lark pressed a hand against the pocket where she had wrapped the *sgian dubh* Adam had given her, wiped clean. "Can we go inside where there is some light?" The heaviness of the dark made it difficult to draw breath, making her words sound weak when she very much needed to be strong.

"Aye," Adam said. "We will start a fire. There is peat inside?" he asked, his words taking on the authoritative tone of a father asking his son if he'd done his chores.

"Aye, 'tis taken care of," Callum said.

"And the roof?" Rabbie asked.

"Mostly," he answered. "Ye arrived a few days before expected."

Lark felt Adam take her hand firmly. Did he think she would run away screaming? Well, if it wasn't pouring, lightning, and terrifyingly dark, and she wasn't stuck on an island, she might run away cursing.

Lightning hit close by, making her jump, her heart pounding. "I am not staying out here," she said and pulled away from Adam's hand. At her tug, he let go, and she trudged out into the storm. The rain was cold and blew directly into her face. The bailey was quickly turning to mud, and her slippers squished as she ran across the bailey, skirts raised high. To think she'd jested that she danced in the rain.

Lightning flashed, illuminating the dead tree. Its evil tendrils lashed out toward her as if trying to catch her. She squeaked and dodged around the churning limbs. With her shawl clutched under her chin, Lark bolted up the steps that led into the stone dragon of a castle. The door latch gave way, and she rushed inside…into more darkness. *Holy Mother Mary!* It was like being blind.

She headed for an arched doorway and a soft glow of torchlight. She halted just inside, her ruined slippers leaving a muddy puddle on the wooden floor. The cavernous room rose to two-story rafters. Beams, some split and some whole, ran overhead, supporting the walls of gray stone. A faded tapestry hung lopsided across the far wall next to a cold hearth coated black with soot. Another tapestry hung by one corner against a second wall. Flaming torches sat in two sconces near a long wooden table covered with dirty plates, tankards, and bowls as if left over from a drunken celebration. The smell of stale spirits twisted Lark's stomach with memories.

Two men jumped up, drawing their swords, faces fierce

and stances battle-ready. "Who are ye?" one asked, his hair hanging to his jawline, framing narrowed eyes.

The other lowered his sword, his lethal stare turning to shock on his boyish face. "'Tis a bonnie lass. I claim her as mine."

The frowning man still held his sword. "Are ye a kelpie or a witch?"

"Neither," she said, her voice breathless.

"She is Lark Montgomerie Macquarie." Adam's deep voice filled the shadowed great hall. "And she is *mine*." Lark opened her mouth to retort that she was no man's but stopped herself. Hadn't she pledged to be Adam's before a priest? *Good Lord.*

The frowning man lowered his sword. "Ye are back?"

"Obviously," Rabbie said, pushing his way inside. He shook his head like a dog, spraying rain out from his bushy hair and clothes. "And Adam found himself a wife. Now light the hearth and find us some ale."

"A wife?" asked the one who'd claimed her on sight. He had a swath of light-colored hair that fell over his forehead into his eyes.

"Aye," Beck said. "The oldest daughter in a family of five *lasses*." He nodded as if that meant something.

Lark crossed her arms, her fingers curling into the wool of her shawl. The room grew lighter with two more sconces lit. One of the men threw a torch into the hearth for it to catch the dry peat. Light pushed back the shadows, revealing floating cobwebs and a few broken chairs stacked with some bedding along the stone walls. There was nothing soft, new, or clean in the whole space.

Before her stood Adam, Beck, and three other large men while Rabbie shuffled down the table checking tankards until he found one with something in it. The men were about the size of Adam, large with muscular arms and wide shoulders.

They stood with legs braced apart as if they could plunge into battle whenever needed. They stared at her, making Lark's knees wobble behind the folds of her gown, and she glanced at Adam. He wouldn't let anything befall her there alone and nearly defenseless with five formidable men. Her gaze slid back around to them, and she inhaled to steady her nerves. "Who are all of you?"

Adam nodded to Beck. "Ye know Beck and met Callum out in the barn. Beck is the second brother under me. Callum is the third."

"I am Callum's twin, Drostan," said the frowning giant. From the candlelight, she could see that his hair hung lower than Callum's, but they looked quite similar otherwise. "I came into the world second that night, so I am the fourth brother."

"Greetings, brother Drostan," she said.

"And I am Eagan," said the one who had claimed her. He smiled openly.

"The babe of the group," Drostan said, making Eagan's smile fade to an annoyed frown.

"With Lark here, we have something to celebrate," Beck said and set the whisky that Lark's father had given them as her dowry into the middle of the table. Eagan laughed deeply, and Callum knocked his fist hard on the table as if cheering.

The sharp rapping startled some birds roosting in the rafters. Lark tipped her head back to watch them fly around, their wings disturbing dust that filtered down. She took a backward step toward the wall behind her, hoping one wouldn't shite on her. The way her day was going, she was a certain target.

"I will find a tap," Rabbie said and strode off into the dark, perhaps toward a kitchen.

"Aye," Eagan said. "A woman on Wolf Isle. This calls for a celebration."

"A woman on Wolf Isle?" Lark repeated, her gaze snapping to Adam. "What does that mean?"

The three newly introduced brothers turned to Adam, too. "Ye have not told her?" Drostan asked, his jaw slack. "Fok, Adam."

"There was no time," Rabbie said, a tap in his hand, which he held up as if in victory. "Ye sots left one in the hall." Were they also heavy drinkers? Like her father? The thought of six drunken men shot a knife of panic through Lark, nearly knocking the wind from her.

She swallowed deeply, turning her thoughts away from her nightmare to focus on her anger. "We have been traveling for days," Lark said without taking her gaze from Adam. "And you said nothing?" Hearing the question out loud strengthened her spine. She tried to remember exactly what Adam had said when he took her aside to speak with her before their brief exchange of vows. *A lot of work. Ill-used castle. Not many people.* He'd failed to mention that there were no women *at all.*

Adam inhaled fully. "Rabbie thought ye might not come with us if ye knew."

"Knew what exactly?" Cold, tired, confronted by five huge men who liked to drink, and bound to a husband who had not taken the time to explain the reality of her new life, Lark's anger blasted through her initial fear.

"That we are the only ones living on Wolf Isle right now, and ye are the only woman," Adam said.

"And," Callum said, holding up a tankard, "the isle is cursed."

Bloody hell.

Adam ran a hand through his rain-damp hair. Why

hadn't he told her everything on the way there? It had been a rapid journey and an unpleasant discussion. *Bloody poor excuse.*

"The isle is cursed?" Lark repeated, her gaze sliding to each brother, one by one, as if they would tell her more. "What the hell does that mean?" She finished with a pointed glare at Adam. "And I am the only woman here? And you six." She threw her arm out to encompass them. "Are the only men on the whole isle?" She looked up. "And we might not have a roof, and there are birds roosting in the great hall, and there are no hearth fires or lights in the village because we are the only breathing things on this rock sitting in the ocean." Her voice had risen as the questions and words tumbled out.

Callum tipped his head. "Well, there are other breathing things, sheep and such, and then there is old Grissell living on the south side."

"I suppose she is considered a woman," Beck said. "So that makes ye the second woman on the isle."

"Grissell is a witch, not a woman," Eagan said, crossing his large arms. "We would run her off, but she does no harm." He shrugged. "And she might put another curse on us if we tried."

"A witch is a woman," Drostan said. "A woman who worships Satan."

Lark stared at them, her lush mouth dropped open, her delicately arched brows raised high, as she turned back to him. "I am second to a witch on an uninhabited isle that is cursed." Her gaze moved to the barrel of spirits. "And you all love to drink whisky?"

The damn birds startled again to fly about the hall as if to emphasize the wretchedness of the situation.

"Rabbie and Eagan are the only two who drink so much they pass out," Drostan said, his voice low.

"Says the sot who wandered out into the night swinging

his sword like a drunken lunatic," Eagan said.

"Ye arse, Da had just died. 'Twas his wake," Drostan said, his voice heavy with warning.

"Drank so much, ye puked on your own boots," Callum added, making Adam run a hand down his face.

"At least I did not piss in Lady Grace's garden to be run off by her husband," Drostan said to his twin.

Callum's teasing grin faded at what he surely remembered as a screeching reprimand by the lady, who held back her wee granddaughter, and a fist in the jaw by her large husband.

Drostan shoved the chair before him across the floor, upending it. Its crash was emphasized with Drostan running across the space to tackle Callum to the floor.

But Adam focused on Lark where she had pushed back against the stone wall. Her eyes were wide in her beautiful face, her frown deep, and the *sgian dubh* back in her hand as she watched his brothers roll around like ill-mannered pups.

He sighed, dropping his hand. She looked like a cross between a nervous kitten and a wildcat about to take down anything that came close.

Adam turned toward his brothers, where Eagan was laughing, which added to Drostan's anger. "Enough!" Adam yelled, and the birds flapped down again, landing on the iron chandelier above them that still had strands of cobwebs like wispy garland.

"Fok off!" yelled Drostan as he got in one more kick, the curse seeming to echo in the large room as silence fell.

Adam breathed in through his nose. "First off, there will be no drinking whisky tonight," he said, his gaze moving to pin each of his brothers and Rabbie. "The whisky belongs to Lark, and she decides when it will be tapped. Second, is the bloody roof on above stairs?"

"Aye," Callum said. "For the most part. We are putting in the last windowpanes in the room way down on the left. Then we will replace the old thatch with rock."

Adam looked around at the pallets set against the walls on the stone floor of the great hall. "But the roof over the chief's bed chamber is sound?"

"Aye," Drostan said, touching his cheekbone where Callum had gotten in a punch. "Not too clean, but dry."

Adam turned to Lark. Her slender shoulders were hitched up high, and she pressed back against the stone wall. Her lush lips were pressed into a thin line, and she clutched her dagger in a tight fist. She stood surrounded by darkness and filth, and yet she did not weep or scream like Liam had said a woman would if any of them dared to bring one over to Ulva.

The *sgian dubh* disappeared into a pocket under Lark's skirt. She tipped her chin higher as she stared right back at him and stepped away from the wall. "Third," she said, her voice strong, "someone will find me a bathing tub. And fourthly, water will be brought up to... whatever chamber that has a full roof where I can sleep." She paused. "Without rats."

"There are no rats in the castle," Eagan said.

"No true bathing tub, though," Beck said.

"We have been using a sound trough that we cleaned out," Callum said and wiggled a tooth to see if it was loose.

"We can sit it in your room," Eagan said and jogged out the door. Adam noticed a slight softening of Lark's shoulders, but they still sat too high.

He grabbed one of the enclosed lamps that had oil in the base and lit it from a torch. "I will show ye above stairs." He took up her two satchels and walked toward the twisting stone steps. The workmanship on them had been perfectly stacked, so it had survived with little damage through the ages. Thank God for the meticulousness of the early Macquaries.

"This way," he said and listened to the *squish, squish,*

squish of water and mud saturating her slippers as she followed. The rain had made the night even worse. Was she thinking about escape? Or perhaps revenge? He held the lamp high to light the steps so she wouldn't trip. He opened his mouth twice to tell her how structurally sound Gylin was. That a good cleaning would see the castle right again. That she would help him bring it and his clan back to life. But in the dark, with the rain beating outside the open arrow slits as they passed, any words would likely make things worse.

It was enough that she was following him. At least for the moment.

They reached the top of the curving tower of stairs, and he stopped before the wooden door of the chief's chamber that stood on the right, a long corridor of smaller, empty rooms off to the left. Even though he'd slept below with his brothers, he had planned to move into the chief's room. Although he doubted it would be that eve.

"This is the chamber," he murmured and pushed inside. He held his breath and thanked the lord when nothing scurried or fluttered or dripped as he stood there. "Welcome."

Chapter Five

Lark stood in the center of the filthy bedchamber. Her eyes trailed along a dusty tapestry hung haphazardly on the far wall that was so full of dust and soot, she couldn't see the stitched depiction. An enormous bed jutted out from the wall with the door. Curtains, which probably contained a century's worth of dust, surrounded it.

If she slept in it after her bath, she'd need another in the morning. She was no pampered lady unused to toil, but the Montgomerie House, which she had run, was spotlessly clean. Comparatively, this was a decaying grave of a dwelling. Could spirits of dead Macquaries watch, despising her for intruding? She looked up and released her breath. At least there was a ceiling of timber eves without dripping holes or birds.

Adam said nothing more, as per his usual. Lark's face tightened, her gaze landing on him. "No one else lives on this isle," she repeated from downstairs. "No other Macquaries or MacDougalls? No castle cook or maid or blacksmith or priest. And no women? At all?"

Lark kept her voice even, tamping down her temper with the last of her strength, and walked over to Adam. She stopped in front of him, tipping her head back to meet his eyes. "At all?" she repeated. She waved her hand. "Not including the old woman your brothers have labeled a witch."

His lips pinched together. "Not currently."

She inhaled the dust-heavy air and glanced around the catastrophe of the room. Anger, disappointment, and something that felt like betrayal rolled around inside her. "How long has the isle been abandoned?"

Adam cupped the back of his neck. "The castle...a score and four years. The village...for the most part, a century or more. The town was abandoned because of superstitions, forcing the Macquaries to live on Mull under the hospitality of the Macleans." His words came slow. When silence stretched out, he dropped his arms by his sides and continued. "Many Macquaries married into the Maclean clan, leaving only a few of us left. My father was the last chief. He tried to retake the isle two decades ago. We lived on it for a few years, but then my mother died birthing Eagan. Da moved us back to Mull because my aunt convinced him it was unsafe for his sons."

Lark looked toward the once grand bed. Did his mother die in it? Had anyone cleaned away the birthing or had they all packed up and left that day? She shivered at the thought.

Adam cleared his throat. "Slowly my father's desire to re-strengthen the Macquarie clan grew stronger than his grief for his wife and worry about us. He raised the five of us to one day come back here, to rebuild." His words grew firmer.

"Rabbie MacDougall was his friend and stayed on with us when Da died last winter. The five of us swore to bring the isle back to life when we buried Da here, so we began as soon as the snow melted."

Lark watched the lines of shadow across Adam's face.

He looked...tired. For several long seconds, silence sat between them as her numb mind pieced the bits she'd learned together into a picture. "And you went in search of a wife," she whispered. "Like you said at the festival."

"'Tis time for Wolf Isle to be re-established and the Macquarie clan to grow in number and strength again," Adam said, his hands fisting against his kilted thighs. Determination hardened his face, cut by shadows and firelight from the lamp.

"So...you got yourself a woman." Her gaze slid to a large armoire. If she opened it, would his mother's old clothes still be in there undisturbed from the night she died? Did her spirit haunt the castle? Cold slid up Lark's spine, and she turned in a tight circle, her arms wrapped tightly around herself.

"Not just any woman," Adam said, making her gaze stop on him. "A woman with strength, an instinct for family, someone who can help build a home."

"You know nothing about me." How could he when he'd only met her three and a half days ago?

He took a step closer, and she braced herself not to back up. "Ye bravely handled the bandits," he said. "Ye took care of four sisters after your mother died, and ye ran her home. That all speaks to your abilities and talents, lass." He stopped before her. "And the rest I will learn in time."

Oh, Anna! She missed her and her little sisters even more in the shadow of such disappointment. Lark looked up, meeting his gaze. "And what have I learned about you, Adam, over these two days of silence?" she asked, trying to keep her words firm and strong.

"I have brought the tub," Callum said with a grunt, but Lark held Adam's gaze.

Behind him, his brother pushed an animal trough in through the bedchamber door. Callum set it before the hearth and strode over to where they still stared at each other. He stopped to look between them. "Well...I will leave ye two to keep looking at each other like there may be a murder tonight." He dipped down slightly, his gaze shifting between them. "Adam, from what I see," he whispered, "your bride is winning."

"Get out," Adam said, breaking the stare to glare at Callum.

"We have the water," Drostan said as he, Eagan, and Beck marched in with three large buckets of water.

Lark turned to the tub. It looked damp from what she hoped was a fresh scrubbing.

"There is a heating cauldron in the trough," Callum called. "Come on." He waved his brothers to follow him out, the floor creaking with each step. "Let us leave the newly-married couple to themselves." The door shut behind the last of them, and Lark could hear them stomping down the stairs.

Did they think this was humorous? This trickery to bring a woman to the isle?

You demanded that he marry you. She closed her eyes on the painful truth. Her head dipped, and she let her face rest in her hands, letting out an audible sigh.

Adam strode over to crouch before the hearth, and she turned her face to watch him. His shoulders were broad, the muscles in his biceps pressing against the confines of the rain-dampened tunic he wore. Even performing a menial task of starting a fire, the man was brawny. Her cheeks warmed as she remembered the way they had touched each other the night before. Would being stranded with no one but him be all that bad? Right then, exhausted and angry, she could not decide.

It took him long minutes to get the damp peat started, but he didn't curse, just kept working until he had results. Adam stood, turning toward her, the growing fire behind him casting him in darkness. "It should heat the room and the water."

She walked toward him to reach the fire and held her hands out to the growing flames. "Adam?"

"Aye?"

"Where will you be sleeping?" she asked, turning to look at him across the room.

The light cast him in dim gold. He looked pained as he met her gaze. "I hope one thing ye have learned about me, Lark, is that I will not touch ye unless ye wish it."

She met his gaze. "You could have warned me, Adam. On the ride…while we ate at the fire…before you…before we kissed in the tent."

He knocked his fists together, one on top of the other. "Rabbie thought it best not to tell ye anything more in case that made ye run away from us on the journey here."

"And you thought listening to Rabbie was the wisest course of action?" she asked, her voice rising despite her wish to remain calm and uncaring.

"Nay," he said and dropped his hands. His gaze penetrated her own. "Do ye… Will ye leave here now that ye know? Seek an annulment?"

Leave there? How exactly could she? "I am surrounded by water." She flung her hand out toward the dark window flanked by heavy curtain. "Where would I go?"

"If ye wish, I will take ye back to your father," he said.

Her heart sped, and she swallowed against the terror wedging itself into her throat. She would never return to Roylin's house. And her neighbors would not take her in after what he had spouted while drunk. They would say that Adam had turned her out. That she'd begged him to wed her, and then he'd turned her away when he discovered her past.

Adam's face was grim. Could she ask him to help her find a safe place to live on her own? *Even prostitutes live in houses with other ladies. No Montgomerie lass is living alone.* Roylin's words twisted inside her.

"I could speak with Tor Maclean about finding ye a place at a cloister, or perhaps my aunt could take ye in," he said. They stared at one another, Adam waiting for her next words and Lark waiting to figure out what they should be.

She had said she was used to hard work, vowed to be his wife until death, and begged him to marry her. She drew a deep breath. "I will stay until I can figure out what to do." And see how big an omission Adam had made.

Rap. Rap. They both turned to the door, which slowly opened. "Lark?" It was Beck. His gaze went from her to the tub, touching briefly on Adam. "Callum forgot to ask…"

"Any of you could have asked," came a voice from behind.

"She and Adam were having a conversation," said another.

"They were not even talking when I walked in." It sounded like Eagan.

"It was a silent, staring, frowning conversation."

"Ye see," Beck said, raising his voice over the others in the hall. "We would…I mean, we usually take a bath in the order oldest to youngest. Of course, ye can go first. Not that we think ye are older than Adam," he finished quickly.

"Not that Adam is old," one of the brothers called. "He is the perfect age for a husband."

Lark saw Adam's eyes go to the ceiling like he was beseeching help from the angels. The brothers, her brothers now, thought to use the bath like her sisters did, one at a time to wash in the same water. The difference here, though, was that instead of her bathing last because of her servant status in Roylin's house, she was afforded warm, unmuddied water.

She sighed and glanced at the rafters above. No angels sat amongst the cobwebs.

• • •

Whoever said things looked better in the morning had never visited Wolf Isle. Lark finished plaiting her still-damp hair as she looked out at the heavy clouds over the white-capped ocean.

The wavy glass panes in the window kept out the wind and rain but not the feeling of isolation and imprisonment. She was on an isle, surrounded by angry sea, trapped with six men. "And one witch," she whispered. Restless sleep in a room, in the very same bed, where a woman had died, made the weight of the morning feel even greater.

She rubbed her hands down her face. *I can laugh or I can weep.* "Or I can stab someone," she said to the empty room. With the dawn, she'd crawled from the heavy blankets. They were relatively clean considering the twenty-five years of neglect coating the rest of the chamber. And there had been no evidence of birthing, thank the good Lord.

She walked to the hearth that she'd stirred back to life and ran a finger along the intricately carved mantel. The line through the dust revealed a deep, polished oak with vines and flowers carved within it. She sighed. "What beauty lies beneath all this dirt?"

Her gaze drifted about the room. With the increasing light of morning, she picked out more carvings: along the bedposts, the headboard, a heavy trunk made of beech wood, and the wardrobe.

Lark dodged the tub where her brothers had bathed after her while she waited on the steps, the water now a cold, murky pool to be emptied. Stopping before the wardrobe, she tugged the worn knobs, and the hinges creaked with misuse. Several gowns hung there, likely Adam's mother's. She could alter one to use. Lark had hemmed and cinched her own mother's gowns for her sisters.

But the item that brought a smile to her face, the first one since setting foot on Ulva, was a pair of boots tucked in the corner. Pulling them out, she examined the well-worked, soft leather. She hurried to sit on the bed, shaking them upside down first to make sure nothing lived within them, and forced them onto her stockinged feet. They were only a little snug and would stretch with further wear.

Laced up, she stood and grabbed her shawl. "Best to see how bad it is," she said. Despite the dread that had enveloped her in her exhaustion last night, she was curious. An abandoned village? What treasures might lie in it like the carvings under the dust of the mantel? Even if her marriage sat on the shifting ground of omission, she could forge ahead to find answers for herself. Her mother had taught her to go undaunted into life, making the most of what she had and striving for happiness despite the ugliness around her.

The turning stairwell was dark with only a few window slits around every second turn. They were open to the outside, letting in the dank coolness of morning. She would inspect the situation today. Then what? Adam had offered to take her to Mull. She could ask for an annulment. Could she buy a cow and make butter to sell? What other talents did she have? Reading, writing, and taking care of children. Did Mull need a teacher? Would they let her live alone unharassed?

Letting a deep breath out in a whoosh, she entered the great hall but found it empty. Pallets were stacked along one wall. "At least they are not still abed." She walked around the room, inspecting the two tapestries that clung to the stone walls like exhausted prisoners chained there. *Take outside and beat.* Her gaze shot into the hearth as a list started to form in her head. *Sweep and fix the grate and spit.* She straightened, her gaze going to the cobwebs in the chandeliers and in each of the wells around the windows. Cut through and paned, that sat way up high. *Dust and sweep everywhere.* Hands on her hips, she turned slowly, her gaze dropping to the entryway at the far end. Her inhale stopped.

Adam stood there, watching her. "Have ye eaten?"

"No." It was then she noticed that there were two oat bannocks on a plate set on the table, and the dirty dishes from the night before had been removed.

He indicated a cup next to the plate. "The milk is fresh. Eagan traded for a milk cow while I was gone."

I can make butter. The thought was a mere whisper against the tether of Adam's gaze.

"Did ye sleep well?" he asked, pushing off the wall where he'd been leaning to walk to the table. "The bedding should have been fresh."

"Yes," she said, keeping her spot near the blackened hearth. She was definitely not telling him how she kept the covers over her head and listened for spirits.

"I will send my brothers up to empty the bathing trough, but we have no servants to see to the privy pot and washstand."

"I have never had servants, something I think you likely deduced by meeting my family at the festival," she said. "'Twas what you were searching for, was it not? A woman who could work hard for you without complaint or lofty expectations?" Lord, she sounded like a shrew.

Adam picked up the plate and cup and walked it over, stopping before her. "Ye chose me."

Heat surged up Lark's neck into her cheeks as her anger erupted. "To escape. Yes, I was desperate and foolish in gambling to win my freedom when in fact..." She spun around, her arms wide to indicate the room. "I have landed in prison anyway." Her voice had risen until the birds overhead were startled enough to fly and flap. *You chose me.*

She caught her face in her hands, a hollow feeling inside at her own selfish-sounding tirade. Taking a deep inhale, she turned around and froze. The look on Adam's face... It was as if he'd transformed into the granite that surrounded them, hard and severe, yet there was something like pain in the tightness of his eyes that made her chest feel hollow. A movement at the edge of her gaze made her glance to the archway where Beck, Callum, and Drostan stood. How much had they heard?

Her gaze returned to her husband. "Adam…"

He set the plate and cup on the floor at his feet since there was no table nearby, pivoted on his heel, and walked to where his brothers waited awkwardly.

Beck nodded to him. "We need help setting the window in the tower room, but the roof is nearly finished." His voice was solemn, devoid of his usual cheerfulness. *Blast it.*

Lark felt her shoulders sag, and she exhaled. As the Macquaries turned away, disappearing into the darkness of the arch, she sunk to the floor, crouching on her heels to pick up the plate and cup. But she stayed there, bowing her head as she held them.

He should have said something on the way here.

• • •

"Thank the good Lord she picked ye," Beck said after the four of them finished climbing silently to the hall above.

"At least she is not weeping," Callum said. "I never know what to do when a lass weeps."

Drostan plopped his hand on Adam's shoulder and shook his head. "I do not see any bairns coming along soon."

"Hold your tongues," Adam said, his voice low in warning. "None of this is your concern."

"I suppose it is if we want to repopulate the isle," Callum said with a grin. He was asking for a fist in his bloody smile.

Drostan removed his hand and nodded to Beck. "I guess ye better be finding a wife soon then."

Beck frowned. "No need to tie ourselves to wives in order of oldest just because Adam fell into the trap. I may start sailing with Cullen MacDonald."

"'Tis a bonnie trap, though," Eagan said, glancing behind him as if he wished Lark stood there.

"Enough," Adam said, going over to grab one side of the window frame.

"I suppose if ye have not consummated the union yet, one of us could woo her," Callum said, his foolish smile tipping Adam over the edge. He nearly dropped the window, its iron frame banging on the floorboards. In two strides he had his fist under Callum's chin as he rammed him backward into the plastered wall.

"No one is trying to woo Lark. She is my wife. If ye so much as wink—"

"Fok, Adam, I was jesting," Callum said. His wide eyes narrowed. "It takes more than a jest to make our serious chief-brother lose control of himself."

Adam pushed a little harder and dropped his fist. He glared at Callum, the biggest rogue of the family. "So much as a wink," he said, leaving the consequence off.

Adam walked back to the window, the muscles in his back stiff. "That goes for all of ye." He ignored the looks shooting between his brothers. Let them think what they wanted, but Lark was not someone they should notice as anything other than a sister. Unfortunately, she was unavailable to him as well. *Bloody hell.*

Chapter Six

Lark washed her hands at the stone-encircled well set in the
bailey, her gaze following a flitting bird. It looked as if the
brown sparrow might settle on the dead willow tree, but then
it swooped higher, avoiding the snapping reach of its leafless
limbs.

Drying her hands in a tattered apron she had found,
Lark walked around the tree, staying outside the dancing
curtain. Her shoulders raised high as hairs on her nape rose.
Although most of the trees outside the castle walls had green
buds or leaves, the willow had none. Black knots sat where
buds should have been sprouting.

She peered closely at a black-handled dagger that was
stabbed into the trunk. The metal protruding from the slice
was gritty with rust. She'd have sworn the tree was dead
except sap still ran down from the wound, making it look
very much like the tree was bleeding. A shiver gripped her
shoulders as she stared.

"I would not touch it," came a voice, making Lark leap
back, her hand slapped over her galloping heart.

She twisted around to see the youngest brother, Eagan, standing with his arms crossed. "Holy Mother Mary, you gave me a fright."

"Apologies," he said, brushing his hair from his eyes. "Just..." He tipped his head toward the tree. "The blade is still sharp."

"Why is it stuck there?"

His lips pinched tight as if he were afraid an answer would jump out. He met her stare for a long moment, waiting for her to look away, but she didn't. Lark had inherited her mother's penetrating gaze along with her red-hued hair and did not back down easily.

"A witch put it there a century ago," he said. "It killed the tree."

Another witch? She turned back to the tree. "Why?"

"We think the blade was bewitched with poison."

"I mean, why would a witch stab your tree?"

"It is said that the willow was big and green and beautiful." He shrugged. "To her it represented our clan, so she killed it."

Lark looked between the tree and Adam's brother. "A witch walked in here and killed your tree."

"Aye."

"Well, there has to be a reason she did that. Is that why everyone moved away?"

More birds flew overhead, avoiding the dead tendrils. Eagan turned away from her. "Ye have a lot of questions."

"Questions are good," she said, following him across the bailey. "I think we should all be asking more questions. Such as, should we bring women to our isle before the roof of the castle is whole?" Brows raised high, she pointed back at the tree. "Or why don't we cut down the dead tree with a bleeding knife wound in the middle of the bailey?"

"We cannot cut it down," he said, without looking at her.

"Why?" she asked. "Does it scream?"

"I…I do not know," he said, picking up a bucket. "Ye need to ask Adam."

At the moment, she didn't want to talk to Adam. She might say something foolish like "I am leaving" or "Kiss me again." Both demands had been jumping around in her thoughts all morning.

"Where is he?" she asked.

"Finishing up the roof in the last room."

Good. Lark traipsed to a door set into the wall. It was only big enough for a man to go through. A heavy wooden bar sat across it, but she put her weight into heaving it across to drop on the ground and yanked the door open.

"Where are ye going?" Eagan called.

"You cannot answer my questions, so I cannot answer yours." Yes, she was being spiteful, but her irritation at the lack of explanations was making her into a shrew.

"Rabbie and Callum hid the rowboat," Eagan yelled down. "And the barge is too heavy for a lass to push."

More anger licked up inside Lark as she traipsed down the path. "'Tis a good thing I know how to swim."

So Adam did not expect her to keep her wedding vows. Blasted man. He thought she would run away without a word.

Clutching her skirt high as she marched toward the village behind the castle, she calmed herself enough to appreciate the way the recently found boots gripped the pebbles and damp boulders. *Thank you, Lady Macquarie.*

Lark glanced over her shoulder several times to see if anyone followed. So far, the path through the grass was deserted. Gylin Castle rose high, perching on the edge of the sea. Even with years of neglect, it was impressive, a formidable defense against…who? There was no one here. She huffed and continued, swinging her arms to help propel her up the rise. Stopping at the top, Lark surveyed the sprawling village below.

Air left her lungs slowly as her gaze scanned the remains

of nearly forty dwellings nestled in the shallow valley along a winding pebble road. Thatching remained on a few, but most were missing their roofs, except for a handful she could see that had stone covers.

"There must be things to salvage," she said to herself, clutching her shawl around her shoulders. At least she could pick out the chapel, its simple cross still in place on the apex over the open door. Perhaps she could find a cottage for Anna's bakery. Maybe she and her sisters could come right away and live in the village. Would Roylin let them go? Pressure in her chest made it hard to swallow. *I miss you, Anna.*

The first rows of time-worn cottages loomed up on either side of the path, hiding the rest of the town from view as she walked cautiously. The wind blew between them, scattering last winter's decay in small gusts. The loneliness of the empty village made her miss her sisters even more. She stopped, blinking back tears. *I will write Anna a letter today.*

A whistle made Lark jerk around. "The wind," she whispered, her voice sounding odd in the hauntingly vacant place. She straightened her spine and peeked inside a roofed cottage at the wooden floors, some of them yanked up along the back wall. The dark hearth looked sound enough. Leaves lay scattered inside, and one of the windowpanes was broken. Was it a happy home at one time? Laughter and smiles, the aroma of fresh tarts baking and a da bouncing a wee one on his knee before the fire? She stared wistfully, bringing forth the old fantasy she used to create in her head.

She closed the heavy door of the cottage to walk on. Three more dwellings flanked her, their empty windows like eye holes in skulls. Something banged with a gust of wind, making her jump. "A broken shutter," she whispered. But then her breath caught, a gasp perched on her tongue, at the sound of...giggling.

Lark's gaze shifted, her wide eyes scanning the broken

cottages. "Who is there?" she called, but her voice in the wind-washed silence just added to the tickle of unease teasing her nape. It had sounded like a child's laugh. But what child would live out here amongst cottage bones? Could it be Grissell, the witch? "Come out," she called. The shutter banged again several paths over, making her jump.

She spun toward Gylin, but halted on the balls of her feet, as a white cat ducked into the old church. Had a family of felines remained after Adam's father had moved them back to Mull years ago? If so, the cottages would likely be filled with cats.

"Kitty?" she called, her voice sounding intrusive amongst the broken and abandoned.

Meow. The soft cry coming from the old church called her forward. "Kitty, kitty," she said, her voice softer as if she did not wish to disturb any restless spirits. Giggling restless spirits.

The roof of the church was still intact, the windows blocked, making it pitch black inside. Lark held onto the open doorframe and leaned in, blinking for her eyes to adjust. "Where are you?"

Meow.

Hands before her, Lark took one step at a time inside. The room was even colder than outside, the night air trapped within, and she shivered, gooseflesh popping up under her sleeves.

Meow. Lark turned to the right, her arm swinging out as she caught sight of the cat's white coat dashing between two rows of pews. Her hand caught something hanging in the room. Rough, it scraped along her knuckle, and she jerked back, eyes opening wide, terror lodged in her throat.

There before her, swaying ever so slightly, dangled the wrapped figure of a person.

• • •

Adam jogged down the three steps leading from the keep. Unfortunately, his brothers followed.

"Ye do not think she would actually try to swim, do ye?" Callum asked beside him.

Eagan shook his head, running forward so Adam could see him. "She turned toward the village, not the water, after I told her the boat was gone and she couldn't push the barge on her own."

Bloody hell. "Ye had to tell her that," Adam said, frowning at his youngest brother. How would Lark come to trust him if she thought of him as her jailor?

"Fool," Beck said to Eagan. "Now she really feels like a prisoner."

"I am not the one who wanted to move the boat," Eagan said.

"We can move the boat," Beck shot back, "but ye do not tell Lark about it. She would have seen that it was not moored and come back to the castle."

"She was asking about the willow tree and the blade sticking in it," Eagan said.

"What did ye tell her?" Adam asked, stopping to turn toward the ugly monument to his clan's failing. The long, dead branches blew in the sea breeze that dashed over the walls.

"Nothing," Eagan said. "And that made her mighty mad." He ran his fingers through his hair. "I told her she would have to ask ye about it. When she asked me where ye were, I thought she would go back in to find ye, but she marched in the opposite direction."

"*Mo chreach*," Adam swore and strode to the short doorway in the wall. He stopped in his tracks as a piercing scream tore through the wind, like an arrow shot straight into his gut. It was distant. It held terror. It was Lark!

"Foking hell," Adam yelled, taking off in a sprint toward

Ormaig. His heart thudded in his ears as warrior fire shot through his veins. His boots ate up the distance along the path that would lead to the shallow valley behind the castle.

"'Tis the curse!" Drostan yelled.

Where was she? "Spread out," Adam ordered. "Yell when ye find her."

Adam ran to the first roofless cottage. His hands caught on the doorframe as he leaned in. A sweep of his gaze showed it to be empty. Another scream rent the air, and he threw himself back. "Lark!" She was close, but where?

Up ahead a white cat trotted out of the old chapel. The creature stared at him, its tail high and flicking. Without any logical reasoning, he ran toward it, barely noting its hiss as he stormed into the dark room.

The chapel's glass windows were covered with several layers of old cloth. "Lark?" he yelled, his voice filling the hallow vault.

"I am here." Her voice caught his breath, and his face turned blindly toward the sound. *Meow.* The white cat slid inside along the one wall where an altar still stood. "Watch out for the...it is hanging...I fell. Down here."

Adam turned in a circle, his gaze catching on an object swaying from a rope. He rushed toward it, sheathing his sword to catch the figure there. "Lark!" But the heavy, wrapped shape was cold. He backed away as it swung. "Bloody hell!" It was a body.

Callum ran up to the door. "Is she in here?" But before Adam could answer, his brother saw the swinging body. "God's balls!" he yelled, running in.

"Lark? Where are ye?" Adam asked, turning his back on the macabre shadow. It wasn't Lark. Lark was warm with life. Lark smelled of flowers and fresh spring wind, not decay.

"In a hole in the floor."

"Keep talking, so I can find ye."

"I...I followed the cat inside and saw...whoever that is hanging. I ran to grab the cat and fell. I am on..." Her voice wavered as if she was trembling. "Adam, I think I am sitting on bones."

"Damnit! Light a torch," Adam called to Callum as Beck showed up in the doorway. "Light a bloody torch." Adam's voice boomed in the echoing room. He dropped to his knees as his brothers fumbled with their flint and bit of wool.

Adam scanned the darkness and felt his way forward. The white cat trotted before him, and he followed the bright color where it stopped, hunched as if on the lip of a hole. "Keep talking."

"I...I am sure they are bones," she said.

"Here," Beck called, running back in with a lit torch, dissolving the thick shadows in an instant.

Before Adam was a series of broken wooden slats that had been the chapel floor. Right over his great-great-grandfather's remains. *Och* but Lark was sitting on the broken bones of Chief Wilyam Macquarie.

Lark focused on the light that poured down the hole. She didn't want to look beneath her. When she'd first fallen in, she'd realized she'd broken through a wooden box, but it wasn't until she'd felt the splintered bones that she'd understood it was a coffin.

Heart pounding, she clutched her hands to her chest and focused on Adam's face far above. She'd never been so happy to see another human being in all her life.

"I will get ye out," Adam said. "Do not move."

"Move?" she said. "Where would I move?"

Beck's face appeared next to Adam's. "She broke through a coffin." Behind him another brother cursed.

"Are ye hurt?" Adam asked.

"Your mother saved me," she said, watching Beck's frown grow to match Adam's, as if they wondered if she'd lost her mind. "Her boots…well, I am assuming the boots I found were hers. I hit feet first, and the boots took the brunt of the fall." *I will be sore.* And she would be taking another bath after sitting on someone's century old bones. Although fresh bones would have been more gruesome.

"Please get me out of here," she called.

Adam leaped upright. Behind him, something heavy hit the floor. Lark swallowed hard as Adam looked over his shoulder.

"Who is it?" she called, but the sound of something being dragged outside likely explained why no one answered.

"Use the rope," another brother said, making her shiver. They were going to give her the rope that had wrapped around another's neck. If curses were real, surely it would reside in a rope that hung a person.

"Is there no other rope?" she asked, as it dropped down, nearly hitting the top of her head. No one answered.

She rocked back to get her boots under her, without using her hands, and braced her feet to stand. Her boot heel slipped as one of the bones shifted under it, and she yelped, her hands grasping frantically at the dangling rope. She caught it, clutching it to stop herself from falling back onto the splintered remains.

"Put your foot in the loop," Adam said. Rucking up her skirt, she did. The rope tightened around her foot like it had around the neck of the poor soul above. Keeping her leg straight and holding on with her hands, Adam and Beck lifted her out of the tomb. As her head cleared the floorboards, she realized the rope was long enough to loop over the rafter above the hole, so they were able to pull her straight up. Level with the broken floor, Beck braced himself, and Adam reached out toward her.

"Swing to me," he said.

She caught his gaze. "Do not let me fall back in there."

"I promise I will catch ye."

Did she trust him? It wasn't trust when one had no other choice. She nodded and took a deep breath.

"Lift your feet back and forth in the air," Beck said where he clutched the rope with two hands.

Lark lifted her legs under the skirt and then pushed them back. "One...two...three." Lark swung forward, and Adam's strong hands grabbed her waist. He pulled her against him, holding her there, and she released the rope.

Lark dropped her face to his shoulder, taking deep breaths to calm her heart. The faint smell of rosemary soap and leather came from his neck along with warmth, making her realize how cold she was. She didn't even know where her shawl had fallen. If it were down in the crypt, the skeleton could keep it.

Adam carried her outside, and she squinted against the bright daylight breaking through the clouds. "Are ye hurt?" He sat her down on the cap of an old well.

Lark blinked, focusing to stare directly into his stormy gray ones. They were growing familiar to her, and when he looked so intensely at her, a nervous energy rose into her belly. "I am well," she said.

"Ye should not have come here alone."

His words made sense, but the reprimand in his tone blew against the tendril of anger that still smoldered inside her. Lark shoved both of her palms hard against Adam's chest where he crouched before her. "And *you* should have told me that someone could be hanging in the village."

She hit him again. The force probably stung her palms more than it hurt the muscular wall of his chest, which only made her angrier, and she hit him again in rapid succession.

"That there were graves to fall into..." She grabbed his shoulders as if to shake them but realized that she wasn't able to move the mountain that was Adam Macquarie.

"Bloody hell," she yelled, letting fury override her trembling. "Is there anything else you need to inform me about? Anything at all?"

"Adam, come see this," Drostan called from where he knelt over the body.

She poked Adam's chest with her finger. "Omission is lying. You are going to answer all my questions and even ones I do not ask."

He gave a small nod and rose to walk over to the body wrapped tightly in a woolen blanket. How could someone hang themselves while all wrapped up like that? Or had a second person done it? The body was small. Could it be a murdered woman or, worse, a child?

Adam and his brothers crouched around the prone figure, pulling the blanket away. Beck stood, looking down. As the brothers sat back on their heels, Beck looked her way, his face still grim. "It is a poppet."

"What?" she said, hurrying over even with the soreness in her knees. She stared down at the painted face of a doll. The blanket lay open, exposing sticks and clumps of peat tied together in the shape of arms and legs. Stones sat inside the blanket, giving it the weight of a human body. Grasses were braided, to look like hair, and tied to tanned leather that was painted to look like a face. Even though it was not a person, the figure was gruesome, and goose flesh rose again on Lark's arms.

"Why would someone do this?" Callum asked, staring down at the doll.

"A better question is..." Lark lifted her gaze to Adam. "Who would do this?"

Chapter Seven

"Ye should take her back to Mull," Callum said where he ate across from Adam in the great hall. "It was definitely a warning against women being on the isle. Grissell must have heard that we are settling the village and castle again, looking for wives."

Adam glanced toward the stairs where Lark had gone after he'd walked her back from the village. She'd been above for two hours. "We are six strong Scotsman," he said. "And yet we would let one insane old woman stop us from rebuilding our clan?"

"Damn, Adam," Callum cursed and looked back down at his plate. "It was bloody creepy."

"And she pulled up the floorboards of the church to find Wilyam Macquarie's grave?" Beck asked. "How? It was built under the church so the witch couldn't desecrate it. 'Tis consecrated ground."

"We found other holes dug throughout the village," Drostan said. "Like she was looking for him even though his marker was in the church."

"How the hell could an old woman dig holes or get that thing tied up in the chapel?" Callum asked.

"Help from the Devil?" Eagan asked, but a slight grin made it more of a jest.

Callum's brows rose. "'Tis a possibility. We should have a priest come here to bless the isle and village."

Rabbie passed the sign of the cross before him. "We need to carry Grissell off this isle."

"And what?" Adam asked. "Burn her to keep her from coming back?"

"If she is a witch," Rabbie said. "We can find a witch hunter to check her."

"They accuse and doom anyone who is different to the flames or water," Adam said. "I will not rebuild our clan on the blood of an old woman." He let his gaze slide to each of his brothers and Rabbie, looking for a challenge. Only Rabbie looked obstinate. "We will find out why and how Grissell did this then reason with her or exile her."

Rabbie stared at the brothers. "Ye think ye can handle carrying one old woman off the isle?"

"Not if she poisons us with a touch or calls demons to carry us away," Callum said and bit into a bannock.

Adam gathered some oat cakes and smoked fish onto a plate. He pushed back from the table.

"If ye are going up to Lark," Beck said, "ask her if she knows how to bake tarts. I am getting bloody tired of bannocks." Eagan, the one brother who had any sense in the kitchen, threw one of the bannocks across the table, smacking Beck in the forehead. It exploded into oat crumbs to pock his face and lodge in his hair.

History predicted a messy brawl would ensue. Adam walked toward the dark stairs. He didn't know what he'd say to Lark. Certainly not, "Can you bake tarts?" But he needed to make sure her trembling had stopped. *Damnit*. Despite her slapping at him and poking him in the chest, she had been shaking like a sparrow who had been dropped by a cat. Did Lark worry that the poppet was meant to be her?

He paused before the chief's door. *Rap. Rap.* "'Tis Adam."

"I am well," she said from inside.

"Can I enter? I have food and drink."

"You can leave it outside the door, or you can enter if you also have answers to my questions."

Releasing a full breath, he pushed the door inward. The muted sun from the windows made it light enough to see even without a fire. Lark stood at one, peering out through the wavy glass panes. She had taken a shallow bath and fixed her braid that had been snagged falling into the crypt. Dark water spots, where she'd scrubbed, marked her dress.

Lark turned to him, her face firm. A few fiery red curls framed her high cheekbones.

"I heard giggling right before I saw the cat in the chapel doorway," she said, making him stop halfway across.

"Giggling? Laughter?" He still held the wooden plate of food.

"Yes, like a child. There was a banging sound, a shutter, I think. It was several cottages over. I convinced myself the laughter was the wind, but..." She walked to stop right before him. "Are there children on this isle?"

"None of which I am aware."

She took the plate from him and set it on the bed, which was still the cleanest part of the room.

"Unless Grissell, the witch of Wolf Isle, can break through floorboards, dig holes, and hoist a heavy poppet into the rafters by herself, the crone has help," she said. She picked up a dry bannock and bit off a piece, chewing. Swallowing, she set it down.

"Callum thinks she conjured help."

"Satan would not bother to play with poppets."

"Agreed," he said. "I will be riding to her cottage on the south side of the isle to talk with her."

"I am coming with you," Lark said, dropping her arms. Her mouth was firm, her face determined as if ready to argue if he refused her request. But he would rather have her with him than leave her back at Gylin Castle by herself.

"Aye, perhaps she would be more willing to speak with a woman. The few times we have come across her, she has fled or chanted as if to throw a curse on us."

"An act," Lark said.

Adam shrugged. "Cursing the cursed seems unnecessary."

Lark's frown relaxed a bit. "I thought you said you do not believe in curses."

"I believe people make curses real by believing in them."

She nodded. Thank God she did not seem frightened. Aye, Lark was made of sterner stuff. "Ulva Isle needs strong lasses, and ye are very brave."

She crossed her arms. "But not brave enough to try to swim across to Mull."

Mo chreach.

"Am I trapped on this isle?" she asked when he said nothing. She studied his eyes as if to catch any lies.

"Nay," he said.

"But the rowboat was hidden. Did you order that?"

"Nay."

"Did you know about it?"

Damn. "Aye."

"So, I am trapped on this isle."

"Nay, but Lark, I ask that ye give the isle a chance to grow on ye. It has so much potential. But I need people to believe in her."

"Her? Wolf Isle is a woman?"

"Nay," he said and glanced around, noting how time

and emptiness had saddened the place that used to be his parents' bedroom. "The land is fertile, the fields bonny, the bounty plentiful. Aye, I suppose it is a woman." He dropped his hands. "Life cannot flourish, and our clan cannot grow without a woman, Lark."

Her voice was low although she met his eyes. "This is what should have been happening on the journey here."

Did she mean instead of ravishing each other in the tent?

"Trust is the one thing I must have in a marriage. I told you that."

He nodded. "I will not lie to ye, lass."

She seemed to weigh his words. "You have said that there are no women on the isle but not why. Did Grissell scare them away with this curse?"

Adam walked to the hearth and looked up at the spot where his great-great-grandfather's sword rested. One of his brothers must have hung it back up. It belonged to Adam now as chief, although there was not much honor in the blade.

"Three generations ago, our great-great-grandfather wooed a lass on the far side of the isle. When he wed a different woman to form an alliance with another clan, the lass hung herself. Her mother blamed our ancestor, Wilyam Macquarie."

"The remains under the church floorboards?"

He turned to her, leaning against the mantel. "Aye. They were buried there so she could not desecrate his grave."

"And Grissell is keeping the threat of a curse alive? Why?"

"She is the dead lass's great-granddaughter."

Lark shook her head. "How could she be if her great-grandmother killed herself?"

Adam rubbed at the back of his neck. "'Tis a gruesome story, Lark."

"I doubt it is as gruesome as picking the dust of someone's

brittle bones out of my fingernails," she answered, holding her hand up, the flats of her nails toward him. "How is Grissell a descendant of Wilyam Macquarie?"

"The sorrowful lass was pregnant, large with child, when Wilyam left her to wed another, and she hung herself. Her mother found her soon after. The lass was dead but not the child moving within her. The woman lowered her daughter down and cut the bairn from her still-warm body. She raised the wee lass to hate the Macquaries, the same with every generation since. As far as we know, Grissell is the last one. She has no offspring."

"Unless they are hidden, running around and giggling while digging holes and hanging warnings about."

"It is possible, but they would be grandchildren by now."

Lark glanced up thinking. "So, Grissell has Macquarie blood within her. She is part of your clan."

"She does not take our name even if the blood is there."

He watched Lark nibble on her lip, the white edge of her teeth showing. "And the curse was against all women?" she asked. "It seems the grieving mother was punishing the wrong sex."

"She wanted Wilyam Macquarie to suffer the loss of his wife and clan. 'Twas worse than death. The people believed the curse when Wilyam's wife and daughter died in childbirth within the year. They began moving off isle. The Macquarie clan all but died out, intermarrying elsewhere. Even off Wolf Isle, lasses did not risk taking the Macquarie name in fear that the curse would follow them, killing any daughters born to them. It is possible that half the people on Mull are more Macquarie than Maclean."

Lark bent to pick up a second bannock and a piece of salted fish. "Fear is powerful, making people act irrationally. Love and pain can do the same." She shook her head. "Killing herself and almost her unborn child. There was more than sadness there. My mother cared for a woman once who lived with sorrow even when her life was far from desperate. It is an illness as deadly as consumption."

Lark ran her hand lightly over the large bed's coverlet as she walked toward the door of the room. "What will you do with Grissell when we find her?" Her eyes widened enough to show her concern. Did she think he would strike down an old woman?

"Exile if she will not listen to reason. Off the isle, and we would guard against her return," he said and watched her blink, her shoulders relaxing. He stopped before her. "Ye do not know my character yet, but I do not judge and execute someone unless they are trying to kill me or my family." Like the men from Captain Jandeau, whoever the devil he was.

She stepped out into the hall. "Will I ride my own horse?"

"I haven't a mount for ye yet."

She shrugged. "I have not ridden since I was small." She stepped lightly down the turning staircase. "So…what is your favorite color, how old are you, and do you like having cats about?" She turned to look up at him as he followed.

Adam breathed deeply, his shoulders relaxing. "Blue, nearly a score and ten, and no."

"Hmph," she said, turning forward again. "That will have to change."

"Very well," he said. "Green."

The light, brief chuckle he heard from her opened his chest and relaxed his tight mouth more than any cup of whisky. Such a small sound, but within it sat something so powerful. Hope.

• • •

Lark felt every shift and brush of Adam's body behind her as they rode across the open field of spring grasses. Even though he'd slept elsewhere, he'd touched every part of her in her dreams, leaving her achy when she woke.

In her sheltered life, Lark had only ever known men to try to take things from her. A kiss, a fumbling touch, her hand in marriage. Adam had taken her away when she'd asked, and he'd given her a taste of passion that now tormented her. But he had kept so much from her.

Will you tell him your secret? Anna's question twisted inside her. Lark's past was a plague upon her. Adam had kept secrets, and so would she.

They entered another copse of trees. Except for the trees near Gylin, most of Ulva was grassland moors and rocky outcroppings with small clusters of oak, beech, and evergreens. "I see no other willow trees on Ulva," she said, her words caught in the wind that shifted and swirled about them.

Adam let his horse wind among the tree trunks, his hands slowing its gait, letting his brothers ride farther ahead. "It is said that Wilyam's grandfather brought the small willow tree from the mainland when he built Gylin. Wilyam's father nurtured it, as did Wilyam. The long green foliage that the wind caught reminded the clan of the waves of the sea surrounding the isle. The Macquaries felt they were more of the sea than of earth. The tree reminded them of their freedom from the quarrels of France, Spain, England, and Scotland."

"And then it was stabbed and died," Lark said softly. She twisted in her seat to look at him. "Eagan said it cannot be cut down."

His gaze raised over her head. "Wilyam tried to chop it down when his wife and daughter died, then many Macquaries after him. It became a right of the new chief to come over to Ulva and try to yank out the knife and rid the isle of the dead willow until my father forbade us from trying."

"Why?" Lark couldn't imagine Adam, with his huge biceps and strong back, not being able to chop down a dead tree.

His gaze met hers. "Each person who tried ended up not being able to father a single child, lad or lass. Our grandfather tried to chop it down when my father was five years old. He never had another child. Each time, the ax would pitch chunks of wood out from the cut, but the chopper could never reach the middle of the trunk or push it over. It is said that by morning, the cuts would be healed. Our father made us swear an oath not to touch the tree or dagger."

"How much of that story is mere legend born of retellings and exaggeration?" she asked.

He shrugged his broad shoulders and met her gaze directly. "The tree is still standing even though it is a hated reminder of the fall of our clan. If it could be felled, it would have by now. Yet something keeps it standing in our bailey."

"A curse you do not believe." She watched the lowering of his brows. His eyes, in the light of day, were a deep gray color that looked almost green as they rode under the spring leaves. She could get lost staring into their stormy depths at the flecks of blue like tiny shards of blue glass.

"Nay, but I believe in my oaths to my father," he said. "I will not touch the tree or dagger until I have a brood of children." She watched him swallow, and he gazed back down at her. "I promised my father I would resurrect our clan here, and I will do what I must to see it happen."

Lark turned forward again, her gaze following the movement of a hare through the grass. "Have you and your brothers fathered any bastards or would you consider that?" She held her breath as he brought his mighty bay to a stop inside the tree line, his brothers ahead halfway across the wide moor.

"Lark," he said, his voice a low rumble. He waited, and

she knew he would wait until she looked at him.

She turned and he held her gaze, a small ache of awareness growing in her middle as he spoke. "I have no bastards and will have none. I *cannot*." The way he emphasized the last word strummed a chord of worry inside Lark.

"So you are trapped in this marriage if I choose not to have bairns," she said. "Because I forced you to wed me at Glencoe."

The horse began a slow walk as if they had all the time in the world to enjoy the spring afternoon. Adam's brothers had completely disappeared up ahead.

"When I was a lad of five, I decided to live in a tree," Adam said.

Apparently, he did not want to talk about her trapping him. "I thought you could not touch the tree," she said.

"'Twas another tree on Mull. I was angry at my ma for making me apologize to my aunt for telling her she was a mean old woman."

"Was she?" Lark asked.

"She still is and lives on Mull." Lark heard him inhale. "I left home and climbed a tree. My da told me to come down. So did my ma. A storm came up, and even Beck climbed up to try to pull me down when our ma said I would be struck dead by lightning. The rain came, yet I remained in the tree for two days before I decided I wanted to come down."

She glanced back at him. "Two full days? No food or water?"

"There was plenty of rainwater, and I had planned ahead to pack some bread and cheese, but pissing from the branches at night grew tiresome."

She snorted softly. "You must have driven your mother to throw cabbages at you."

"She almost did. Da said I had a determined streak that would see me living a long life. Ma thought I was a stubborn fool who would fall out of the tree and die at five years old."

"What does this have to do with me forcing you to marry me?" Lark asked.

"My parents were both right. I am determined and stubborn, and no one can ever make me do something that I do not want to do." She turned, and he met her gaze without blinking. "If I had not wanted to wed ye, I would have stolen ye away instead. So ye would not have to wed or take a nun's vows."

Her brows rose high. "With Fergus and Giles raising a party to go after you?"

"I am not afraid of jackanapes." She watched his gaze move out across the meadow. "I would have seen ye away and set up where ye wished to go. Instead, I married ye."

Her heart squeezed. "Why?"

His gaze dropped to her eyes, his eyebrow rising. The look bordered on seductive, and it increased the warmth growing in her middle. "I liked the way ye churned butter," he said.

She thought back to how she plunged the cream, fast and hard, and a flush rose up her neck. He looked back out over her head. "But if ye wish to leave here, I will petition for an annulment. Despite the boat being hidden, ye are not trapped on Ulva."

Not trapped? She'd been trapped her whole life. What did it feel like to have choices?

Callum called to them as his gray horse broke from the forest ahead. "There is smoke rising from one of the stone cottages on the edge of the south shore."

"Grissell," Lark said and leaned forward as Adam pressed his bay into a canter.

Adam slowed them to a walk when they reached his brothers before the cottage. He circled it once and stopped near the front door. The dwelling had a curved stone roof that made it look like a giant mushroom. The front door was rounded to match and remained shut as if trying to keep out the world. A large, well-tended garden sat off to one side where it would catch the southern sun. Flustered chickens hurried into the woods, flapping their useless wings. A milk cow and two sheep stood in pens, but there were no barns to be seen.

"I will talk to her," Adam said.

"And have her spit, chant, and disappear again?" Lark said. "'Tis time to try something else."

Adam dismounted and helped Lark down. "Grissell," he called. "Come out to explain your actions against the Macquaries." His voice was like thunder, full of power and vengeful promise.

Eventually, the door opened inward. A hunched woman with a long white braid over her shoulder walked out using a carved tree limb as a crutch. She definitely looked like a witch with her bent frame and weathered face. But it seemed she could barely lift herself, let alone a doll fashioned of rocks and peat.

The woman's milky eyes fell on her. "Mighty brave, lass," she said and smiled to show surprisingly intact teeth. "Coming to the cursed isle of wolves."

"There are no wolves here." Lark's arm swept out toward the cow and sheep. "For your pens would do little to stop them from eating your animals."

Adam stood beside Lark. "And there is not a curse on this isle. What there is, however, is a woman who continues to hold a grudge over wrongs committed over a century ago, wrongs that have nothing to do with the current Macquarie clan."

The woman met Adam's lethal frown with one of her own. Such bravery. She stood alone before five large Macquaries and one fit MacDougall without flinching as if she had weathered much worse.

"My great-grandmother's curse stands," she said. "Until Macquaries learn the truth about love."

"Witch!" Rabbie yelled. She smiled wickedly in reply.

"What truth is that?" Lark asked. "There are many regarding love. Love is patient, love is kind, love gives instead of taking, love requires sacrifice and compromise and trust. I am certain there are more." She felt the Macquaries looking at her, but she kept her gaze on Grissell. "Which truth must they learn?"

Even Grissell looked unsure for several heartbeats until her face relaxed into a toothy grin. "All of them for the curse to lift."

Lark shook her head. "But how will you know if one is learned?"

"I do not lift the curse," Grissell said. "It lifts itself when the payment is met."

Lark let her arms go wide and looked around the clearing. "So this curse…it hovers around and watches us to see if one of these descendants learns all these truths?"

Grissell frowned and waved her one free hand. "I do not know how it works, but Macquaries will not have a strong clan again until these five, the great-great-grandsons of Wilyam Macquarie, learn all the truths about love."

"We should make a list, then," Lark said. "So they can cross them off once completed." She looked at the brothers. "I suppose you will all need to find women, then, in which to fall in love."

"To break the curse?" Rabbie asked, his voice stilted.

Lark nodded. "It seems the logical plan." She pointed at Rabbie. "Lucky for you that you are a MacDougall." The old man's eyes blinked shut for a moment as if relief robbed him of his Scot's strength.

Lark turned back to the woman. "The Macquaries want

to build a strong clan but cannot with a curse scaring people away." She flipped a hand toward the brothers. "Mistress Grissell says the curse will lift once all five of you learn about love, and it is not going to happen with just me on the isle. So yes, wives would be a start." She frowned, glancing between each of the large brothers. "Unless any of you want to take the holy vows of a priest. Then your love would be only for God." She looked back at Grissell. "It should exclude him, would it not?"

They all stared at Lark. Eagan cleared his throat. "I…I do not want to be a priest."

"Nor I," Callum said.

Drostan and Beck shook their heads, pinched expressions in place.

Lark smiled. "Then wives for all, and you, Mistress Grissell, will stop trying to frighten people away from Wolf Isle." Lark looked at Adam. "Maybe you should stop calling it Wolf Isle."

"I have done nothing to frighten anyone away," Grissell said, her gaze steady as she met Lark's.

Lark's eyebrow rose. "You have not made a doll to look like a hanged woman? Or dug holes to find the bones of Wilyam Macquarie?"

Grissell lifted her chin. "I can barely tend my chickens or walk away from my bit of isle."

"I would see inside your cottage," Adam said.

Grissell turned to the side. "Do as ye wish."

Lark followed Adam to the doorway. Small windows, with four panes each, were open, allowing in light under a freshly thatched roof. The cottage had a privacy screen, large bed, cooking hearth, and shelves of crocks and bunches of dried herbs. It looked like an apothecary shop or a witch's kitchen.

Adam glanced under the bed and behind the screen but

didn't find anyone hiding.

"It is me, my animals, and my cats," Grissell said.

Lark looked about but didn't see any. "White cats?"

"Aye. I have two. They prowl about the isle on their own."

"One was in the old village yesterday."

"Likely Saint Joan. She has been moussing for days now," Grissell said.

"You name your cats after saints?" Lark asked.

"So ye did not go to the village and hang a doll?" Adam asked at the same time. He looked too large in the one-room cottage.

Grissell ignored him. "My cats do not like people. I am surprised you are not scratched."

"Answer the question," Adam said.

"No, I did not go to the village. I am but an old woman, living alone. I do nothing to encourage the curse. It is up to ye and God and my ancestor to bring it to an end." With her final words, Grissell pointed a finger, bent and bumpy, toward the door.

"Be warned, Mistress Grissell," Adam said. "If ye do anything to endanger my wife or my clan, ye will be exiled from this isle."

"Be warned, Chief Macquarie," Grissell responded, "if ye and your brothers do not learn the lessons at which your ancestors failed, your people will completely die out. There will be no Macquaries left to bring sorrow on Eve's women again. Respect your women. Bring no bastards onto the isle. Learn the power in love."

The old woman's words ticked away inside Lark. *Bring no bastards*. Grissell turned on her heel, her gaze going directly to Lark. Her cloudy eyes seemed to delve into her, seeking out the secrets Lark had tried to leave behind.

Lark caught Adam's fisted hand, feeling dizzy. She tugged him to gain his attention. "Help me up onto the horse," she whispered. What did she mean by bring no bastards onto the isle?

"Are ye well?" he asked.

She nodded. "I just… She has nothing more to say." And Lark certainly had nothing to say. Curses were not real, and secrets should remain tucked away.

Adam led her over and cupped his hands for her to set her foot in, lifting her high to straddle the horse. Her legs were sore from her fall, but she kept her groan inside. He climbed on behind her, bringing the horse around as the old woman watched them leave. Weaving through the few trees behind his brothers to the shoreline, Adam rode along the rock-strewn beach where a half-broken dock jutted part way out into the sea.

Adam stopped, his brothers pulling even with them.

"There was no one in the house?" Beck asked. "Someone who could drag that wrapped poppet to the village?"

"Nay," Adam said.

Lark looked back toward the cottage tucked into the woods. "Someone definitely lives with her."

Adam nodded his agreement.

"Are ye certain?" Drostan asked, twisting in his seat to peer through the trees as if a person might show themselves.

Lark looked at Adam. "The bed is large. A woman living alone has no need for a privacy screen, and the jars on the top shelf were dusted. No cobwebs in the rafters, either. On a good day, Grissell might be able to reach those with a broom. But not to dust the jars without knocking them off." Lark nodded.

"The thatching was fairly new, too," Adam added.

"There is definitely another person on Wolf Isle," Lark said, thinking back to the wind blowing through the abandoned village. "A person who giggles."

"Giggles?" Drostan asked.

"Lark heard a laughing child before she found the hanging poppet," Adam said, his face grim.

"A child?" Rabbie squawked. He turned in a circle as if trying to spy one.

Beck shook his head at the old man. "No need to panic."

Lark watched their faces, all of them pinched with worry. Even Adam looked grim. "If there is a child, I would hardly think there is need to panic," Lark said. How could such large warriors be worried over a child playing pranks?

"Grissell has never wed," Callum said.

"The child could be without wedded parents," Drostan said.

She swallowed. "And what does that matter?" Her voice sounded small before the men staring at her.

"A bastard cannot be on the isle," Rabbie said, his hands moving wildly with each word. "'Tis part of the curse."

Lark looked back toward where the cottage was hidden in the trees. "But Grissell was probably born out of wedlock."

"Another reason to exile the witch," Eagan said.

"'Tis her ancestor who cast the curse," Adam said, shaking his head. "I think Grissell is exempt. But we guard against other bastards coming onto the isle and will not bring one into the world ourselves." All four younger brothers shook their heads in unison. The comicalness of it would have made Lark laugh if she had not lost all her breath.

"Aye," Rabbie said. "If we are to save this clan and make this isle our home, no bastards are allowed. Damned from birth for the sins of their parents." He shook his head, making his wild hair stick out even more.

Sparks started to appear in Lark's periphery, and she made herself inhale. "No bastards," she repeated, her whisper hardly heard. Even left a hundred miles away, her secret had followed her with tenacious cruelty.

Chapter Eight

"All of you stand still," Lark said as she inspected Adam's brothers.

They wore clean shirts and crisp wrapped plaids about their hips with swords polished and snug in their scabbards. They looked like a small military force ready for parade before the queen. "Hands out," she said, and one by one, they put out their hands, palms down.

"Lasses will not be looking at my fingernails," Beck said with a wicked grin. "Not with all this." He puffed up his chest.

Callum snorted. Adam stood apart from his brothers, looking deliciously impressive in his kilt, the end of the long length of wool sashed over his broad shoulder to cross his chest. A circle of twisted silver pinned the sash in place. The Macquarie brothers were handsome in a raw type of way, but Adam, with his serious intensity, was by far the one who would attract the most lasses if he were still unwed.

Unwed. Lark tamped down the wild thoughts that had plagued her since their trip to see Grissell three days before. She hadn't invited Adam into the bed in the now clean chief's room, at least not in the flesh. But he stroked her thoroughly in her extremely vivid dreams.

They'd all been busy scrubbing Gylin castle, and she had climbed the stairs exhausted and alone even though she'd felt his gaze, as if he waited to see which way her favor swayed. And with each day they worked side by side, righting the tapestries and washing the beauty back into the castle's carvings, she swayed more and more toward him. But if she laid with him, consummated their marriage, would she be thoroughly trapping him in it? Trapping him and destroying his chance to rebuild his clan?

I will tell him after the Maclean wedding today. What exactly? That she wanted an annulment? That she would bring down the curse on his isle?

"Are we presentable?" Eagan asked, his light-colored hair shorn so it stayed out of his eyes.

Lark blinked, forcing a steady inhale. "One last check," she said and walked along the line, checking their hands and shirts for dirt. "We are not going to a festival but a wedding. Cleanliness is important, and if you want to find wives, you do not want anything to frighten them off."

Like a secret that could destroy their lives. *I do not believe in curses.* Adam's words seemed so distant now.

Drostan huffed softly. "If the curse does not keep them away, I doubt a bit of dirt will."

Lark held up a finger. "If anyone mentions the curse, you smile and make light of it, saying that you have seen no signs of darkness on Ulva."

"So...trick the lasses?" Callum asked, his brows high. "I would think being a lass who was tricked into wedding our big brother, ye would not condone something of the sort."

"A swollen lip or black eye will also keep the lasses away," Adam said, his legs braced and arms crossed. The Macquaries, without a mother about, had grown into a rough and tumble sort of family. It was different from dealing with her squabbling sisters, but overall, siblings aimed to hit each other in the most sensitive area.

"Blacken his eye after the wedding. They are finally clean and dressed," she said as if they were recently breeched lads. She turned her gaze on Callum. "Complete honesty about the perceived curse must be revealed before any wedding can take place, but at the start, 'tis best to let the ladies find they like you."

Her gaze moved to each brother. "So no fighting or talking about hanging poppets and undug graves, or there will be no more tarts like the ones you sampled this morn. Understood?"

"Lord help me, I would sell my soul to Satan for a lifetime of your tarts," Beck said, his easy smile wicked.

"Then you should stand near the dessert table at the celebration and find out which lady baked your favorites," she said.

"Clever," Drostan said, nodding in approval. "I will watch the lasses dance. The ones who laugh have a happy disposition." Happy disposition? Of all the brothers, he frowned the most, his greenish eyes a soulful mix of sadness and discontent.

"A kiss is all I need from a lass to choose one for a wife," Callum said with a broad smile through his neatly trimmed beard.

Lark exhaled. "God help us."

Rabbie chuckled. "Glad I ain't needing a wife."

Lark turned to the elderly warrior. "You need to remind them to behave or else this isle will never prosper, curse or not. I would not let my daughter wed into a family of fools."

Lark felt Adam walk up beside her, and her heart beat fast as she inhaled his fresh scent that reminded her of the open sea and wild moors. He presented his arm, and she lay her hand upon it. "Ye look quite bonnie," he said near her ear. She was wearing one of his mother's gowns made of fine, thin wool in the same red and green plaid from which their kilts were made. For good or for bad, they would certainly stand out as Macquaries.

"The tarts," Lark said, and Adam grabbed the large basket she had packed with the raspberry, honey, and blaeberry tarts, which she'd been baking over the last two days. "It is heavy," she said and then realized how ridiculous that sounded. She'd seen him training that morning with his brothers before they all went to wash in the freshwater pond east of the village. Adam had muscles that mounded and stretched like a legendary warrior. What would it be like to touch that strength? To feel that strength touch her?

"I will take care," he said, the edge of humor in his voice. His bicep mounded through the crisp white tunic he wore as he easily lifted it with one hand. The obvious strength made her breathless, and she looked away. *I will tell him on Mull.* Then he could decide if he wanted an annulment before she did something foolish.

His brothers strode ahead, disappearing through the door in the wall, which Adam had fit with an iron lock. With the portcullis down and the door locked, only Grissell's white cat, who continued to keep close to the castle, could climb in and out of Gylin while they were away.

"You say your aunt on Mull has the family Bible where the curse is written," Lark said, avoiding a puddle from the night's rain.

"Aye."

"I would like to see it. Sometimes handed down information becomes skewed and misinterpreted. Not that I believe the curse," she said as lightly as she could, "but your brothers and definitely Rabbie do."

"Aunt Ida will probably come to the wedding," Adam said, studying her. "I will ask."

Thank goodness she could read. Never before had she needed to read something so urgently.

. . .

The ceremony was short and the celebration loud with smiles abounding. Even with the presence of the MacLeod Clan, who were related to the groom marrying Liam's sister, Adam remained lighthearted. 'Twas true Lark had not invited him to her bed, but she had not insisted on an annulment, either.

Adam led Lark over to the table where her tarts were being devoured and Callum was tasting and complementing every bonnie baker. Chief Tor Maclean and his wife Lady Ava stood to one side, chatting with their daughter, Meg Maclean, who was of marriable age. She had beauty and wisdom from both her father and mother. But would the chief let his daughter marry into a family considered cursed?

Meg hurried off when the bride waved to her, and Adam came before them. "Chief, Lady Ava, this is my wife, Lark Montgomerie Macquarie."

Ava reached both hands out to take Lark's, smiling with genuine warmth. "So nice to meet the woman who captured the chief of the Macquaries." Even after twenty years in Scotland, Lady Ava still possessed an English accent, but Lark smiled back warmly and bobbed her head in greeting.

"You have a lovely home here," Lark said. "And such a prospering town."

Tor snorted. "As long as the damn English keep to themselves."

Ava frowned his way. "That is no way to talk at a wedding."

"I completely understand," Lark rushed to say. "King Henry will not be cowed by our hatred. It seems to make him push even more for the Queen Mary to unite with his son, Edward. Scotland must band together to meet the English threat."

Tor's eyebrow rose as he considered her. "I agree." He looked to Adam. "A wife who is bonnie as well as intelligent." He nodded and put his arm around his own wife's shoulders. "It is a blessing and keeps things from ever being dull." He kissed his wife's head.

Ava smiled up at him and then reached out to catch Lark's arm. "I am certain we will be close friends. Here, let me introduce you to my sister, Grace. Do not mind the ferocious look of her husband. Keir growls but will not bite. Unless they threaten Grace. Oh, and Adam's aunt, Ida Macquarie, is over there," Ava said and leaned in conspiratorially. "Now that lady might bite."

Adam watched Lark walk away. The gentle swing of her hips in the Macquarie plaid was like a beacon, drawing his gaze. Her wavy, red-gold hair dipped and curved down her back from the ribbons where she tied some up on top.

"Once ye finish ogling your wife," Tor said, "I need to talk with ye."

Adam turned in time to see Tor's smile fade. "What about?" Did the chief of the Macleans have an issue with him moving his clan back to Ulva? The Macleans had used the isle for grazing their sheep before, but otherwise, they had left it alone.

"Cullen Duffie spotted a ship without colors sailing toward Ulva a few weeks ago. He thinks it is the same ship that he has seen numerous times over the last six months. I sent a group of my men to my southeast shore, and they've seen the ship sailing toward Ulva's southern shore, close enough for a landing party to row over."

Adam's forehead tightened. "I have not seen the ship, but several of our sheep have gone missing. Perhaps they are pirates." For if they sailed without flags or colors, they represented only their own affairs.

"Ye have not seen anyone else on Ulva?" Tor asked, his

frown as grim as Adam's. "Perhaps French? They seek a base to attack England." Henry VIII's son Edward was next in line to rule England. Even though Scotland's Queen Mary was only five years old, the English king was determined to see her wed to Edward, unifying Scotland and England into one country. But Mary's mother, Mary de Guise, was French and preferred her daughter marry the French king's son, Francis. King Henry had declared war on the Scots, sending troops into their country to force Mary Queen of Scots' regent into signing the wedding contract.

Adam shook his head. "Grissell is the only one living on Ulva. Although we think someone lives with her, helping her."

Tor's mouth quirked to the side. "I doubt the woman would house French pirates." His gaze slid across some of his warriors walking down by the docks below the hill. "I can send some men back with ye to protect Ulva."

The word "protect" grated on Adam's pride. For generations, his family had sought protection from the Macleans of Mull when the Macquaries had fled Ulva in the wake of the curse.

"I appreciate the offer," Adam said thoughtfully. "I will send word immediately to Mull if they come ashore with evil intent. But I think my brothers and I can handle it."

Tor smiled and gave a nod. "I thought ye would say as much. Ye are a strong chief, Adam Macquarie. Yer father would be very proud of the work ye are doing to bring back your clan."

"Thank ye," Adam said. The Maclean chief was wise and strong, even as he aged. No wonder his people were loyal to the last breath. "I have grown up with a good example to follow." He obviously meant Tor Maclean. Even though he loved his da, John Macquarie had given up on the clan when his wife died on Ulva. He had given into Aunt Ida's demands that he bring his sons back to Mull, certain that the curse had stolen her sister's life.

Adam watched Cullen Duffie, chief of Clan MacDonald on the neighboring isle of Islay, walk up, his easy smile absent. He nodded to them both. "Ye told him about the ship?"

"Aye," Tor said. "He has not seen anyone, but some of his sheep are missing."

Adam exhaled long, realizing he hadn't told Tor everything. "And…someone made a doll to look like a woman and hung it from a noose over the dug-up bones of the original Macquarie chief that brought the curse to Ulva."

Both chiefs turned to look at him, their bearded jaws dropping open. Cullen's eyes opened wide. "Well now. Ye may not want to tell any of the marriageable lasses, whom your brothers are circling, about that."

"And my Meg is not marrying one of them," Tor added, his thick arms crossing his chest as he looked past Adam to where his daughter spoke with Lark and his wife.

Cullen frowned. "And neither is my sweet bairn, Camilla." His gaze moved to his own bonnie daughter, who had inherited her mother's French beauty. Ava was introducing Lark to her, and Beck sidled up to them as he chewed a tart.

"Excuse me," Cullen said and strode directly toward them, a da bent on chasing off a suitor from a cursed isle. Adam exhaled.

"Ye did not mention that part earlier," Tor said. "Sounds like ye do need assistance over there."

"I think it was Grissell trying to frighten us, with the help of whomever is living with her. Curses are not real."

"They are if people believe in them," Tor said.

Hadn't he said the same? Adam gazed off toward the west where his isle sat, lonely and waiting to be filled again with life. "Good thing I do not."

Chapter Nine

No bastards can be born on the isle.

Ida Macquarie's words played through Lark's thoughts as she watched the fires being lit and sipped on honey mead. The woman had been sharp and frowning, her gaze judgmental as Ava introduced Lark.

It took only a handful of words from Ida to make Lark certain she could not live with Adam's aunt if they annulled their marriage. However, the words she remembered from the family Bible were encouraging. *No Macquarie can father a bastard.* It had nothing to do with permitting bastards on the isle. Still, she would like to read the words herself, but it seemed no one had to know that Roylin Montgomerie was not Lark's father. Not even Adam.

The mead caught in her throat. *Trust.* Honesty created trust, which was the one thing she told him that she must have in a marriage.

A set of pipes played along with two fiddles. People gathered in small groups, laughing and raising their cups for the happy couple as they made their way amongst them.

Lark breathed deeply. No one here knew anything about her, about her birth, about her life, about her shame. And she could keep it that way, not risk their judgment if somehow it got out. The thought made her clutch her shawl tighter about her shoulders.

If she kept her secrets to herself, forgot they even existed, she could stay wed, have legitimate children, and help rebuild Ormaig, Gylin, and all of Wolf Isle at Adam's side. Her life could be full of purpose and maybe even love. Her gaze drifted to Adam across the field where he spoke to Beck. Her husband was the perfect combination of intelligence, rugged good looks, and brawn, and yet he did not lord his position over people. And he had been patient and gentle with her. Could Adam give her acceptance, a true home, and maybe even love? Her heart raced with hope.

As long as no one finds out about my past.

"Iain MacLeod has not shone his ornery face," Beck said next to Adam and raised his tankard to toast the observation. "Although having that handful of MacLeods around is bloody irritating."

"The groom is a MacLeod," Adam said, his gaze following Lark as Meg and Ava walked over to her. The presence of their rival clan had been plucking at his brothers' tempers all day, and he'd had to remind them several times not to start a fight, for the sake of the bride, Liam's sister. And for Lark.

Beck frowned. "I thought Julia knew better than to tangle with them."

Adam watched Lark with the ladies, her head turning to the shadows where couples were starting to wander off to find privacy.

"The only MacLeods I have met are ornery sots," Beck

said and took a drink of his ale.

Adam watched Liam Maclean stop next to Lark, pulling her aside. He spoke, and her gaze slid out, stopping on Adam. He gave her a nod. "If I am not back," Adam said, cutting Beck off, "ye are in charge of keeping our brothers peaceful. Do not come looking for me."

Beck laughed softly. "Aye. Best bed her, brother, for ye cannot think straight until ye do."

He kept his gaze fastened on Lark even as she looked to Liam. When she turned back to Adam, her smile had fled. *Damn.* What was he saying to steal away her smile? Liam was against them moving back to Ulva. Was he telling her that he believed the curse was real? That it was dangerous for her and any children they had?

As if noticing his rapid stride, Liam suddenly turned and walked away as if on an important mission. "What was he saying?" Adam asked, stopping before her. "Ye were smiling and then ye looked like a mad hornet."

"Well…he was telling me how the isle is cursed and that I could sway you to abandon it because you seem to like me more than all the lasses you've bedded before."

"*Mo chreach*," he cursed under his breath. "He has never been in favor of us moving back."

"Maybe he likes your company here on Mull," she said, her gaze following another couple who walked off into the growing night, hands clasped. "So…you have slept with a lot of women? Anyone walking around here that I should know about?"

Adam rubbed a hand over his short-cropped beard. "God's teeth, Lark. Do not listen to bloody Liam. He is an arse." Adam was going to make Liam listen to *him* when he caught up to him.

Adam met Lark's hard stare as the silence between them lengthened and grew awkward. Was she jealous? The thought warmed him enough to stop him from walking off to pummel his long-time friend. He took hold of her shoulders. "I know we are learning to trust one another, that it is the most important thing to ye in a marriage. I will not step out on ye, Lark."

She studied him. "Because you will not allow yourself to father bastards?"

He frowned. "I have managed to do that without remaining celibate." She looked away. *Mo chreach!* He huffed. "I have no idea what ye want me to say."

Her shoulders seemed to sink, and she glanced up at him. "What is the most important thing to *you* in a marriage?"

He knew better than to say anything about tupping, even if after a week of dreaming each night about Lark writhing and moaning his name had made it instantly jump forefront in his mind. He looked up at the darkening blue that was quickly changing to black in the moonless night sky. "I suppose trust, too. Honesty, so there is no need to worry over what the other one is thinking." He rubbed his chin. "And being able to work together toward a goal."

"A goal of bringing life again to Ulva," she said. Her brow furrowed as if she thought hard on a matter.

He reached up to smooth the worry lines on her forehead with his thumb. She pulled back, and he dropped his hand. "Aye. I would have ye work next to me to do so."

She turned her face toward the flames. Adam breathed deeply. Even past the harsh tang of woodsmoke, she smelled warm and sweet. "And to be honest with ye, lass, I would also have us lay next to each other like we did in the tent."

Her face turned to his. "You do?"

The softening in her face stirred him with hope. "Aye, lass, very much."

Beck was right; he couldn't think straight without taking Lark to bed. He slid his hand down her arm and captured her hand. "Lark—"

"I think several of the ladies would like to visit Ulva," Ava said, walking back over with her daughter on her arm.

Damn. There were too many people on Mull.

"Thank you for bringing it up with them," Lark answered, which was good since he was suddenly surly.

"Thank ye," he repeated.

His sudden impatience roughened his voice. "It is getting late, so we are leaving soon," Adam said as Drostan walked up, his gaze on Meg.

"No," both Ava and Meg said at the same time. Ava smiled. "We were hoping you would all stay for tomorrow. There will be contests between the clans, a small festival in honor of the wedding." Ava lowered her voice. "And I am certain you and your brothers would like to show the MacLeods they shouldn't try to raid Macquarie property again."

Meg reached for Lark's free hand, and for a moment, Adam felt like tugging her away. "Adam and you can stay in Aros Castle with us. There is an extra room ready since Cullen and his wife, Rose, went back to Islay. Their twin boys are a handful, and they dare not leave them overnight. Lark, you can have a warm bath here." She glanced at Adam. "In a bathing tub, not a horse trough."

"A warm bath would be wonderful," Lark said.

Och but he would look like a brute to refuse her. Adam exhaled slowly and turned to Drostan. "Let the others know we are staying the night."

"Aye." Drostan glanced at Tor's daughter and walked off into the dark. Would he try to find Meg later? Adam should warn him that her father might just put a blade in his gut if so.

"Wonderful," Ava said. "One of Tor's men is always on watch and will lead you to the empty room. I will ask for the tub to be moved in there, along with several buckets of water to be warmed."

"Thank you, milady," Lark said, excitement lighting her tone.

Adam stood patiently, listening to them discuss coming over to Ulva to clean until some of Ava's friends drew them away. He clasped Lark's hand so she wouldn't follow. "A word," he said. Glancing side to side, to see no one approaching, he pulled Lark gently over to the other side of the fire next to the chapel where the shadows were thick.

He cleared his throat. "Do ye like to dance?" He nodded toward a group of laughing ladies forming a ring about one of the fires.

"Sometimes," she answered and took another sip of honey mead.

What should he say next? *Can I share your bed in the castle? Can we put aside the ridiculous idea that you might still want an annulment?* How did one woo a virgin? One who might still be angry with him? Adam made a straggled noise, and she glanced his way. He straightened his shoulders, his legs set naturally in a battle stance as he grew determined to say something, anything.

"I am not...I do not woo lasses like Beck. My whole focus has been on starting our clan over, building it up, so I never learned to be clever while talking to lasses."

"You do not need to be clever," she said, her mouth softening as she turned toward him. "Just say what you are thinking."

The shadows and shards of firelight played over her high cheekbones and lovely chin. Lord, how he wanted to run his finger over that soft skin. Say what he was thinking? *Can I throw up your skirts right here and kiss every inch of your lush body? Then carry you into that castle and make you scream my name as you burst with pleasure?*

He opened his mouth and paused. "Uh...are ye hungry?"

Bloody hell.

"No," she said with a shake of her head.

"Do ye need to use the privy?"

She shook her head again, her lips turning up slightly.

They stared at each other for another breath, and he curled his hand around her small one. It felt fragile in his large palm, and yet he knew how strong Lark was. "Can I kiss ye?"

The world around him vanished into darkness as he waited for her answer. She gave a small nod, and he inhaled. Stepping into her, his lips bent toward her, and he waited to see if she would pull away. Lark kept her head tipped up to him, her eyes open, and he pressed a gentle kiss on her soft mouth.

The heat of her body soaked into him. He wasn't sure if he'd pulled her into him or she'd melted forward, but his arms were around her so that he could feel the softness of her curves pressed into him. Softness to mold against his hardness.

The feel of her, the delicious smell of her, mixed with the detailed memories of his dreams, erupted a firestorm within him. He stroked down her back. She trembled slightly, and Adam caught her face with one hand, guiding her against him to deepen the kiss. She was letting him touch her! *Slow. Keep it slow. Do not ruck up her skirts and rut with her against the chapel wall.*

His rational thoughts faded quickly to fragmented whispers. He'd been so close to her, yet she'd been untouchable, for days and uncomfortable nights. But now…now he would touch her. "Lark," he managed to say against her lips as she spread a trail of fire with her fingers down his chest to the hardness beneath his kilt. Through the wool wrapping, she stroked over him. He inhaled swiftly, her touch robbing him of his mind.

Pent-up raw want funneled through Adam as he held her to him. She fit him perfectly, and the fact that she hadn't pulled away at the feel of him released his worry over bedding a virgin. Lark was brave and soft with a good dose of wild.

Lifting her against him, he stepped back until the shadows of the chapel swallowed them. Along the side of the building, they were out of sight from the revelers. As her hands began to explore him again, he caught the edge of her petticoat, catching it as he rucked it up until her bare arse lay in his hands. The skin was soft, and he stroked lower, seeking the wet heat between her splayed legs.

"Do you not want an annulment?" she murmured against him.

"What?" he asked. "Nay, I never have," he said, kissing her as he bent forward, surrounding her with his body.

"But you do not know…about me," she said around shallow panting. "Who I am. Where I come from. What if…" Her words turned into a whispered moan as he found the spot he sought. As the sound grew, he caught her mouth in another kiss.

Yet a moan still filled his ears, a moan that was not from Lark. He felt her stiffen in his arms.

"Oh God, yes," came a woman's voice from the dark. "You know right where to touch me, Keir."

A low growl came from the back side of the chapel.

Adam slowly let Lark's skirt drop into place and held her close where they leaned against the chapel wall. Adam leaned his forehead against Lark's as they both breathed, and he tried to summon enough strength to pull away from her. But the noises coming from the couple were so filled with passion, they boiled his blood even more. From the way Lark clung to him, she might be having the same reaction.

"Right here against the chapel," the woman whispered, her voice coming in pants.

"Aye, my wanton *Sassenach*."

"God may strike us down for sullying his house, but Lord I want you inside me now," she said.

"We are wed, Grace. God wouldn't mind me tupping ye inside, spread upon the altar."

Fok. They were listening to Keir MacKinnon and his wife, Grace. Without a word, Adam grasped Lark's hands and silently led her back the way they'd come in front of the chapel. Before stepping out into the light, he tried to adjust his raging jack, but it would take a dousing from the North Sea to tame it.

"Oh…" Lark whispered, her hand going to her mouth. She was flushed, the bun on her head toppled to one side, and her gown askew. He bent toward her. "Ye look ravished."

Her hand went straight to her hair. "So do you," she whispered.

"Best we get ye out of the light and up to the castle," he said, catching her chin for a lingering kiss. When he pulled away, she stared at him with a look of confusion and almost pain. Was she on fire inside like him? She opened her mouth.

"Adam, ye need to come." Eagan jogged up to them, making Adam pull Lark slightly behind him to shield her rumpled appearance.

"I am seeing Lark to the castle. She is tired."

"Bloody hell, Adam, I mean it. The MacLeods are starting trouble, and Beck and Drostan are about to begin a clan war with them."

"Dammit," Adam said.

"You need to go stop that," Lark said, her voice shaky.

Only the threat of all-out war could tear him away from his warm wife who seemed to have forgiven him. He spotted Meg Maclean striding across the road.

"Meg," he called, and she waved, coming over.

"Have you seen my aunt Grace?" Meg asked. "My

mother is looking for her."

"No," Lark answered quickly, glancing at the chapel that hid the lovers. "Maybe she needs to be alone for a bit."

Meg rolled her eyes as if Lark had told her exactly what Grace was doing. "Like my parents, Aunt Grace and Uncle Keir are always finding places to be *alone*. It is quite scandalous."

"Adam," Eagan said, his voice heavy with warning.

"Can ye take Lark up to her room at the castle, Meg? I have to stop a clan war from starting."

"Lord, no blood spilled on Julia's wedding day," Meg said and took Lark's arm, her gaze taking in her appearance. She smiled. "And we will get that bath set and ready." She looked over her shoulder at Adam. "The room is the third one on the second floor over the main keep."

"Thank ye," Adam said. He met Lark's eyes. "I will find ye." For he would after this mess was cleaned up. His damn brothers couldn't keep the bloody peace for one night.

She walked into the darkness with Meg. Adam turned with Eagan, following him past the fire.

"Your jack is tenting out your kilt," Eagan said.

"If ye had a wife as bonny and curvy as mine, yers would be, too," he answered, his words surly as they trudged across the clearing.

"Get the fok out of my face," Iain MacLeod yelled as Drostan stood directly before him. A small group of onlookers included his other brothers, more MacLeods, and…the priest who had married Lark and him at the festival. The cleric wore bland monk's robes and a slight grin, his large hand wrapped around a tankard. How and when had he come to Mull?

Adam shouldered his way through the Macleans gathered on one side. "Drostan, stand down."

"He poured his ale on me," Drostan said, shaking his damp head.

Adam stepped straight up to Iain MacLeod. He was stout and crass and always ready for a fight. His brother was the chief of their clan that was trying to re-establish themselves on the Isle of Skye. Being brother of the clan chief made Iain think he could raid and cause trouble without getting his arse kicked or throat slit.

Adam slid his sword free of his scabbard, the hum of steel singing in the cool night air. The MacLeods behind Iain drew their swords as well. Adam didn't see the groom there, but he would hear of it if there was a bloodbath on his wedding night. As much as Adam would like to see it done, he wouldn't curse Liam's sister's marriage if it could be helped.

He held his sword out to the side, point down, and opened his hand. The blade dropped, piercing the ground. The length quivered where it stood with its tip embedded. "I suggest," Adam said, his voice low in warning, "that ye walk away knowing luck was with ye tonight. Or has your brother told ye to start a war with the Macquarie Clan?"

Iain smiled coldly. "Ye mean all five of yer clan?" He leaned close to Adam. "And an old man and a doxy to share between ye."

Before Iain could even blink, Adam clenched his fist and brought it across with the strength of his shoulder, slamming it into Iain's nose. The idiot howled as he fell, arse first to sit on the ground in the puddle he'd made by turning a full tankard of ale over Drostan's head.

Adam yanked his sword from the ground and kicked Iain in the chest, making him fall backward flat, his men jumping to get out of his way. The lethal end of Adam's sword pricked the valley at the base of Iain's hairy throat. "If another word about my wife falls from your foking lips, MacLeod, I will slice your head from your shoulders." Even though Iain's fool posse stood with their swords before Adam, he knew his brothers stood more than ready at his back.

"*Stad!*" Rearden MacLeod strode up with Tor following him, both of them looking like they were about to rip into someone. "Not on my wedding day," the groom yelled. "What the bloody hell, Macquarie?"

Adam looked in the fault as Iain lay back, sword at his throat and blood gushing from his already crooked nose.

Keir MacKinnon walked out of the shadows from the direction of the chapel. His shirt was untucked, and he definitely looked like he'd been tupping, but he didn't seem to care as he stepped before Rearden and Tor. "The fool on the ground started the fight and then slandered the Macquarie's wife."

Tor stepped around Keir. "Adam, stand down. He is not worth the mess. Beat him in the contests tomorrow."

Damn. Iain deserved more than a punch in the face for his words about Lark. The MacLeod, who had been only a pain in Adam's arse, was now an enemy.

Adam breathed deeply and lowered his sword. Taking two steps back, he glanced at the large crowd that had witnessed his response. So much for his legendary control.

The idiot stood up, spitting into the dirt, blood-smeared face screwed up in a snarl. "The Macquarie Clan's days are numbered," Iain said and jabbed a finger at him. "Ye are cursed. No women will survive it to make more of ye."

He turned away, and Adam realized he held his sword ready once more, but words and foolish curses could not be killed with a sword.

Chapter Ten

"If you care for a little whisky to help..." Meg paused as she pointed to a jug and cup on a small table near the bathing tub. "Help with anything, I suppose." She smiled. "Like if you have trouble sleeping. It is smooth," she said as if she were an expert on the potent brew.

"Thank you," Lark said. "For everything." Meg nodded and shut the door behind her.

Lark turned in a tight circle, her gaze stopping on the caldron they had placed over the hot fire in the hearth. *Sweet Mother Mary. What the bloody hell do I do?* Now that the raging wildfire that had consumed her in the shadows by the chapel had cooled a bit, her sense of integrity was screaming loud and clear.

She dipped her fingers in the cold water already in the tub. "I should have told him," she whispered to the concentric circles that radiated out from the drips of water hitting the surface. Her secret could not stay secret, even here on the western isles.

I do not believe in curses. Adam had said it more than

once. And neither did Lark.

No bastards can be born of the Macquaries descended from Wilyam Macquarie. Ida must know the exact wording of the legend.

But what if Lark said nothing and terrible things happened on Ulva? What if her past became known by his brothers and Rabbie? What would they think? What would Adam think?

And now, Adam was coming up to join her, alone. Her eyes turned to the large bed surrounded by rich curtains. Pillows, fur throws, and soft quilts seemed to beckon. A perfect nest for lovers. "Sweet Mother Mary," she repeated out loud and took a steadying breath, her gaze moving to the whisky jug. She had tried some at her mother's wake, and she remembered the heat and how she'd not cared what the villagers thought of her, at least for the night. Had it been courage or drunkenness?

"Just a sip, then," she whispered. "For courage to tell Adam." Should she tell him everything? Or just that she'd been born a bastard? Her heart fluttered hard like a bird caught in a snare. Yes, a single mouthful of whisky would loosen her tongue. It certainly loosened Roylin's tongue.

She poured some into the cup, and before she could rethink, she swallowed the draught. The whisky went down, but she opened her mouth to breathe out the fumes and coughed, her eyes open wide. Fire of a different nature tore down to her stomach, warming her middle. "Bloody hell," she said, coughing again, the back of her hand against her lips. She rinsed her mouth and chewed some of the mint that Meg had left for her to clean her teeth. How anyone could enjoy the taste of whisky was a mystery. Although the heat in her middle was potent and pleasant.

Not knowing how long Adam would be, Lark found herself looking at the door as she added the heated water to the tub. "God's teeth," she swore softly. She did not plan to give up her bath, but it would be best if she were not naked when he arrived. Meg had left a small mound of soap that smelled of summer strawberries, two bathing sheets, a hair comb, and a fresh smock to borrow. Aros Castle was filled with thick area rugs, clean water pitchers, and dust-free surfaces. It was sweet comfort after living in Gylin this past week.

Lark worked the comb through her tangled hair quickly. "Wood smoke and dirt," she said in the empty room. Before they left the next day, she was going to find another bathing tub to take back with her. That was if she was welcome back. If she told Adam, would he tell Lady Ava and Meg why they annulled their marriage? *Maybe they won't care.* But the thought of losing her new friends twisted tightly inside her.

Eyes pinned to the door and ears alert, Lark dropped her unlaced gown, shook it to hang over a chair, and yanked off her stays and smock. It was cold in the room, and she nearly leaped into the bathing tub, her breath catching at the warm water as she sunk in, her skin puckering with sensation. The heat of the water seemed to meet with the heat from the whisky.

"Oh yes." She sighed. If she bent her knees enough, she could submerge her breasts underwater, her chilled nipples pearling hard with sensation. She took up the strawberry soap, inhaling the summery smell, and ran it over her limbs, scrubbing it in with the small ball of wool Meg had pointed out. Legs, feet, toes, arms, back, neck, face. She dunked herself to rinse, inhaling when she rose. With her eyes closed, she could imagine herself in a sunny meadow surrounded by strawberries. The luxury almost made her forget her troubles. Almost.

Honesty and trust. They built the foundation of a solid marriage. But why bring trouble into it if no one could ever know? Lord! The whisky wasn't helping her decide anything.

Lark washed her breasts and then down between her thighs, her fingers moving across the ache that had been there since Adam's kiss. Worry had barely dampened it. Washing and touching herself was nothing new but, with the knowledge that Adam could be stroking her in her most intimate nooks, made her breathing shallow. *Only if you keep your words to yourself.*

Sliding down in the wooden tub, she dunked her head under to fully wet her hair. She surfaced and scrubbed the strawberry soap through it, working out the remaining tangles. Before, being the last to bathe meant the water was always dirty and cool, so the warm bath in the large tub was truly bliss. She sighed as she sank deeper, her feet perched on the rim at the end. With a full breath, she slid all the way under, her fingers working the suds out of her long strands of hair. If Adam threw her off Wolf Isle, it might be a long time before she had another warm bath. Lark doubted that nuns were afforded such luxury. And certainly, Ida Macquarie did not look like the type to take pleasure in anything.

No. I cannot live with her. Water filled her ears, the warmth cradling her. Was this what peace felt like? She let her lips break the surface to take in another inhale only to submerge once more, her eyes shut, her knees and shins out of the water at the far end. Her hair floated about her like a cloak or a mermaiden's hair. If only she could stay submerged in warmth where her past could not reach her. No worries. No judgment. No shame.

I do not believe in curses. If she could hold onto Adam's words, if he truly did not believe, then her past could not hurt her at all. She could almost hear him calling her name.

Splash. Rough hands grabbed her arms, making her gasp, her limbs flailing out before her. She opened her eyes to murky water as she was yanked up out of the wet serenity.

"Lark! Lark, lass!" Adam's voice bellowed through the room, but Lark was too busy sputtering and coughing out the water she'd sucked in to answer.

His large hand pushed back the hair from her face. Water was everywhere across the floor and Adam as he grabbed her to him, almost shaking her. "Lark, speak," he demanded.

"Give…me…a bloody chance," she managed to yell. She rubbed the sting in her eyes and squinted one at him, taking in the wretched concern pinching his face. With his white teeth bared, he looked tormented.

"Ye were under the water, unmoving, even when I called your name."

"I could not hear you under the water." Hand fisted before her, she suddenly realized that she was completely naked and dripping. Without any sheet nearby, Lark stepped into Adam as if he could cover her. "And there is now water all over the floor."

"I do not give a shite about the floor," he said, but his voice had come down in volume. How the hell had she not heard him even with water in her ears? Everyone in the castle could likely hear him.

He held her close. When she looked up, his hand was rubbing hard at his forehead as if it pained him. "I thought…" He trailed off.

"What?" She frowned at the torture on his face.

Shaking his head, he looked down at her. "Stupid threats from MacLeod smashed my common sense."

"He threatened me?" Her brow rose. Was the man dead then? Julia would never forgive them.

"Nay…he said the curse would kill Macquarie women, and then I saw ye under the water. Eyes shut, floating there."

She stared at him, feeling a weight grow along her limbs. "You do believe in the curse," she whispered. Even if he refuted it, she could see it in the concern lining his features.

"Nay," he said, his gaze roaming over her face as if checking that she was truly breathing. "Baths...they are dangerous, and ye did not respond."

She raised one hand to his bristled jawline. "I have been taking baths since I was a wee lass. If I am to drown, it will be in a wild ocean or murky loch."

"That does not make me feel better."

She sighed a long release. "Because you believe in the curse."

His mouth opened and closed before he said anything. "Perhaps a part of me does, but not a large part."

He was being honest, and so should she. But not while she was naked in his arms. She glanced toward the bathing sheet on the chair, very aware that she was pressed against him. "The back of me is getting cold."

His eyes slid past her face to the swell of her breasts where huge watermarks darkened his shirt. She felt his gaze like a caress, and warmth from within pushed against the cold penetrating her skin. *Cac!* She should have been out and dressed before he came.

He began to pull away, but she held herself to him and stepped her bare feet onto his boots so he wouldn't stomp her toes. "Walk me over." She wasn't ready for him to see her completely, head to toe, naked when she was wet and cold, with her hair like dripping seaweed. His tight mouth relaxed into a half smile as he rocked back and forth as they moved forward.

"I was wrong," he said.

She kept her eyes level with his chest. "We agreed on that a week ago."

"When I said ye should roll in mud or go around soaking to keep suitors away." She glanced up to see him shake his head, his gaze dipping along her hair and swell of breasts. A slow grin smoothed the worry from his face. "Mud or dung perhaps, but wet…" He leaned into her hair. "Ye look even more enticing."

The warmth of his breath strummed through her, making the juncture of her legs clench in anticipation. She squeezed them shut. "I…" she started to say and stuttered. "I need a moment, Adam. We need to talk." She felt slightly more relaxed than when she'd arrived in the room. Perhaps the whisky was giving her courage.

His face grew serious. "Certainly."

"Do you want a bath?" she asked as he released her and turned his back so she could dry and throw on the clean smock. "Although most of the water has splashed out."

"I stopped to wash in the creek that runs next to Aros Castle," he said. She watched the play of muscles in his back through the thinness of his shirt as he crossed his arms. The bottom edge of his wool wrap allowed her to see the well-turned cut of his calves above his boots, and his biceps bulged where he crossed them in front. Her mouth went dry with want.

"I am sorry for having to leave ye with Meg," he said, still turned away.

"Is everything all right?"

"The MacLeods were trying to start a fight with Drostan. Keir MacKinnon and Tor came to keep things calm." He ran his hands through his hair. "Tomorrow will be a test of our patience during the games."

Tomorrow. Just the thought of what could be happening the next day made her stomach flip. Rabbie could be yelling. Drostan shaking his head. Eagan staring open-mouthed. Callum demanding she be exiled. And Adam…he might be finding a priest to start the annulment so he could send her back to her sisters. And Roylin Montgomerie.

"I know what ye are thinking," he said, making her breath stop. He glanced over his shoulder to see her dressed and turned around.

"You do?"

"I will speak with my brothers about not fighting."

"Oh…yes, no fighting," she said.

They stared at one another for a moment. Where to start? "I spoke with your aunt, Ida," she said.

"I apologize for whatever she said."

Lark's mouth relaxed. "She did frown quite a bit, and I can see why you decided to live in a tree instead of saying your apology for calling her mean."

A small chuckle escaped him. "It is a wonder she was my mother's sister. I remember Ma being as sweet as Ida is sour."

"Ida has the Bible about the curse," Lark continued.

"Aye."

"And she reads it more often than you or Grissell."

"I suppose," he said, his brows furrowing as if he tried to decipher where she was going.

"She says the curse says no bastards may be born to Macquaries descended from Wilyam, not that no bastards can live on the isle." He did not say anything, only stared at her. "So what Grissell said about no bastards being allowed on the isle under the curse is not true."

Adam stepped closer. "We are wed officially by a priest, Lark. Our children will not be born bastards."

One hand clutching the drying sheet, Lark's other hand flipped around in the air. "What I mean is you do not need to worry about a bastard moving to Ulva. That is all. I…I would think it would be awkward to ask those coming to live there if their parents were wed."

He took another step closer until she had to tip her head back to meet his gaze. "I do not believe in curses," he said again, tucking a soaking strand of her hair behind her ear.

"Except when you think I have drowned in my tub," she whispered. Holy Mary, he was close, close enough for her to smell the soap that he'd used to wash.

His eyes closed momentarily with remorse, and she grimaced. *I do not want to bring him pain or worry.* Lark just wanted to bring that roughish smile back to his handsome face.

She reached for him. "I bring luck to your isle," she said, sliding her hands up his chest. The feel of his hard muscles under the thin linen sent a spiral of want through her already warm middle, straight down to the ache starting to grow again between her legs. "For I must be lucky."

"Oh?" he asked, his hand sliding down her back to rest in the curve above her buttocks.

"I lost a slipper just in time for you to find it to save me at Beltane. Perfect timing. I must be lucky then," she said.

A hint of surprise showed in his eyes. "I am glad ye see it that way."

Lark realized that she did, and she smiled. "Yes. Yes, I do." She stared up into his face. His kind eyes and lush mouth made her reach up on her bare toes to press her mouth to his. His hand came up to capture the back of her head, and she slanted easily against his lips, opening instantly to the slight pressure.

Adam pulled back, and she blinked her eyes open to see a slight furrow along his forehead. She longed to rub it away. "Have ye been drinking whisky?" he asked.

Her hand dropped back to her side. Would he stop kissing her if he thought she'd had more than a sip? The ache in her argued against the truth. "Only a nip," she said. "To wash my teeth really." She shook her head. "I do not drink spirits." It was not a lie. She had a gulp, but to a big man like Adam, that would be a nip. And many people used spirits to wash their teeth. "I decided to use the mint instead." She made a face. "Whisky tastes terrible. Should I wash my mouth out with water?"

The furrow smoothed. "Nay," he said. "I like the taste of whisky and mint…" He leaned in closer. "And ye."

Her breath caught at the intensity in his stare. The heat within her grew, sending tendrils of sensation everywhere. "Then taste me again," she whispered. "If you wish." She wet her lips, and his gaze dropped to her mouth. "Because…I wish it."

"Ye are sure?" he asked, his voice a rough whisper.

She nodded, feeling the ache coiling in her abdomen. "I have never been surer in my life," she whispered back, stepping into him.

His muscled arms wrapped around her, and she could feel the hardness beneath his kilt press against her. A thrill vibrated through her. "Lark," he said, drawing her name out. "I am going to taste every little strawberry-smelling inch of ye that makes ye shiver with pleasure." His voice was like the rumbling murmur of water over rocks, pushing out any other thoughts that swirled in her mind.

She swallowed at the promise in the depth of it. His words added to the heat of the whisky and her want, and she realized the words were indeed easier to say. "Find every inch," she whispered and pulled back from him, taking two steps. He let her go, watching her. Gazes locked, Lark lifted the edge of the smock she'd just donned. She felt the fabric slide along her already sensitive skin, tickling the tips of her nipples as she lifted it over her head.

She let it float wherever it fell and lowered her arms to her sides. She was completely naked, the fire at her back to warm her where her wet hair still dripped along the skin of her buttocks.

The sharp heat from the flames burning behind her was nothing compared to the heat in Adam's gaze as it traveled slowly down the length of her form. As if he were savoring the most delicious treat, anticipation was evident in the tightness of his muscles and the hunger in his look. His hands clenched into fists at his sides as if stopping himself from grabbing her roughly to him. The idea caught her breath and sent another wave of tingles across her skin. Her nipples were pearled, her breasts felt heavy, aching to be touched.

Perhaps whisky did give one courage for she felt none of the silly shyness that she imagined feeling as a virgin. She lifted slowly under her breasts, running her thumbs across their peaks. As if she were a landscape, his gaze traveled down from them to her curved belly and hips to the juncture of her legs where he paused. She clenched inside as if he'd touched her there, and her knees felt wobbly. She pushed them tighter together and let her arms lower. His gaze teased her, sending her blood racing. What would his touch do?

"Och, but ye are absolutely beautiful," he said, his voice raw with honesty. His hand opened, coming up to slide slowly down her arm from her shoulder. She closed her eyes as the touch sent more sensation coursing just under her skin like a gentle kind of lightning teasing her body. When he let go, she opened her eyes.

Without looking away from her gaze, Adam stripped off his wet shirt. Lord, her husband was magnificent with broad shoulders and muscular biceps. A light sprinkling of hair curled across his tanned chest where little scars, white and crisscrossed, marked his skin. One slash sat on the dip of his waist like an enticing trail to follow below his kilt. They showed evidence of his experience in battle even though he'd not spoken of it. Her gaze slid along his skin, and she wanted to taste every single one of them.

Her damp hair made her shiver. "Wait by the fire," he said, striding to the large bed. She watched as Adam lifted under the thick feather tick and mass of blankets strewn there. Lark froze at his display of strength as he raised it all in one scoop. Like a mountain moving, he carried the bulk to the fire. Stepping around the tub, he dropped the nest of extravagant comfort several feet back from the flames.

He grinned, melting away the solemnness that usually rested in his features. "Comfortable and warmer to dry your hair."

Lark walked over to him, lifting her free hand to his chest, her stomach fluttery. "I have a feeling we are about to get warmer even without a fire." Where were these saucy words coming from?

The gap between them was small. Instead of dragging her into him, his knuckle slid gently along her collarbone. Her lips opened as if she could not draw enough breath, her heart beating a rapid rhythm.

She raised her finger, touching him, running it gently along the puckered skin of the scar on his jaw. "It must have been very painful."

"More uncomfortable." He met her gaze, and she watched his lips move over the deep burble of his northern accent.

Her hand slid down his warm skin to stop at the edge of his kilt. "Then we should find pleasure when we can." Being wed to a man like Adam Macquarie would surely bring her pleasure.

He caught her hand and brought her palm to his lips, kissing it in a gesture that made any other thoughts melt away. Her muscles tightened and relaxed, and the ache below made her legs shift.

Adam caught her face between his hands. His kiss met her inhale, and she slanted immediately against his warm mouth. Eyes closed, she surrendered to the taste of him, the clean smell of him, the feel of his hands as they slid from her face to her shoulders to caress a trail down her spine. The caress came forward to rest on the slope of her naked hips. He kissed from her lips, across her face, to her ear. "Everything about ye is soft and lush with curves," he whispered.

Lark tipped her head back, clinging to his shoulders, as his lips branded her neck, and more shivers lit through her body. It felt wanton and amazing and perfectly right.

"Your trust honors me," he whispered, the deep rumble of his voice like another caress.

Trust? It seemed she was supposed to trust him with more than her body, but at the moment, all other thoughts fled her. She swallowed, feeling the tightness in her breasts and below, as if her body anticipated things that she knew little about. Instead of leaping upon her, it was as if he was giving her time to get used to being naked with him. She rested her palms on his chest. His words made her brave, and she took a small step back, raising her arms to thread her fingers through her damp hair. The hair around her face had begun to dry, creating curls that brushed her cheeks.

"See what you have won with this marriage," she said softly. "A barrel of whisky and..." His gaze left her face, following her hands as they slid from her breasts down her side and over her hips, one hand skimming the skin of her gently rounded abdomen. She shivered at the intensity of his eyes.

An appreciative growl came from low in his throat. "I have no need for whisky, but my thirst for ye is sinful."

She smiled. "We are wed, Adam. God would not mind if you tupped me in a church, spread upon the altar," she said, repeating the heated words they had heard from Grace's husband.

He snorted softly with his grin, his unhurried gaze traveling across her skin, until his grin faded, leaving such primal lust on his face that the crux of her legs clenched with heat. He stepped forward, his lips coming back to hers for a kiss, a kiss that barreled right into ravishment.

Lark lifted onto her toes, and Adam cupped her bare backside for a moment before setting her down. She drew gulps of breath, watching as he pulled his leather belt open. The heaviness of his kilt dropped with a thud to the floor.

Adam Macquarie stood before her, naked and glorious in his masculine beauty. As chiseled as a Greek god, his proud jack long and lifted. He stalked toward her, and they backed up until Lark stepped into the middle of the nest of quilts and furs on the floor.

"A lovelier sight I have never seen," he said, closing the distance to kiss a path of heat along the side of her jaw and down her neck. She raked the side of his narrow hips gently with her nails, sucking in a gasp as his mouth closed over her nipple, teasing it into an even higher peak. It was as if her breast was tethered to the heat between her legs, an ache that demanded to grow. Like a taut wire, plucking one tightened the other into a coil of desperate need.

"Adam, oh god," she moaned as he switched to the other breast, his callused hand sending shivers as it slid down the curve of her lower back to cup and squeeze her backside, lifting her against him. His jack was hard and hot against her abdomen.

Lark slid her hand between them, rubbing the thick muscles of his thigh. The more she moved closer to his length, the harder his muscles clenched. Boldly, she closed her hand around him, and he groaned, a growl-like release of breath from deep in his chest. Hard and thick and long. A virgin's fear tried to break into the passion flooding Lark. But she pressed on with the delicious ache strumming through her, stroking him up and down.

"Aye, Lark," he groaned against her lips and lowered them to the bedding.

She gripped his broad shoulders, built strong by swordplay, and leaned back. He knelt before her, watching her with hunger to mirror her own. Gaze sliding down to his thick jack, she watched him stroke along it from root to tip and back. The pure male ease in the action made her mouth drop open.

She knelt up before him, sliding her hand down to meet his, and rubbed the juncture of her legs against his thigh, brushing the sensitive nub there. It pulsed with want, and she shifted it against the base of his jack.

"Bloody aye," he said and lifted her with both hands under her backside to fit her intimately along his length. His mouth descended back to hers, their kisses turning instantly wild and open until Lark swore the taste of Adam was seared into her memory. Honey ale and mint.

To keep her balance, Lark hitched one leg up around his hip, opening herself. His fingers dipped low. Her breathless inhale turned into a low moan as he touched her, the pressure spiraling up through her charged body. Gentle but insistent, he explored every nook, rubbing and grazing. She moaned into his mouth, pressing into his hand, as he slid inside, his fingers finding all her sweet spots while his thumb worked against her. "God, Lark, ye are wet fire," he murmured. "I want to taste ye."

"You are," she said, kissing him. Breathless, she pressed against him as his fingers moved within.

"I would taste your heat."

Her body clenched at the passion in his words. "Lie back," he said, moving over her so that she reclined into the pile of quilts and pillows. Propped on her elbows, she watched his gaze slake her bare body, taking in her full breasts perched on her chest. "Good Lord, ye are a goddess," he rasped and lowered his head to kiss her stomach, making it flutter under the heat of his breath.

"I ache," she said, her hips rising to brush against his chest. The muscles clenched inside her, and she reached below to touch herself. He lifted his head to watch, and she spread her knees for him to see how much she needed him.

"*Mo chridhe*, Lark," he murmured and met her gaze. "Aye, lass, give into the ache," he said, and Lark watched the dark waves of his hair as he lowered his mouth to cover her, sucking and swirling around her most sensitive nub as his fingers slipped back inside, working her flesh.

She gasped at the wet heat completely engulfing her as he loved her with his mouth, tongue, and fingers. Never could she have imagined such thirst within her. "Yes, yes," she called, not caring how loud she called out as her body spiraled higher and higher. "Oh god, yes," she yelled as she shattered quickly, and waves washed through her, making her bones feel soft and muscles contract and release.

Adam slid up her body, his fingers still within her, stroking every last swell of sensation. His arms came on either side of her head, and she felt his thick length seeking her. She pulled her knees up, angling so he could find her.

"Lark?" he said, meeting her gaze. So much shone in the depths of his eyes as he waited for her answer.

"Yes," she said, and he thrust into her.

Pain tore through her remaining pleasure, making her squeeze her eyes shut. They both breathed fast for several heart beats, and she blinked open. Adam held himself poised above her, everything in his body taut and waiting. She glanced down to see him fully embedded in her body. They were joined, fully husband and wife, fully committed to whatever was to come. She raised her eyes and grabbed hold of his shoulders, pulling him down onto her body. Clasped together, his strength all around her and within her, she'd never felt so safe in her entire life.

"Has the sting ebbed?" he asked behind clenched teeth.

"Yes," she said at his ear. "But you sound...tortured."

"Ye have no idea," he said, making her smile.

Still clinging to him, Lark tipped her hips, pressing into him, and heard his swift intake of breath. She did it again, and he groaned.

"I am giving ye time to adjust," he said, his breath tantalizingly hot against her neck as she recalled where his mouth had been, bringing her pleasure. The image of his head bent between her legs fanned the spark within her. He pulled back slightly to study her face, his eyes serious and assessing, the line of his brows furrowed.

"You have split me in two," she said. "Time to set me aflame again." She tugged his head to her lips. Kissing, he slowly moved within her body.

He palmed her breast, teasing her sensitive nipple as he slid the smallest amount. Heat washed down through Lark again. He was huge, but her body accommodated him, clenching against him. When his fingers wove a path lower to strum against her sensitive spot, she thrust against it as she kissed him, opening her mouth. Back and forth, he teased, blowing upon the coals of fire within her, igniting the sparks back into the inferno she welcomed.

She slanted against his mouth, giving and taking, tasting and reveling in his heat. Her fingers curled into the large muscles of his biceps. He was so hard everywhere, powerful, rugged, and wild yet gentle with her. The feel of his muscles made her shift restlessly under him.

Sliding in and out, the movement was smooth, their bodies fitting perfectly together. Giving and taking, they found a rhythm that fed them both. Adam moaned, and Lark swallowed it with her open-mouthed kiss. Spreading her legs even farther apart, Adam sunk in completely, his growl filling the room as he increased the tempo as they strained against one another. His fingers worked their magic across her, his teeth teasing her bottom lip and nibbling a way to her ear where he breathed wicked words. "Do ye like the feel of me plunging into ye, lass?"

"Oh god, yes."

"Ye are wet fire, like nothing I have felt before," he said.

She wrapped her legs around his waist, tipping her pelvis higher until her ankles locked to ride against his perfect arse. Together they thrust over and over, building higher until Lark felt her body start to reach for release again. "Now…it is coming now," she yelled and heard Adam growl loudly as his body strained against her, exploding and filling her with more heat as they rode out the storm together, holding each other tightly.

Nothing could make me let go. Not curses. Not her past. Adam was where she belonged, whether he was on Wolf Isle or in Aros Castle. As long as she was with him, Lark had found home.

A shiver ran through her as she realized that she was starting to give her heart away. A heart was a fragile thing.

She nuzzled her face against Adam's chest, breathing in their combined scent. "Hold me," she murmured.

"Aye, Lark." He rolled them to the side, their bodies still entwined.

Please do not let go.

Chapter Eleven

Adam strode across the sun-filled meadow where the Macleans had set up several events, including the caber toss and axe throwing. Tables laid out with sweets, cider, and mead were draped with brightly colored cloths.

He whistled a tune he hadn't heard since he was a child and realized it had been one of his father's favorites before his mother died. He smiled at the memory of John Macquarie escorting his wife around a festival on this very hillside. She had made his eyes twinkle and his smile easy.

Now Adam would be able to escort Lark. He'd left her sleeping after a night of loving. When he'd seen Meg Maclean below, he'd asked her to have a maid wake Lark if she did not rouse before mid-morning. He continued the jaunty melody, the sun seeming to smile down on him.

"What the bloody hell is coming out of your mouth?" Beck asked, sullen as usual in the early morning. His hair was sticking up, and he had a small towel and ball of soap.

"Heading to the creek?" Adam asked.

"Aye, Callum says I stink of whisky and ale." He narrowed

his eyes. "I have never heard ye whistle."

Adam shrugged, watching a bird fly overhead. "I think I will start." He smiled. "Da used to."

Beck's brows slowly rose as his eyes opened wide. He glanced at the castle and then back at Adam, and a wicked grin tipped up one side of his mouth. "So, ye finally made that marriage real, eh?"

"Go take your bath. No woman is going to wed a man who stinks of whisky and ale."

Beck walked off chuckling as Callum jogged up to Adam. "I have signed us up for the caber toss. There are a number of lasses I intend to impress."

Adam chuckled. "Make certain they know about Ulva before asking them to wed."

Callum snorted, his smile sharpening into a wry grin. "Everyone on Mull already knows about the curse."

Adam watched another bird soaring in the breeze above them. "I will talk to Tor Maclean about the curse being broken with Lark coming to the isle. We need to convince a few Macleans to come live there."

"Broken?" Callum said. "What about the hanging poppet and unearthed bones that ye told him about yesterday?"

"'Tis the work of an old woman who plays pranks," Adam said as they walked up to Drostan on the meadow above Aros.

"Grissell could not even walk to the village, let alone dig holes through it until she risked entering the church to find Wilyam Macquarie's bones," Callum said. "And why go to all that trouble to find them and then not take them?"

"Why the bloody hell are ye talking about that here?" Drostan asked in a gruff whisper. He looked slick from the sword practice that Adam had forfeited that dawn in order to make Lark yell out his name one more time.

"Adam bloody told Tor about it yesterday," Callum said.

Adam crossed his arms. "I gave Tor my oath to tell him everything about the isle as we resettled it. He can send warriors over to help us remove a single old crone if need be."

"A witch," Callum said. "Not just a crone, and a bastard at that."

"Again," Drostan said sternly as he nodded to a group of giggling lasses wandering by. "Why are ye talking about this out here? Are we not supposed to be finding lasses willing to come live there?"

Adam glanced about but saw no one that could overhear them. Still, he lowered his voice. "Lark spoke with Aunt Ida after the wedding. She says the curse says nothing about bastards living on the isle, just that we cannot father any on the isle."

"How about off the isle?" Callum asked.

Drostan hit him hard in the arm. "No bringing bastards into the world at all."

Callum rolled his eyes. "I was jesting. Da told us that enough that I practically hear it every time I glance at a lass." He looked at Adam. "Speaking of lasses, ask Lark to invite some of her new friends to Ulva," Callum said. "She must want more women on the isle with her. Ye know, to do things that lasses do together."

"Such as?" Drostan asked.

Callum shrugged. "Baking, watching us train, making delicious tarts for us, fluffing bedding and picking flowers. Oh, and making tapestries. We need more on Gylin's walls."

Drostan snorted and turned toward the road. He let out a low exhale, his lips forming an *O* as his brows lifted. "Lord, Adam, ye may want to stay by Lark's side today."

Adam turned to see Lark walking along the path toward the field. She was still far away, but the new gown she had borrowed from Tor's daughter fit her form well, cinching her waist in a deep green, the color of ferns in the summer forest.

Curls cascaded in red glory down her straight back, and as she nodded and passed several Maclean men, they stared, several of them catching up to her on both sides.

"She has a bloody wedding band on her finger," Adam said, his words like a growl. *Damn randy fools.*

"I do not think they are looking at her finger," Callum said, making Adam's fists clench. He left his brothers on the field, striding away like a slide of rocks down a mountain. Several glanced toward him and retreated, leaving one lad smiling foolishly down at her.

"I will be tossing the caber in a bit," the lad said. "Can I have your favor for the contest, a ribbon perhaps for luck?"

"The only man she will be favoring is her husband," Adam said. The lad blanched as he caught Adam's look.

He nodded, gave Lark a tight smile, and hurried off with the rest of his fool friends, several laughing at him.

"He was only being kind," Lark said, her smile softening her tone. The swell of her breasts teased the edge of the lace smock poking up from her bodice worked in green plaid. She took Adam's arm.

"He was leering at ye," Adam said, his irritation still high. "Even though ye wear my ring." He looked down on Lark as they walked. From his height, he could practically see down her bodice, or at least imagine that he could. His jack agreed. "I will find a shawl for ye," he said.

"I do not want to cover up the lovely costume Meg brought me to wear. I wonder if I can purchase it from her."

"Ye look too bonny this morning," he said, his frown relaxing as he leaned in to place a gentle kiss on her lips. "I thought ye would sleep longer," he whispered near her ear. "Ye seemed fairly exhausted after ye screamed my name right before dawn."

A slight flush pinkened her cheeks, but she smiled mischievously. "And you fell asleep within minutes of roaring my name."

The side of his mouth went up in a half grin. "We will head back early to Aros to catch up on our sleep. A nap will do us both good."

"Sleep? Really?" she drew out with a wry smile. "Somehow I do not think I will feel like sleeping when you come to nap with me." This teasing between them was easy and comfortable. Aye, marriage was good. A bonny, sweet wife would bring forth a brood of children and a settled isle. Lark was brave and lush and would help him see his clan established and his oath fulfilled. Trust, the most important aspect of marriage to her, was already growing between them.

Beck strode across from the stream, his hair wet. "Glad to see ye up and happy this morn, sister," he said, a smile tugging his mouth. "Adam was whistling when I first saw him. He has never whistled before." Beck ignored Adam's frown and trudged off toward the field where warriors and lasses were gathering for the start of the contests.

"Maybe I can sign up to throw my *sgian dubh*," she said and patted her leg as if she had a weapon tied beneath the petticoat.

"We will head over after the caber toss. Callum signed us up," Adam said, his gaze scanning the circle of warriors. Liam stood talking to the priest from Glencoe who had wed them.

"I heard you won the toss at the Beltane Festival," she said, her words low. "Impressive." He turned, meeting her smile, and felt a lightness in his chest.

Colorful tents were set up, and the bride and groom, from the wedding yesterday, were heralded onto the field with cheering. Small clusters of visiting MacLeods stood nearby. Had the groom ordered them not to start trouble? Liam's sister, Julia, seemed happy about the marriage even though she would move off Mull to the MacLeod's territory on Skye. Perhaps the groom was an exception to their foolish warring nature.

"My mother used to take me to festivals with my sisters," Lark said as they walked. The wind tugged at her curls, making them dance down her back and across her slender shoulders. He remembered kissing the smooth skin between them, inhaling her sweet scent from under the silky mass at her nape while she slept.

"I had heard…that she had died," Adam said, and her smile turned sad.

"Two years ago from consumption."

"I am sorry."

"Thank you," she said and inhaled, squeezing his hand where their fingers were intertwined.

Ahead, all four of his brothers waited for them, nodding a greeting to Lark. Adam pointed across the field. "There is Meg. Ye can stand with her, and then we can sign ye up for tossing daggers after the caber toss."

"Come on," Eagan said. "They are lining up, and lads are inspecting the logs."

"Those are MacLeods over there," Lark said, frowning at his brothers and then Adam. "No fighting. Slicing off heads at a festival will not attract wives and will surely upset Julia."

"See," Callum said. "Lark wants more lasses on Ulva, too." He looked at her. "So don't ye go telling them about the hanging poppet and falling on bones."

"Only if it comes up in conversation," Lark said without cracking a smile.

"Good morn," called a foreign-sounding voice. Adam turned to see the priest, but what pulled his attention was the sudden weight against his side.

"Lark?" he said low. "Are ye unwell?"

"I…I am surprised to see anyone I recognize," she said haltingly. A flush had covered her chest and neck, and a look that could only be described as dread washed over her features.

Before Adam could question her, the man walked up to their group, nodding to Beck. "I thought I recognized you two yesterday when that MacLeod was trying to start trouble." His gaze slid to Lark, and he smiled. "And the lovely young Beltane bride given away by Roylin Montgomerie."

"Father Lowder," Lark said. "I did not know you traveled this far north or onto the western isles."

"I travel to many lands to bring the word of God." He reached inside his robes. "And sometimes to carry news. A letter from your sister." He smiled as he handed it to her.

"Thank you," Lark said and tugged it. The letter didn't come away from his fingers, and he grinned as if playing a game until he finally let go.

"From where do ye hale?" Adam asked, frowning at the slight tremble he glanced in Lark's hand as she unfolded the parchment. "Your accent is like nothing I have heard." Was she frightened of the priest or what news he might bring?

The vicar smiled, his teeth bright in his tan face. "I grew up on the continent, but my father sailed the seas, and I went with him. I suppose I picked up the accent of the heathens on the southern isles."

"I imagine ye have vastly interesting tales of adventure on the sea," Beck said.

Lowder laughed. "That I do."

"And now ye travel across Scotland marrying Beltane brides?" Adam asked.

Lowder's chuckle sounded lofty. "As of late. There are a lot of blessings needed in this trampled country. The damned King Henry of England stealing from Catholic churches down there and sending troops north." He shrugged, his shoulders broad under his robes. "I do what I can to help."

"I have a question for ye, Father," Eagan said.

Adam watched Lark as she unfolded the missive, her eyes scanning the words. There had been no seal on the parchment, and Adam looked back to the priest. Would a man of God read a letter not meant for him?

Lowder smiled at Adam's youngest brother. "What is it you wish to know, my son?"

"How does one break an evil curse?" Eagan asked.

"The curse is not real," Adam said.

"But if it is," Eagan said, "we need to know how to break it. And ye have not asked a priest about it as far as I know." He had not. Any cleric that their father had asked had said the isle was tainted with evil but that he could give rights of it over to the church to see it cleansed. He eventually stopped asking, fearing that all of them were corrupt.

"A curse?" Father Lowder asked, his brow rising.

"Aye, on Ulva Isle." Callum pointed. "West of Mull. It was cursed by a witch a century ago, and no women have thrived on it since."

"There is a witch living on the isle, too," Drostan said. "Aunt Ida told Lark that the curse only states that bastards cannot be born of us on the isle, not that one cannot live on it."

"We still do not know the specific details," Beck said, frowning. "What if we father a bastard off isle and bring it on the isle?"

"That is what I asked," Callum said.

Adam cut a sharp glance to Callum. "It is superstition." Was this talk making Lark worry? But she didn't seem to be listening as she continued to read the letter, finally looking up, her gaze far away.

The priest's face scrunched as if he were thinking hard. "Satan's evil cannot touch a woman of purity and virtue, one with a clean heart and body, a woman with a godly past. With God's protection, she could thrive, and her virtue could break the curse."

One by one, his brothers turned their faces to Lark. As if suddenly hearing the priest's words, her frown sharpened. A clean heart, purity, and virtue? What husband would want that in his bed? Not he. Lark had been like fire undulating under him last night, teasing him with her touches and impure words, heating his blood and joining him as they came together. He wouldn't pray, ask, or wish for anything else.

"Perhaps ye should come to Ulva," Eagan said. "And bless her... The isle, that is."

"I would be happy to visit," Father Lowder said with a beaming smile. He turned to Lark, holding out an arm. "I can escort you over to Lady Maclean and her daughter, to watch at a safe distance, milady."

Lark felt stiff next to Adam. "I will take ye over," he said.

"'Tis no trouble," the priest said, grinning. "I am headed there now." He held out his arm.

When Lark did not move forward, Adam began to walk with her on his own arm. Meg met them halfway and took Lark's other arm. "I will take you over to stand with us," she said. "Adam, you go off and show us how you throw the cabers." Meg smiled almost wickedly between them. Had she heard Lark's cries of bliss through the walls of Aros?

"I am well," Lark said and gave him a tight smile. The priest had walked on and now stood talking to Lady Ava. Adam nodded and returned to his brothers.

"He has the build of a warrior," Beck said, shaking his head. "A shame he's a priest and won't take up a sword."

"We will need a man to hold mass in the chapel on Ulva once we *resurrect* it," Eagan said and snorted at his own humor while Adam continued to watch Father Lowder. Was it a coincidence he had come up this way? Perhaps when he found out Anna Montgomerie wanted to send word to Lark, he had traveled north to Mull with the MacLeods attending the Beltane Festival.

Adam's frown grew as he walked with his brothers up to the line of cabers. *Bloody damn hell.* Iain MacLeod stood beyond, watching them. He had dark circles under his narrowed eyes from Adam's punch last eve. He and his men were dressed in crisp kilts and had removed their shirts. Maclean lasses lined up to watch them while the lads pretended not to notice.

Liam Maclean walked along the line of cabers. "Ever since ye kicked his arse on Ulva, he wants ye dead," he said to Adam.

Adam turned his glare on Liam. "Speaking of kicking an arse, why the bloody hell were ye telling Lark I'd slept with many women?"

Liam's smile dropped away, but he didn't have time to respond.

"Damn, Macquarie," Iain yelled down the slope. "I am still surprised ye aren't dead on that cursed isle of yours." The lasses bent their heads together, whispering.

"How is your beak feeling this morn?" Callum asked, thumbing his nose at him.

Iain frowned, his lips curling back like a hungry mongrel. "'Twas an unfair punch," he said and looked to Adam. "Shall we take another go at it?"

"What was unfair about it?" Adam asked. "Ye tried to start a clan war, and I broke your nose. Seems like an even trade."

Iain slammed his fist into his palm, his scowl showing clenched yellow teeth.

"Feeling brave with your pack of cousins here to back ye up," Eagan said. There were at least ten MacLeods on the hill, outnumbering them easily.

Iain shot his hand in the air, his thumb caught in a

rude gesture, but looked to Adam. The group of shirtless MacLeods shifted, letting one press through them. Adam recognized Fergus MacLeod from the Beltane Festival, one of Lark's tenacious suitors, hatred evident in his glare. Had he followed her there, bringing Father Lowder with Anna's letter?

Iain *tsk*ed. "I hear ye tricked a lass into wedding ye."

"Foking tricked her into giving up her life to work on your cursed isle," Fergus added as he stalked closer.

Iain crossed his arms over his hairy chest and nodded to where Lark stood across the field. The bastard was going to get his damn nose punched again. But Adam wouldn't be the one to start the fight even if he would surely finish it. *No fighting.* Lark's reminder kept his boots rooted to the ground.

Iain turned to look at the row of women behind him. "Be that a lesson to ye, lasses, not to believe anything the Macquaries say to ye."

Drostan took two strides uphill, but Beck stopped him with a hard clasp on his shoulder. "Adam told her everything about Ulva before he wed him," Beck said. Not completely true, but Adam had tried. Even so, the comment was like a thin needle twisting in his gut.

Several of Iain's cousins moved to stand before each of his brothers with Iain and Fergus confronting Adam together.

"Ye fools thinking to impress the lasses by picking a fight, MacLeod?" Adam asked, his face blank with apathy. His brows rose slowly. "Because they will not be thinking much of ye with missing teeth, broken faces, and a pint or two less blood."

Iain smiled crookedly while Fergus held his scowl. "I am heartily glad the curse hasn't finished ye off already," Iain said.

Drostan chuckled, the sound tinged with dark contempt. "Ye afraid of curses? Because I am certain that many of them have been placed against your life, Iain MacLeod."

Iain spit. "Ye letting your wee brothers talk on their own? They will get themselves into trouble that way." The belligerent arse must wish for an early grave. Adam's *wee* brothers were as tall as he, which meant taller than any MacLeod there, and twice as toned and talented with a sword.

"Shut the fok up," Eagan said, and Callum stepped in front of him to stop him from charging into the line of war-ready clansmen. His brothers were always hungry for a chance to battle the slander said against their diminished clan. It was both their weakness and their strength, their fury feeding their frenzy for vengeance.

No fighting. Mo chreach.

Iain grinned. "Aye, keep the rascal under control else he will end up dead on this isle instead of on yer own. Isn't that where Macquaries go to die? Wolf Isle?" He laughed, and his men joined him. Adam breathed evenly, his temper kept in check with the discipline he worked hard to hone. A chief must rule his wants with wisdom, which required a level head and thoughtful restraint.

"'Tis a shame ye've wed," Iain continued, his gaze slid past Adam to settle on Lark. "She will end up as dead as your mother and then no lass will step foot on your cursed isle."

Snap. It was as if the iron chain Adam held on his rage ripped apart. One, two, three steps, and he caught Iain's collar in his fist. War erupted around him as his brothers leaped forward, attacking the other MacLeod cousins. But Adam was intent on slamming his fist into Iain's gut. *Foking bastard.* Leering at Lark and thinking of her dead, blaming it on him for bringing her to Wolf Isle like his father brought his mother. *Bloody foking bastard.*

Fergus charged forward to grab Adam along with a third, but Liam Maclean jumped in, slamming the other man with a well-aimed fist while Adam threw Fergus to the ground. He followed his momentum with a kick, sending him sprawling into the dirt before turning back to Iain, who held his nose that once again dripped blood. Adam lifted Iain up around the middle, propping him above his head to spin him in a tight circle.

"Put me down! Ye are a foking dead man!" Iain yelled, his blood flying out from his nose with the force of the spin. Adam threw him like he was a boulder in the stone throwing contest, his body thudding against the hard ground followed by a groan.

Adam pivoted back to see that several Macleans had jumped in, as well as Rabbie, to support his brothers, making the sides even, and he surged forward to help. Fists flew, and large bodies were shoved, falling amongst the shrieking women who had lined up to watch the caber contest. A pack of dogs ran amongst them, barking and adding to the chaos. Drostan and Callum each had a MacLeod in the air over their heads while Beck defended them against several who ran forward. His brothers threw the MacLeods onto the heavily laden tables of sweets and drinks. Dishes crashed to the ground as the table broke under their combined weight, and the entire tent shifted, falling over.

Everywhere, men wrestled, most Macleans joining in to help the Macquaries like they had all their lives. Without the Macleans, the other clans would have wiped the Macquaries out decades ago. Why then did their help strum more anger inside Adam?

Half covered with jam and honey ale, the two MacLeods hurled themselves back into the fight, attacking Callum and Drostan, who grappled with them to end up clasping them in wrestling holds around their thick necks. Luckily for the MacLeods, no swords were drawn.

Eagan's anger made him swing wildly, taking down a MacLeod with sheer battle frenzy, but his youthful anger made him take risks. Adam ran to him, guarding his back and shoving away two other MacLeods bent on knocking Eagan into the ground.

"Enough!" Tor Maclean's voice cut through the grunts and curses of battle. "I said enough," Tor yelled again. He and Keir MacKinnon stood on the outskirts of the brawl. Tor grabbed several MacLeods from the clutches of Adam's brothers, as did his tattooed friend. "'Tis a friendly competition, not a bloody war."

Adam's arms lowered, his fists unclenching, and he wiped blood from his hands on a cloth he carried tied to his belt. His gaze ran down the line of his brothers. Eagan had a broken lip that would need to be stitched, and blood leaked from cuts on all their knuckles. Rabbie was sitting on a caber, sweat over his face but very little blood. The MacLeods looked worse by far.

Iain clutched a rag to his nose as he drew in fast breaths and pointed at Adam. "He threw the first punch."

"Because ye said his new wife would die like his mother did on his isle," Liam yelled.

"We can add a public flogging to the games," Keir added, his tattoos of little crosses and Celtic circles adding to the promise of pain in his even voice. How the man had convinced his sweet, mild wife, Grace, to marry him was a mystery.

"As much as ye'd like to, Keir," Tor said, "I would not taint Julia's wedding with screams and more blood."

Liam wiped his lip with a swipe of his finger. "Appreciated. For Julia's sake, let's keep the public displays of blood at a minimum. My sister is squeamish." He took a deep breath and looked at the mess of broken dishes, tables, and scattered food. "As it is, she is going to cry at the loss of her favorite tarts. Damn, and her stack of wedding buns." The white pastries lay scattered in the grass where several of the older women tried to salvage them.

As if on cue, a wailing began, and they all turned to see Julia Maclean MacLeod run up the hill toward them, her groom, Rearden, chasing after her. Lark, with Meg Maclean, were following briskly, menacing frowns in place.

Beck huffed in resignation. "Shite. Here comes Lark."

"Damn, she looks mad enough to stab us," Callum cursed, his voice low.

"Ye should have seen how she handled those thieves on our journey here," Beck whispered, his hands folding in front of his ballocks.

Lark marched toward them, her eyes snapping with fury. She cut them all a look of pure reprimand and bent down to help console Julia, who wailed over the toppling of the confection in white sugar work. Tor's wife joined in, all of them helping to pick the little cakes up, brushing them gently. But there was no whole table on which to set them.

Eagan tried to help, but when he dripped blood on one, and Julia started crying louder, he retreated to Adam. Beck and Callum went forward to help while Drostan glared at the MacLeods, waiting for them to dive back in.

"Find a whole table," Tor ordered, and four of the Macleans ran off.

Adam stepped up to Tor. "Chief Maclean, apologies."

Tor's face was as hard as Adam's, but his mouth softened as he met his gaze. His voice lowered. "A settled spirit in a man keeps his head level." He exhaled. "Ye have the dedication of your father. Do not let others divert ye from your goals." He shook his head "Men like Iain MacLeod create diversions." Tor glanced toward Iain where one of the Maclean lasses peered up his nose. "Ye should wonder what the reason is behind them."

Adam nodded to the wise chief. "Thank ye for your loyalty to the Macquaries and for letting us live amongst ye for generations."

"Ye are always welcome," Tor said. "Although…" He nodded to the mess and wailing behind Adam.

"Bloody Macquaries," the groom yelled out as he drew his bride into his arms, anger flashing in his eyes as he stared across at Adam.

Lark stepped up. "I am so sorry, Chief Maclean, for this mess. Thank you for the invitation to Mull and Aros," she said, her voice even. "We will be departing now to prevent any further disturbance within the families representing the couple." She nodded and turned on her heel to walk away.

Beck's mouth dropped open. "We have not competed yet."

"He says we are still welcome," Eagan said, his lip dripping profusely.

"Adam was but defending your honor," Drostan called after her.

Fergus MacLeod leaped forward to follow her, dirt smeared on his ruddy cheek. He grabbed Lark's wrist, swinging her around. "Your bloody da meant ye for me or for anyone he could sell ye off to. But not a cursed Macquarie."

That foking devil!

"Adam, hold on," Tor said, his hand braced on Adam's shoulder.

"Ye will lose your hand and your bloody tongue," Adam yelled at Fergus.

Fergus's meaty hand still held Lark's wrist. "Your father wants ye back, ye know. Sent me to fetch ye for him," Fergus continued. "He cannot stop talking of ye. Drinks himself into a fit and says—"

"He is not my father," Lark yelled. With a jerk and twist of her arm, she yanked her wrist free. Drawing the *sgian dubh*, her glare pierced Fergus. But Adam didn't give her a chance to stab the arse. He walked up behind Fergus and slammed one hand into the man's shoulder. Fergus swung around with the force, and Adam's fist smashed into his jaw, knocking him on his arse as Lark jumped back.

Fergus was sprawled on the ground, his eyes barely able to focus, so Adam crouched low. "Never touch or speak to my wife again." Fergus spit, glaring, the sounds of another fight in the background.

Lark spun away from the scene. Not her father? What did that mean? Who was Lark's father? She flew down the hill, Meg chasing after her. Adam exhaled a smothered curse.

"Enough!" Tor yelled behind him, but Adam continued to watch Lark hurry away. "Or ye all will be thrown off the Isle of Mull."

Lark gave the bride a hug where she still cried on the path then said a few words to Ava Maclean and Meg. She shook her head when Father Lowder approached, the curls still tumbling down her back, looking silky and fragrant. Lark glanced back at him, her face blank, and turned to walk toward the docks.

Drostan ran up to him. "Do we go then?"

"Aye. See to the barge," Adam said. *Sell her off?* What did Fergus MacLeod mean by that? Who was Roylin Montgomerie if he was not her father? Why did she live with him, and why would he want to sell her off and then send Fergus to fetch her back?

The questions around Lark were adding up into a bigger mystery than Wolf Isle.

Chapter Twelve

Lark stood on the shore as Adam and his brothers tied the ferry securely to the dock on Wolf Isle. The sun was not even high, and they were already back.

Waking up, her body had been deliciously sore from such passionate loving with Adam. She had firmly decided to let her past stay in the past. But then she'd seen Father Lowder. And then she'd read Anna's letter. And then she'd yelled before everyone that Roylin Montgomerie was not her father.

The brawling, hysterical bride, and bruised wrist from Fergus's grip added to her already twisted worries.

"Are ye well?" Adam asked. His deep voice made her close her eyes as her heart leaped into a frantic trot.

She forced an even breath and looked up at him. "The bride was distraught, all of you are bleeding, and we may not be welcome back onto Mull." But none of that mattered in the face of her secret. From Anna's letter of warning, Roylin had been revealing all her secrets, real ones and ones he imagined in his sick mind.

"Tor will have us back," Adam said. "Perhaps not the

MacLeods."

She glanced past him to where his brothers tied the ferry secure. They all had blood and dirt smeared on their white tunics and bruised knuckles. Callum had a swelling eye, and Eagan's lip needed stitching.

Adam's eyes held questions, and worry snaked through her. The whisky did not help her open up to him about her shame. It only made her more open to his caresses.

She glanced down at the damp grass. "I am embarrassed for our family." Like it or not, she and Adam had consummated their marriage several times, and she was part of their family. An annulment would be nearly impossible. Would he petition for divorce?

Adam looked away, his shoulders rising one at a time as if they ached. "Iain is an arse, and I should not have reacted."

"The arse threatened ye, Lark," Callum said, striding past them, his gaze trained on the ground as if he searched for something. He turned to walk backward and nodded at her. "Adam was showing him how painfully foolish his tongue was."

Her tongue was equally foolish. No one had immediately asked her about her confession on the stilted ride across the water. Her brothers did not seem to want to look at her. Were they ashamed of themselves or wondering about her?

"Eagan definitely needs his lip stitched," Beck said as he strode past.

She'd been wielding a needle since she was five years old and her mother was seeking a way to make her valuable in the household. "I will see to it up at Gylin," she said. Their knuckles would all need attention as well, and Rabbie had been unusually quiet, his face pale.

Drostan crouched down, his finger on the ground. "There are extra footprints on the beach," he said, glancing up at Adam.

"I cannot tell if these all are ours," Beck said near the dock.

"Go on up to the castle," Adam said. "Keep your eyes open." His brothers drew their swords and hurried up the path.

Adam grasped Lark's arm and moved before her, dipping his head to look in her eyes. "I am sorry, lass." His voice was quiet, and her body remembered the timber well. A wave of sensation slid along her skin, making her lips open to draw in breath. He caught her chin in his fingers, and she remained looking into his eyes. They were clear and bright, not bloodshot or blurry or filled with pain and shameful want.

"I wish the fight had not tainted our night together," he said. "And…" She held her breath, waiting for his questions. "…the letter from your sister," he said. "I hope all is well with her."

She wet her dry lips. "As well as can be expected." She met his gaze. "You have likely figured out that life in the Montgomerie household was not…easy."

He touched a curl hanging down the side of her face, his thumb grazing the skin. "I am beginning to see that." He frowned, but his touch made it feel like concern. "Perhaps someday, when ye want, ye can tell me about it."

She almost turned her face into his hand to kiss it but nodded instead.

He brushed his thumb over her cheek. "Roylin Montgomerie is not your father?" There it was. Of course he had heard her; everyone had. She drew in breath.

"Adam!" one of his brothers yelled from way up the path. "Adam." Callum jogged down the path, his eyes wide. "Adam, ye need to come."

"What's happened?" Adam asked, turning, and Lark released her breath.

Callum glanced at Lark and then Adam, shaking his

head. "Ye just need to come."

Adam grabbed her hand, and they hurried after his brother through the trees, racing toward the castle. Had someone attacked it while they were away? What mischief could have been done over the course of one day?

As they rounded the curve in the path, they slowed as the other three brothers and Rabbie stood before the gate. Adam and Lark hurried forward, and the men stepped back. There in the center of them stood a woman, her stomach protruding in the late stages of pregnancy. She had straight blonde hair and bright blue eyes, her gaze going straight to Adam. She glanced at Lark and then gave him a scalding look that made Lark's insides toss.

"Adam Macquarie," the woman said and laid her palms on her round stomach. "This child is yours."

. . .

Adam walked the length of the table away from where the overly ripe woman sat eating some bannocks that Callum had found in the kitchen.

Lark stood across the room by the cold hearth. She'd said nothing since the woman's proclamation and did not look at him.

"Your name just happens to be Elspeth," Drostan said. "Like the woman who originally hung herself after finding herself with child by Wilyam Macquarie."

And like then, Adam was married to someone else. The fact that the woman was lying made it likely someone was using the legend of the curse to prevent his clan from settling the isle again, but why and who? The woman could not be working alone. He studied her. She looked vaguely familiar, but he did not remember ever talking with her, let alone tupping her.

"You will be cursed if you do not do right by me and this child," Elspeth said, hugging her protruding belly. "Having a bastard on this isle will keep it in ruins."

Adam hadn't been close to any pregnant women, but she looked to be about done, like the bairn could drop out of her at any moment. "As I said, I do not know ye. The child could not be mine if we have never slept together."

She waved off his comment. "You were drunk on whisky."

He had never drunk enough of anything to make him forget his actions. Even the night his da died, when the man had wrung a promise from him to see Wolf Isle settled. He recalled everything that night, even the guilt that he hadn't done enough to help his father in his quest to move them back to the isle.

We have a house, but we have no home here on Mull. Be the Macquarie to break the curse and build a home on Ulva. His father's words showed up often in Adam's nightmares, usually the ones where he was too weak to hold a sword.

"Where did ye say this," Beck waved his hand at the woman's stomach, "happened?" All of Adam's brothers had asked the woman the same thing.

She closed her eyes. "Like I said five times before, it was at a festival on Mull. I was visiting with my da, and all of ye were into your cups, and I had taken a nip, and Adam and I kissed behind the barn—"

"Which barn?" Rabbie asked, eyes narrowed.

"I do not know," she said, glaring at him. "I had taken some whisky and was unfamiliar with Aros."

"And who is your father? Where is he now?" Callum asked.

"He was Henry Sinclair, and he is dead."

"How?" Drostan asked.

Lark pushed away from the wall where she'd been standing. "I think Elspeth has answered enough questions for now." She walked over to her. "Let us get you settled in a bedroom so you can rest."

"And ye rowed over here yourself?" Eagan asked, his words muffled from the rag he still held against his lip. "With that belly?"

"And your boat happened to float away?" Drostan asked, his arms crossed.

Lark helped the woman stand. "There is a room above that you can share with me."

Share with her? *Damn*. Did Lark believe her lies?

Elspeth walked slowly, her roundness making it look awkward and bloody uncomfortable. How did women do it? Men were foolish to think women weren't strong when they could grow life within them, carrying it until birth and longer still as a needy infant.

Beck came up behind Adam when they disappeared up the stairs. "Have ye ever seen her before?" he asked, his voice low.

Adam turned to meet his brother's gaze and noticed the questions on all his brother's faces. "She looks slightly familiar, like perhaps she has been on Mull. But I have never even talked to her."

"She is lying," Drostan said. "But why?"

"To have someone support her and the babe?" Eagan said and grimaced at the pain his talking shot through his lip.

"But why pick Adam? Who even gave her his name?" Callum asked. But they had no answers.

"I do not, for a moment, believe her name is Elspeth," Adam said, turning back to look at the dark steps.

Rabbie set his tankard on the table. "The extra set of footprints on the shore are too big to be hers. I went down to check and did not see any small prints except one set, which was Lark. The woman's footprints came from the village."

Drostan crossed his arms, deep frown in place. "So a man

came from the sea, and the woman came from the village or beyond. Are they connected?" Silence settled in the hall for a moment.

"What did Lark mean about Roylin not being her father?" Rabbie asked, scratching his bushy beard. His eyes narrowed with obvious suspicion.

Roylin had signed the marriage certificate as Lark's father. Perhaps her mother came to the marriage after her first husband died. Roylin would be her stepfather. "I do not know," he said.

"Well, ye better find out," Rabbie said, his words sharp.

• • •

The woman was settled amongst the quilts of Adam's large bed, the fire crackling in the hearth as it consumed the peat. Elspeth fell asleep almost immediately. Lark hadn't asked her any questions, and the woman hadn't provided any answers.

Adam's child? The look on his face made her want to believe him that he didn't know the woman at all. But why would she lie? Why use Adam's name? Was she desperate to wed before the child was born so it would not be a bastard? Bastards certainly had a more difficult way in the world.

Rap. Rap. A light tap on the door made Lark jerk her face from the flames. *Adam.*

Opening, she found him standing there, hands braced on each side of the door. Without a word, she stepped forward. It took him a moment to step back, allowing her out into the hall to close the door behind her.

He looked into her face in the dim light of the candle he'd set in a window nook. "Ye know it is not my bairn, that she is lying," he said.

"You are certain? Men can do stupid things when full of whisky." Roylin had fallen off horses, started brawls, slept in ditches, and told the whole town things about her. "It is possible you do not remember because of drink."

He leaned closer, his face full of conviction, his brows lowered. "I have never been full of whisky. An honorable man does not drink past reason and tup women, Lark. And yet ye think it possible of me. Have I given ye cause to doubt my word?"

She broke the tether between their gazes, looking off into a dark corner that had been dusted free of cobwebs. "No, but I have seen it before."

"Drunk men tupping women?"

"Drunk men doing terrible things," she whispered. "And regretting them afterward."

There was a long pause. "Has that happened to ye? Terrible things?" His voice was a rough whisper in the darkness.

Blurry eyes and a drunken smile surfaced in Lark's mind. Rough hands and the sour smell of whisky. *Ye look like me wife.* Her entire body tensed at the memory.

"Lark," he said. "Has anyone hurt ye?"

She turned her gaze back to his. His face was hard, his jaw clenched, as he studied her. For a moment, her heart beat hard like a panicked bird in the clutches of a hawk. Could he know the truth? But no one was allowed inside her head to see the shame cowering in the darkness there. "Was someone drunk around ye, a fool who did terrible things?"

"I…I came to you a maid last night."

"Aye, but has someone harmed ye?"

She shook her head, rubbing her wrist. "We need to do something about Elspeth," she said, redirecting him. "She is certain you are responsible."

He exhaled. "The woman looks slightly familiar, as if she attended an event on Mull years ago, but I do not recall even speaking to her before. And I highly doubt her name is Elspeth. Someone told her to use that name to make the curse seem real."

"Who else knows about the curse?" she asked, the tension unknotting in her back as they moved farther away from questions about her past. *I should have told him last night.*

"Most on Mull to start with," he said.

Of course, rumors would run amongst the people like a plague. All of Mull would likely speculate about what Fergus had said and how she had answered. Would he reveal everything Roylin had said? Lark tried to shake off the dread curling in her stomach. "Who would know the name of the original pregnant woman who hung herself?"

"Anyone who has read the family Bible or asked about the specifics of Macquarie history would know the name Elspeth."

"Grissell would know?" Lark asked.

"Aye." Adam's frown deepened. "And ye said ye thought someone was living with her in the forest."

Lark nodded and looked back at the door. "Attacking the woman with questions is not going to get her to talk. We will keep her here, especially as her time grows near. The babe is an innocent in all this."

She watched him carefully, his gaze rising above her head as if thoughts moved rapidly within him. "The child is almost certainly a bastard if she is blaming me," he said.

The word "bastard" sunk inside Lark, like a lead ball thrown into a frothy loch. "You keep saying that you do not believe in curses, and yet I see you do."

"The curse is real for some," he said, looking back at her. "Rabbie. My brothers. They have been taught all their lives that darkness will envelope Ulva if we bring a bastard to it."

She shook her head, swallowing hard. "From what Ida told me, the curse just says that Macquaries cannot father a bastard. It has nothing to do with one visiting the isle. If Elspeth does not have a husband, but her bairn was fathered by someone other than a Macquarie, the curse does not apply." Anger welled up inside her. "Bastards are not lepers or demons, Adam. They are babes who are innocent of the sins of their parents."

When he glanced down at his arm, she realized that she'd grabbed hold of it, her fingers curling into the tunic. She slowly released him.

"Aye," he said, his eyes narrowing to study her in the low light. "'Tis wrong to think a bastard is any different than a bairn coming forth from a strong marriage." He rubbed a hand through his hair, still studying her. "My father beat it into our heads that we were never to father a bairn outside the sanctity of marriage, because of the curse, which he believed with all his heart. Despite what the family Bible says, he told us time and again that no bastards should even set foot on the isle."

Lark dropped her hand and stepped back until the wall held her up. "What would happen if you did father a babe out of marriage? Would the curse want you to kill it?"

"Nay," he answered quickly, his brows pinching low. "Ye think I could murder a child?"

Lark breathed past the thumping in her chest as they stared at one another in the cold shadows. She shook her head. How could she think something so terrible of him? "No." She shook her head again. "I do not think that."

She let her breath come out in a small gust. "We should ask a midwife to come from Mull to see the woman," she said. "I attended a few births with my mother and can help, but we will need her services."

Adam rubbed a hand down his face. "Of course. And to stop Rabbie from harassing her, we should move her to Mull, so she gives birth off Ulva."

"It should not matter if the child is not yours," she said, her words a hoarse whisper.

"We need to read the family Bible again, just to make certain. It will keep my brothers and Rabbie satisfied." He watched her closely, and she could almost hear the tangle of questions swirling in his mind. "Lark...ye said that Roylin Montgomerie is not your father."

Lark swallowed and breathed deeply, unlocking part of her confession that she should have confided in him before they came together last night. "My father died before I was born. He was an English soldier. My mother and he fell in love." She looked past his shoulder, not wanting to watch his face, her words soft. "They did not marry before he was killed. She came to her marriage with Roylin Montgomerie with me." She swallowed. "A bastard." She breathed deeply and bravely met his gaze. "You have created no bastards, Adam, but you married one."

Adam's face remained pinched, the lines in his forehead deepened from the slant of the shadows in the corridor. "Ye did not tell me."

The heavy, teetering yoke that Lark always felt balanced on her shoulders, shifted as if it would crush her. "I meant to, last night, before..." Her words broke off as she ran out of breath. Standing against the wall in the curved tower, she felt a cold fall over her and wrapped her arms around herself. She waited.

"I will have Beck fetch the family Bible from Aunt Ida when he talks to Lady Maclean about helping with the birth."

Her heart pounded. "What if what is written is exactly what your father said?"

Silence.

The silence stretched. "You said you do not believe in curses," she reminded him.

"And ye said that trust was the most important thing to

ye in a marriage."

She opened her mouth and closed it. Twice.

"Trust goes both ways, Lark."

What could she say? She had kept the secret of her birth her whole life, just like Adam had been told to believe the curse his whole life.

Adam's face smoothed into an apathetic mask, making her stomach knot. He looked past her toward the door of the chief's bed chamber. "We know nothing about this woman except that she lies," he said. "'Tis unsafe for ye to sleep in there with her."

She gave a little nod. "I will check on Rabbie and tend to Eagan's lip." She looked down at his large hand in a splash of light from the torch. It was strong, with calluses from his sword and work, fingers that had touched every inch of her last night. "Your knuckles, too," she said, her voice low.

His eyes focused on his hand. "Aye, thank ye." The tone was flat, almost defeated. She almost preferred anger.

"Should I sleep on the barge on the water, until you have had a chance to read Ida's Bible?" She took a quick breath. "Although, then I suppose we would need to put Elspeth out there with me."

"Nay, Lark," he said, his tone crisp. "Ye will sleep with me here on the isle."

"Rabbie and your brothers may have a problem with that."

"Aye," Adam said, his voice heavy. "They will."

Her fingers slid against the rough wall from granite stone to granite stone as they descended. The castle had been there for hundreds of years, hands and fingers skimming these exact rocks. Even a reputed curse hadn't toppled them. If only she could be as strong.

Chapter Thirteen

Bastard? Adam had brought a bastard to Ulva, something he swore to his father he would never do.

It was dawn, a new day, but he had no idea what to expect of it. He closed the door to the room that had been a nursery in Gylin where he and his brothers had slept as bairns. It was the only other one that currently had a real bed in it. Lark had shared the smaller bed with him but had laid way on the other edge. It was a wonder she had not fallen off.

He'd hardly slept, listening to her mumbled words and watching her face pinch as if she grew afraid. He'd nearly woken her, demanding to know what demon she fought. But then she'd quieted, and he'd lain still, wondering if the demon looked like him.

Why hadn't she told him she was a bastard? If she'd planned to do so before they came together, why hadn't she? Did she really think he would try to get rid of her because of her inauspicious beginning? *Would I?*

"Nay," he murmured as he reached the bottom of the tower stairs. How would the isle or Grissell even know that

Lark's parents had not wed? They may have wed under God's law anyway. Lark said they fell in love.

There was no one in the great hall. Good. His orders to his brothers the night before were to start early. He wanted answers and that Bible as soon as possible. Last night, with his sour disposition and Lark being present, they had not asked him about her revelation on Mull.

Adam stepped out into the bailey. Beck glared at him as he stuffed a flask into the satchel he was taking. Was it just the morning that made him look full of fury or had they been talking about Lark after they left them last night?

Beck coughed and tugged on the strap to close it. "The Bible, fabric, a midwife. Anything else I should retrieve from Mull?" he asked. "Brides for all my brothers, perhaps, and that priest to marry us?"

The wind blew the thin, whip-like limbs of the dead willow tree in a dance. A long tendril snapped close to Adam. *I do not believe in curses.*

"Adam?" Beck said, raising his voice.

"What?" His voice cracked like the leafless ends.

"I said, should I also bring back brides and a priest?"

"Just get the damn Bible." He looked up at some clouds blowing in from the ocean on the west. "And take a tarp. It will rain."

Beck snorted and grabbed his satchel. "Walk with me," he said. Adam glanced back at Gylin, but no one else was outside. Hopefully Lark was armed if she went to check on the pregnant woman. They stepped out the small door in the wall and headed down the path toward the dock.

"Ye should know that Rabbie was talking last night about what Lark said."

Adam didn't respond as he walked along, trying to keep his anger contained. Beck was Adam's brother, best friend, and second-in-command of their clan. He did not deserve

Adam's ire.

Beck continued. "He wanted to know who Lark's father is if the man at the festival, who signed her marriage license, is not. Do ye know?"

"He died before Lark's mother wed Roylin Montgomerie. He was in the English army and was killed."

"English? Bloody hell. That's akin to marrying Lucifer himself," Beck said, but a slight grin on his face showed that he jested.

Adam could weave a tale of Lark's parents being married, but look where deceit had led them so far. He kicked a rock to fly forward along the trail. "They were not wed."

He took two steps before he noticed that Beck had stopped in the path and turned to him. Beck's mouth was open, his face impassive. He swallowed. "They were not wed? At all?" Could one be partially wed?

Adam shook his head and continued walking. He heard the crunch of Beck's boots as he caught up. "Well damn." Beck cursed under his breath.

Adam stepped up to their rowboat and untied the thick rope from the stake in the ground.

"What are ye going to do?" Beck asked, staring at him wide-eyed.

Adam continued to coil and finally raised his head. "I am not divorcing Lark or having the union annulled."

"The priest who did it is at Aros," Beck reminded him of the well-muscled cleric with the lewd smile.

"I do not trust him." He met Beck's gaze. "And I said I am not having the marriage annulled. For all I know, Lark is with child already."

"From one night together?" Beck asked but stopped talking when Adam glared at him. "Pretty damn powerful of ye if she is," he murmured under his breath and stepped aboard the boat. Adam walked over to a wooden chest and drew out a tarp to throw at him.

"Keep this between us," Adam said.

Beck picked up the oars. "Rabbie will ask ye as soon as he sees ye."

"Aunt Ida told Lark that the curse revolves around *us* fathering bastards. It matters not who we wed."

"I certainly hope that is what it says," Beck said, his brows pinched.

Adam turned away to stride back up the hill. What would his brothers think when they found out? Would they react like Beck? He was the most accepting of people, the least superstitious of the lot. Rabbie would likely demand he throw Lark off the isle with Elspeth that very day if he knew. Adam rubbed his clenched fist against the throbbing at the back of his head.

Adam walked up to the gates but did not go inside. His other brothers were already working to finish the roof on the last room, but Adam wanted to follow the woman's footprints that Rabbie had seen in the village. If they came from the south side, she'd probably walked from Grissell's cottage.

He turned at the sound of the door in the wall opening. Lark stepped out, a shawl covering the top of her blue dress, her hair caught in a long braid that laid against her shoulder.

"Is anything amiss?" he asked, striding toward her. There were slight circles beneath her eyes showing her poor sleep.

"No," she said, a hand to her chest as if she'd gasped at his voice. "Elspeth is still in our...your bedchamber. I have eaten and thought I would look for her footprints."

"If they come from the south, she is probably the one living with Grissell," he said.

They began to walk together toward Ormaig, a three-foot space between them. "Elspeth could not have rigged that poppet up in the church rafters," Lark said. "Not by herself in her condition."

The caw of a gull made her look upward, and Adam studied the graceful column of her neck. He cleared his throat. "Did ye sleep well?"

"No," she answered, glancing at him. "And you?"

"Nay."

He and Lark followed the pebbled path toward the village. "Ye were talking in your sleep," he said, and she caught the toe of her boot on a buried rock.

"What did I say?"

"I could not tell, but ye sounded frightened. Do ye remember a dream or nightmare?"

She shook her head. Overhead, more clouds rolled in, and a breeze blew from the west off the ocean. They entered the town, silent without people. Their silence added to the ghostly feel.

"I remember when the village had life in it," he said to break the eerie feel. "Before my father moved us back to Mull." They stopped beside the first building. "It was sparsely populated. My father had only lived on the isle for about five years, slowly convincing what was left of our family and some of their friends to move back over. The soil was rich and fertile, and the isle was without predators so sheep could roam free."

"And they all left after your mother died?" she asked, looking at him as they walked through the twisting path among the lifeless dwellings.

"They felt the curse killed her."

"Unfortunately, many women die from childbirth, but Eagan lived."

They reached the chapel and stopped. "He lived, but Eagan was a twin."

"A twin?"

Adam watched the breeze tug at the curls around her face like errant ribbons. "Our sister died with our mother."

He breathed deeply. "Two Macquarie females at once, descendants of Wilyam Macquarie. People panicked. The two pregnant women left immediately. Then several women died of age and a few ewes became ill. It was enough to make everyone leave."

"Even your father?"

"We were the last to go, but Ida said she'd take us lads with or without him." He turned to scan the silent buildings with their vacant, watching windows. A curtain blew ragged ends with the growing wind.

"'Twas a hard time," he continued. "People blamed the Macquarie curse for every little thing that went wrong. Many even moved away from Mull, taking on the Maclean family name."

Lark did not reply, seeming to take in his words, words he should have spoken on their journey. Maybe she would have told him she was a bastard if he had been honest with her from the start. What would he have done if she had?

He cleared his throat. "I want to search the south side of the village for footprints." They walked that way in silence.

Adam pointed to a structure without a roof. "A woman lived there who baked bread and tarts."

"My sister, Anna, would like to start a bakery," Lark said.

He opened his mouth to say that she could come to Ulva and start one but then closed it.

Lark glanced at him, her lips in a thin line. "Anna is not a bastard. She is Roylin's daughter."

"She is welcome," he said, wishing he had said it before Lark spoke.

"Perhaps you should have wed her."

"She was not the one being forced to wed that night," he said, his voice even.

She stopped walking. "Do you wish to annul our marriage?" she asked, and he turned to her. They stood opposite one another in the center of abandoned, neglected, dead homes. "We can do so after we are certain I am not with child."

Anger that she had not trusted him with the truth fought with an absolute want to be with Lark. He walked closer to her. "Ye are my wife, and I will not walk away from ye." He watched the small flecks of gray in her blue eyes as she met his stare.

"Perhaps I should walk away from you, then," she said. "Would that be easier on your conscience?"

He inhaled fully. The air smelled of rain, and the sweetness of the strawberries was still coming from her hair. "I will hide the boat."

She frowned. "You cannot keep me a prisoner."

"I will until ye believe that ye are not dooming this isle."

"And what happens if crops wilt and ewes die? What then? Will I be abandoned like this village?" There was no self-pity in her strong gaze, just mistrust and determination.

"Ye do not trust me at all," he said and watched her look past his shoulder. She did not reply.

"I have nothing else hidden from ye," he said. "No secrets, no plans that I have not told ye. I did not sleep with that woman." His arm flew out toward Gylin. "There are no more curses of which I know. There is nothing in my past that should matter."

He rolled up a sleeve and pointed to a scar, trying not to recall how she'd kissed it two nights ago before the fire at Aros. "I got this from Iain MacLeod when he raided Ulva several months ago." He lifted the edge of his kilt. "This one was when Liam and I were boys and training like fools with real swords." He touched his jaw. "From the sword of an Englishman who tried to attack Aros a few years back." He yanked his tunic up over his head and off, turning his back. "And this scar," he said, showing the long one that nearly cost him his life, "was from the same battle."

He turned back to her, letting his hands out to the sides. "There is nothing else about me to keep hidden. I have no secrets." He watched her swallow hard. Her beautiful eyes blinked as if she held back tears. "Lark…" He waited. "Lark," he said again and reached out to touch her chin, guiding her to meet his gaze. "I know trust has to grow between two people, but I am asking ye to trust that I will not abandon ye."

She breathed in through her nose and nodded slightly.

He rubbed his thumb across her cheek, marveling in the softness. "Someone has made ye distrust so easily."

She blinked, her gaze centering on his chest instead of his eyes. He dropped his hand.

A white cat, likely the same one from before, scooted out of the cottage where they stood, breaking the moment. Not that he thought Lark would suddenly start talking, revealing all to him. The cat trotted to the chapel.

"I should check inside," he said.

Lark nodded, and he turned to stride over to the chapel. They had opened the shutters to allow in light when his brothers had filled in Wilyam Macquarie's grave with earth. Adam walked around the inside perimeter to the back where the cat slid along one of the pews.

"What were ye thinking?" he murmured at his great-great-grandfather as he glanced where the fresh boards were laid. If the man had known that he would destroy his entire clan by sleeping with the girl he kissed in the woods, would he have let his passion cloud his judgment? Had he feelings for her? Loved her? Had he wished he hadn't married his wife?

"Everything as it should be?" Lark asked, peeking in from the doorway.

He dropped his hands, glad to hear her speaking again. "Aye. With a bit more washing, the chapel could be used."

"That would be a good start for the village," she said and stepped back from the door when he came out.

Adam nodded toward the winding road that was lined with weeds and overgrown bramble and scooped up his tunic. "When I bring in more sheep, they can eat here first on the grasses." The sweeping wind on the isle kept the vegetation low and scraggly with only a few pockets of taller trees about. Somehow talking about the future of the village gave him hope that he and Lark might have one together.

Adam looked to one of the buildings that still had a roof. "We can salvage those with roofs, cleaning them and making them safe from the weather. I will get wood and glass panes from Mull or the mainland."

A few fat drops of rain hit the road, making him look up at the brooding sky.

"Maybe we should return to the castle," Lark said, but before she could finish the sentence, the sky opened like a filled bucket that had been sliced with a claymore. She gasped, her voice higher pitched, and he grasped her hand as the rain plummeted.

She ran with him as he headed straight for a house with a roof, pushing inside. Breathing hard, Lark spun in the doorway of the one-room cottage to stare out at the spring rain dropping like stones beyond the eaves.

"The roof is sound," he said. The cottage was not too battered. It was one that had been inhabited when the isle was settled a score of years ago. A bed with a blanket sat against the wall near a hearth. Slabs of very dry peat sat next to it.

Thunder rumbled, and they watched more lightning splinter across the sky. "It does not seem likely to stop soon," Lark said. She turned around, surveying the room, and walked over to sit on the edge of the bed, clutching her shawl around her arms.

He shook out his tunic and laid it over her shoulders. "A fire will keep the chill out," he said and walked to the hearth. Adam layered the dry peat. He struck the flint he always carried, the sparks caught on the bit of wool in his fingers, and he set it on the peat, watching it catch quickly.

Scratch, scratch, scratch.

He turned to see Lark sweeping with a straw broom left in one corner. She peered at the mantle that had flowers carved into it and stopped to run her fingers along the etching of vines. "Someone loved this little house."

"Not enough to stay," he said, closing the door against the rain that had turned sideways, wetting the floor inside the threshold.

She moved to the window to rub the wavy glass pane to look out. "They were afraid." She turned, leaning her back against the daubed wall, lifting her gaze to his. "Fear makes us do things we regret."

Had she been afraid? "Like asking a stranger to marry ye?" he asked.

"Like not telling your wife that she was responsible for helping you break your family's century-old curse?" she answered.

Like not telling your husband that you are a bastard? Adam wasn't a big enough arse to say it out loud. Especially when he knew Lark was thinking it from the flush rising in her cheeks.

Thunder rumbled as if anger rent the air. A sob broke from Lark's lips, and she ran to the door, throwing it open to dash into the rain.

"Lark!" he yelled, following her. He chased her into the muddy road, both of them instantly soaked with the heavy rain. He caught her shoulders, halting her.

"Let go!" she yelled, but he turned her to him. Anguish pinched her forehead, her mouth open, rain pressing her curls down close to her head.

"Lark," he said, rainwater rushing so hard he had to shout to be heard. Thunder boomed, and the trees on the perimeter thrashed.

"I was afraid," she yelled at him as he held her there in the road at arm's length. "Once I realized how important my birth was to you, I..." Her lips closed to swallow, the rain traveling like rivulets down her face so that he could not tell if she cried. "I did not want to get an annulment." She shook her head, her gaze moving to his throat instead of his eyes. "I even took a bit of whisky to give me the courage to tell you before you came up to the room, but it did not help." She shook her head again, her hands going to her face, covering her eyes. "You would send me...away."

The tempest roared around them, mirroring the storm gathering inside Adam. Lark was afraid, truly afraid, and his warrior blood pounded in a rush to protect her. It hurt that she thought him so dishonorable. He grabbed her hand, pulling it away from her face, and slid his palm along her soaked cheek. "I want ye here, Lark. I want ye with me." Her eyes lifted to his, and she searched his face. "I would rather abandon this isle than abandon ye."

Her eyes opened wide at his words. His father was probably turning in his grave, but Adam realized he meant it. "No more secrets between us, Lark," he called above the rain. "Just ye and me, wife and husband, together."

Her hand came up to squeeze his where it cupped her cheek, her eyes closing as his mouth descended onto hers. Rainwater mixed with the taste of her as he deepened the kiss, pulling her into his arms. Adam felt her hands lift to hold the back of his neck as he curved over her form, blocking the hard beat of the rain.

His hands slid along her form, her gown molding to her curves. Their kiss became wild, their hands stroking through the wet. The storm was like a curtain, blocking out the world beyond them, as if it banished the curse, the talk of bastards, his brothers, and his oath to his father. Only Lark remained.

Thunder cracked close by, and Lark jumped, pressing closer to him. Adam turned, half carrying her back the few steps to the cottage where the door stood open. They ran inside, and he slammed the door shut.

Both of them stared at one another, the fire crackling behind them. Would she turn away again? He would not let her. Not now that he knew she wanted him.

Adam took a step toward her, but she was already moving toward him. They met in the middle of the room, their mouths coming together in a rush of desperation. The fire already growing inside Adam erupted. The kiss turned wild from the moment their lips touched. His hands caught her head as she ran hers down his bare shoulders, holding him as if she were afraid he would slip away. But he was not going anywhere.

The rain pounded on the roof as the storm thrashed around them. Hands touching, exploring, bodies pressed together. Adam felt Lark tremble. She must be chilled. He backed them up toward the fire, and his fingers moved between them, plucking at the laces of her bodice. "Ye are soaked," he said against her lips.

In answer, she shrugged her shoulders to release the bodice. It hit the wooden floor with the weight of the water, followed by the pooling of her soaked skirt. She bent to unlace her boots, bringing her mouth close to his jack, making it twitch. Rising, she balanced with her hands on his shoulders as she toed off the boots and leaned in to kiss him.

"I am lost in the taste of ye," he murmured against her lips, his arms around her, pulling her cold body against his hot skin. Lark yanked the lacing tie on her stays, and they followed, leaving her in a wet, white smock.

He looked down at her. "Ye are lovely, lass," he said,

taking in how the wet linen clung to her peaked breasts.

"I want you," she said, untying the top of her smock. "And this is cold." He helped her find the edge, pulling it over her head.

Adam's breath caught as his gaze fell upon her. Naked, standing in the glow of the fire, Lark was like a beautiful, otherworldly nymph. Her long braid of coppery hair fell over her straight shoulder. A gentle swell to her stomach, curved hips, and full breasts made her lush and soft everywhere. His hardness yearned for all that softness, and she wanted him.

With a tug of his belt, Adam let the sopping woolen wrap around his hips fall to the floor. He stood in only his boots. Lark's gaze dipped to his jack, which stood upright, hard and demanding.

She reached for him. Adam's groan came out like a growl, up from his gut, and he walked her back until she was pressed against the wall, the window at their side. They met in a frantic touching, tasting, giving, and taking. Thunder rumbled outside, but it seemed farther away. Pulling the tie from her wet braid, Adam fingered through the length gently.

"Strawberries," he said against her as they kissed. He dipped his head, sliding his lips along her neck, his thumb strumming her taut nipple.

She moaned softly on an exhale, the crux of her legs pressing against his length. "Touch me," she whispered, her words more powerful than the thunder. The rain still hammered outside, adding to the frantic energy building between them. Lark breathed against his mouth, and he caught her moan as he found her heat. She was soaked with want.

He felt her shudder and looked into her face. "Like hot, sweet honey," he rasped.

Her eyes were closed, her lashes spiked with rainwater. Pink lips parted, she groaned, pressing into his hand as he stroked her flesh. His lips savored the taste of her skin as he kissed down to her breasts, pulling one peak and then the other into his mouth, his tongue swirling to pull another moan from her. Lark's head lulled back against the wall as he played her body. She was gorgeous, the long column of her throat exposed above her full breasts, her body open and wanting, her red hair draping behind her, skimming her slender shoulders like silk cloth.

He turned her to the wall, his hands cupping her breasts and his thumbs tweaking the hard pebbles. He leaned into her, pressing his rigid jack against the soft crevice of her perfectly round arse.

She stilled, her back suddenly rigid. "No," she said, turning abruptly.

Adam stared down into her face. "What is it?"

She shook her head, breathing heavy, and looked up to meet his gaze. "Not that way," she whispered. Her arms went around him, and she buried her face into his chest. Adam held her tightly.

"I want to see you love me," she said.

He slid a hand into her hair and pressed warm, deep kisses on her lips, and she reached onto her toes to wrap her arms over his shoulders. They clung to each other as he walked them to the bed. Their breaths mingled, and she pulled him with her down onto the low bed, the old frame creaking as he followed.

Damp hair spread across the hay-filled tick, her hands lifted under her breasts, and her knees fell open, Lark was the most sensual creature he had ever touched, tasted, or even seen. She was glorious, and she was his. He swooped down to kiss her. He would hold onto her forever. No more talk of annulment, no talk of being a bastard and what that might do to his plans, no holding back from this incredible creature moaning under his kisses. Her hand grasped him, guiding him to her heat, and he pressed forward, thrusting deep.

Her lips fell open on a moan, and she pressed up, her body seeming to pull him farther inside. Meeting his thrusts, a deep and frantic rhythm built between them. The bed cracked and creaked with each meeting of their bodies as they climbed higher and higher.

His hands caught her face, and he looked into her eyes. "We are one, now and forever," he said, the words like an oath as every muscle in his body coiled tightly.

"Yes," came out on her breathless exhale. The pale skin of her neck was flushed, her lips parted, but she kept her eyes open, staring at him as he watched the peak of her passion tear through her. "Adam!" she yelled.

Thrusting wildly, Adam roared as he exploded, Lark grabbing hold of him to ride their carnal tempest out together. Straining, clasped together, the bed under them moved. With a cracking sound, the warped legs gave way. But Adam barely noticed as they clung together, the bed dropping soundly onto the floor beneath them.

Chapter Fourteen

Rap. Rap. Rap. "Adam? Lark?"

Lark jerked awake. The gold waning of the sun shot light through the wavy glass of the window where figures stood outside. "Holy Mary—"

Adam leaped out of their awkward nest of bedding and broken bed. He yanked his sword free of his scabbard where it lay with his abandoned kilt. Hair ruffled and completely naked, he strode to the door.

"Is there anyone in there?" It was a man's voice.

Lark gasped and rolled to the edge of the bed, reaching to scoop up her discarded smock. She yanked it to her exposed breasts as the door swung inward. Ava Maclean stood there with Liam Maclean and Ava's daughter, Meg. Right before Adam.

"Good Lord," Ava yelled, her hands flapping up before Meg's wide eyes. The lady of Aros Castle grabbed her daughter's shoulders, turning her around as they retreated from the door, only to be replaced by Liam Maclean. He glanced past Adam to Lark, his brows raised. "Greetings, milady."

"Callum said you two were down here in the village rebuilding your clan," Ava yelled from where she'd moved into the road.

"I think that is what they are doing," Meg said, making Lark flush even hotter.

"Oh," Ava answered. "So sorry," she called.

Beside Liam, Father Lowder stepped up, his piercing gaze taking in the room. He snorted with a grin when he spied the broken bed.

"Bloody hell." Adam lowered his sword. He did not seem to worry over the fact that he was completely naked and obviously ravished. "A man cannot find privacy even on a nearly deserted isle." With that, he slammed the door in their faces.

"We will be right out," Lark called, awkwardly climbing over the splintered bedframe, coaxing her breasts back into the stays that she'd found on the floor tangled with her petticoat and bodice. They were all cold and wet. She looked at Adam and whispered, "Bloody hell."

His frown softened as he walked over to her, brushing his fingers lightly across her cheek to push her tangled waves behind one bare shoulder. He bent his lips to her ear, and the warmth of his breath teased her. "'Tis nothing to be embarrassed over. We are wed."

She glanced behind her toward the bed. "We will need to fix this," she whispered.

"'Tis a trophy to remember the day our marriage truly began," he whispered back.

The tension in her face relaxed, allowing a smile.

"The ladies met with Elspeth up at the castle." Liam's voice penetrated the cottage wall.

Lark glanced toward the sound of the voices, her smile fading.

"Elspeth and the babe seem to be healthy," Ava called

out. "I would say she will be giving birth within the next two weeks, but one never quite knows."

"We need to get dressed," Lark said, grabbing up her wrinkled petticoat.

"Do we?"

"I think you gave Ava and Meg a big enough shock for one day already."

Adam's gaze remained hungry as he watched her corral her breasts while he re-belted his kilt and threw on his tunic. Clasping her hand, Adam led her toward the door but stopped before opening it. He looked up at the carved lintel, the same flowing motif that adorned the mantel over the hearth. He touched it and looked down at Lark, his eyes full of...something. Hope?

No more secrets. Her stomach tightened. He would not leave her. He promised?

Adam opened the door. Rain dripped off the eaves of the sound little cottage, and the sun, which had been covered so thoroughly before, was casting light from its apex. They must have slept for a couple hours. Lark pulled her hair to the side, fashioning a quick braid to keep the waves under control.

Several Maclean warriors stood beside Ava and Meg where they peered into open doorways several cottages down. The ladies turned toward Lark and Adam, Ava with an encouraging smile and Meg with wide eyes, her gaze dropping down to Adam's kilt and then back up to Lark's face. Tor's daughter may have never seen a naked man before, and Adam was a chiseled mountain of a man, especially without his clothing.

Liam and Father Lowder talked near the chapel, their words kept close between them. Liam had a frown, although the priest held a neutral look and shrugged.

"The town has wonderful potential," Ava said.

"I completely agree," Meg said, walking off to explore.

Ava nodded to their cottage. "Some cottages still have roofs. And the chapel is sound." Excitement lit her eyes.

"It will require work," Lark said, looking out. "But it can be rebuilt into something quite comfortable and thriving again."

Liam and Father Lowder, having finished whatever private discussion they were having, walked over in time to hear Lark's prediction. "As long as the curse does not destroy everything again," Liam said.

Father Lowder nodded solemnly. "I feel evil on this isle."

"Nonsense," Ava said, her easy smile turning downward. "This isle just needs good people, some wooly sheep, a few dogs running about, and children laughing."

Giggling, maybe? Could the mysterious sounds have been Elspeth?

Meg walked out of the nearest cottage, one with half a roof. She held a doll that was stuffed with wool to plump it out, its hair and eyes stitched with yellow thread. For the most part, it was clean and definitely not over a score in years. "I would say there are already children about," Meg said and glanced around as if one might be hiding close by.

A shiver caught Lark, making her rub her arms. Father Lowder strode with authority, taking the doll, his large hand squeezing it. "The poppet has been newly left."

"Elspeth," Lark said. "She must be living with Grissell and, when walking through, left the doll."

"She is too old for poppets," Liam said.

"Maybe that is why she left it behind." Ava's brows pinched. "We can ask her when we go back to the castle. But first I was hoping Lark could show us around the village." Ava smiled at her. "We can make plans to remake this place."

Meg turned in a tight circle. "Ormaig is like a half-built village. It but needs roofs, furniture, and flowers planted about."

"And people," Lark said.

"People will not come if the curse is still working its evil," Liam said.

"It will fade away if ye stop talking about it," Adam said, his voice rough.

Father Lowder held his hands in prayer before him. "I have only recently arrived on Mull, and yet I have heard about it from no less than seven people and even more after yesterday's revelations." He looked directly at Lark, his eyes unblinking. She couldn't look away as he studied her. What had Roylin told the priest? What did Father Lowder believe?

The wind blew, and a loose lock of hair danced before Lark's eyes, letting her break the tether. She pulled in a shaky breath and lowered her gaze to her boots. Turning away, she walked over to the house where the doll had been found.

I know the truth, no matter what Roylin says.

Meg's footprints stood out before the door, but there were smaller ones. The rain had washed away Adam and her own prints, so these were freshly made. They could not be Elspeth's from the other day.

A sound behind one of the buildings made Lark snap her gaze upward, the breeze blowing to scatter the warmth of the sun. Lark followed the weedy path where more of the smaller footprints sat deep in the newly made mud. "Is someone there?" No one answered.

Lark turned to get Adam. She was about to round the corner but heard her name and stopped shy of the cottage's edge.

"But Lark is a bastard," Liam said, his voice rough. "Her presence here will keep the curse going. Ye need to get her off the isle, along with this Elspeth woman. All of ye should go. Let the evil subside again."

Lark's fingers curled into the chipped daub of the house, her breath stopping so she could hear. Did Adam tell them she was a bastard? Her gaze slid to the priest. Roylin had told Father Lowder.

"The two of ye can live on Mull," Liam continued. "Adam, let your sons settle Ulva."

"Or you can send the two women with me to Iona Isle," Father Lowder said. "To the abbey there, to be cleansed of their sins."

"Nay," Adam replied abruptly.

"Nay," Liam added. "Just to Mull."

"The holiness of Iona will cleanse their hearts and bodies," Lowder said, his face hard. "Lark Montgomerie's taint could reach across from Mull."

"Taint?" Adam said. "What the bloody hell are ye talking about? She had no choice in the matter of her parents' union. Any sin is upon them, not her."

Lark peeked around the corner to see them in the same circle she had left them in. Even the Maclean warriors stood listening. "Roylin Montgomerie was a drunk," the priest said.

She held her breath, straining to hear his horrible words, her stomach tight. "After you left the festival," Lowder said, "he drank whisky for days, wailing about how he wanted Lark back. That she was the image of his dead wife and that he would wed her himself."

Lark pressed against the wall, letting it support her. *No. No. No.*

The cleric continued. "It is common knowledge amongst those who know Roylin that the man visited her bed after her mother died. More than once."

Her legs would not hold her, and she slowly slid down the wall to crouch. Only the rugged grip of Adam's mother's boots kept her from falling backward into the mud.

"Get the fok off my isle." Adam's voice was like the thunder that had boomed overhead earlier.

Lowder continued. "Her shame for sleeping with her

father—"

"He is not her father," Ava said.

"And she was a virgin in my bed, not that it is any of your damn business," Adam said.

Lark couldn't bring herself to look around the cottage or even stand.

"She could have fooled you. Women have been known to—" The rest of the cleric's statement was cut off, and Lark buried her face into her hands. The cold from her wet clothes made her tremble, while hot tears leaked from her eyes to wet her hands.

"Let go of him, Adam." Liam's voice overrode the blood rushing in Lark's ears.

"Get the fok off my isle," Adam said. "And if I hear ye speaking of Lark to anyone, I will hunt ye down and cut your tongue from your screaming mouth."

"God's teeth, Adam!" Liam yelled. "Let him go."

"What type of clergyman spreads such lies?" Adam asked.

"Or speaks the secrets of the confessional?" Ava said, her tone furious.

"Roylin Montgomerie spoke it aloud at the festival after you took her away. 'Twas no confession." The priest's voice sounded strained as if Adam had him by the throat. Anna's letter to warn Lark of Roylin's rantings gave proof to all the priest said.

"Get off now before I add killing a priest to my sins," Adam yelled.

Lark heard his sword slide from his scabbard, but she could not do anything but squeeze her eyes shut. Her stomach clenched as memories of Roylin rubbing against her from behind came unbidden, as if the priest's words had unlocked them. All her ignoring and pushing the nightmares down had not diminished the pain and shame. It all roared back into her mind until she felt like she would vomit.

Breath, hot and thick with sour whisky, whispering in her ear. *Ye ain't my daughter, but ye live in my house and care for my girls. Ye look like my Hannah.* He had pressed against her, his arousal obvious and sickening. Even if he'd treated her as a servant growing up, he had been the only father figure that Lark had. His drunken words and pawing were sickening, making her feel such shame.

She'd began practicing how to throw a *sgian dubh* with accuracy, but could she kill him? Whispers and stares had followed her throughout town until it had become unbearable. She had been both relieved and terrified when he said she could not live with them anymore.

"Where is she?" Ava asked. "Lark?"

Her words gave Lark strength to move. She rose and hurried farther into the woods, throwing her arms out before her to push through the narrow copse of forest. She must hurry away, away to…where? She had nowhere to go. The abysmal thought threatened her courage, making a sob catch in her throat.

"Lark?" Adam's voice came from behind her, spurring her forward. "Lark, wait," he called, and she knew he saw her.

She stopped, hand steadying herself on the ridged bark of a thick tree. Her chest lifted as she took in full breaths of wind, tinged with salt and the beginning of low tide.

"Lark," Adam said. She listened to his steps on the mossy forest floor as he walked closer. She didn't look at him. A man of God thought she was tainted enough to doom their isle with her wicked past. Could Adam think she'd ever want Roylin? The thought disgusted her.

She turned, tears in her eyes. "I hated him," she whispered.

Adam's face was tortured. "I will kill him," he said, his voice a rough whisper, and her eyes flooded with tears.

Her lips were numb, but the words came out like poison from a festering wound. "I managed to keep him from…"

Adam took the remaining steps toward her, his arms going around to pull her into his chest. Lark curled into a ball against him, breathing in his scent. He didn't say anything but held her for long minutes, his jaw touching lightly on the top of her head. She heard footsteps and felt him wave someone off who retreated. Ava? Liam? It didn't matter. They all knew her secrets now.

She breathed in, and as if the air coming in forced the words out, she began to talk. "He never thought of me as his child. He treated me like a servant living in his house. My mother trained me to be as important to the running of the family as she was. I worked hard, making it up to Roylin that I wasn't his daughter."

Adam remained unmoving, holding her there as the words tumbled free, words she had kept buried. "When she died, I noticed him watching me as I continued to do all my chores, taking up what my mother had left, caring for my sisters. He drank so much whisky."

She swallowed, growing silent. Adam continued his strong grip around her. The wind blew off the shoreline beyond, rustling the leaves overhead, and Lark whispered. "For the past few months, he'd grown worse. I would wake next to Anna to find him staring at me in the night. Several times he came up behind me, pressing his…and his hands pawing at me. I pushed him away, and he would yell it wasn't fair to be stuck with me looking so much like my mother and yet he couldn't touch me. As if it was my fault."

Adam squeezed her gently.

"I kicked him right before we left for the Beltane Festival, like I did to that thief in the woods. Roylin said he would marry or sell me off so I could torment someone else." She swallowed. "And then you came to the Beltane weddings."

Lark lifted her eyes from Adam's chest, her chin sliding up his tunic to look at his hard face. It seemed wrought from granite as he stared out over her head, but he looked down to meet her gaze, and his narrowed eyes softened.

"I am sorry, Adam, to bring taint and shame to your isle." She closed her eyes, not brave enough to face censure in his gaze. "And now you know all *my* secrets."

Adam's hand came up to cup her cheek. "Ye have no shame in this, Lark. Roylin..." He paused as if the name brought bitterness to his tongue. "That drunkard takes all the shame." His face hardened. "I will kill him if he comes anywhere near ye. Did Anna's letter say he would follow ye?"

She shook her head. "Just...the terrible things he is saying."

Adam's nostrils flared like he was about to charge, slicing through her demons, and she grasped his thick arm. "His lust cannot hurt me here." Her voice dropped to a whisper. "But I could hurt your clan, if I am taint—"

"That priest is wrong."

"What if he is right? What if he tells people on Mull about me?"

"I will cut out his tongue."

"The others—"

"The crimes done to ye are not yours, Lark, even if others find out." He bent to look hard into her eyes. "We build forward."

Lark felt wrung out, her heart laid bare. She took a full breath, letting the cool summer air cleanse her. She stared into Adam's eyes, her fingers curling into the folds of his sleeves as if they were a lifeline. There had been no words of love, but there were definitely feelings between them. He'd said that he wanted to stay married, even knowing her secrets. *I must trust him.*

Lark nodded slowly. "Building forward, then."

Chapter Fifteen

Adam turned at the sound of pebbles crunching outside the gate. Liam and Beck walked up to Gylin Castle from the shore.

"Damn, Adam," Beck said, his face hard as stone. "Liam told me what Lowder said. Are we headed down to find that arse and cut his tongue out?"

"Which one? Lowder or Montgomerie?" Adam asked, crossing his arms. His gaze slid to the castle where Lark, Ava, and Meg had retreated. His respect for the lady of Aros Castle had increased ten-fold when she'd hugged Lark, whispering to her until Lark's shoulders relaxed. What she said was between them, but he was grateful for whatever it was. He knew Ava had endured a difficult past in England. Some even whispered that she was born out of wedlock.

"Montgomerie," Liam answered. "Father Lowder will keep his words to himself. He rowed off in the second dinghy we used to cross over from Mull."

Beck pointed at the mist swirling in, leaving a hazy look to the trees. "He may have to pray his way across. I do not think it safe for Ava, Meg, and their men to row back tonight."

"But, Adam," Liam said, coming closer, "in the morning, I think ye need to come off Wolf Isle. At least for Lark's sake. She will feel worse if things go poorly here. Ye said yourself that ye never truly supported the clan's return here."

"That was before I swore to see it done," Adam murmured. "I will see my clan strong again." He looked to Liam. "Here on Wolf Isle."

"But Lark's taint—"

"Shut your foking mouth, Liam," Beck said. "If anything goes wrong, it will have nothing to do with Lark."

Liam swore beneath his breath, jerking on his short beard, and strode off, passing Ava Maclean as she walked out of the keep. "A word, Chief Macquarie," she said, her hands clasped.

"How is she?" Adam asked.

"Lark is doing better. She is sitting with Elspeth." She shook her head. "I would never trust that priest with a confession. If anyone is going to stain this isle with sin, it would be someone like him."

"He is rowing back to Mull." Adam crossed his arms.

"He likely feared for his life," she said. "I will let Tor know he is not welcome when we travel back." Ava stared outward toward the water. "Likely tomorrow with that fog rolling in." She turned back to Adam. "Lark is worried that she will prevent you from accomplishing your mission to rebuild your clan here. That is your mission, is it not?"

"I swore to my father I would see it done."

"Is that the only reason? Because you swore to resettle Ulva to a dying man?" she asked.

Adam looked over her head toward the dead willow. Somehow it did not look so intimidating. He would build up his clan around it. "My brothers and I have never had a true home, despite the hospitality of Clan Maclean. Ulva will be that home."

Ava touched his arm. "Dirt and stone do not make a home." She looked up with troubled eyes. "I lived in England on a grand estate, but it was not my home. I did not have one until I came to Aros and Tor, and I fell in love. A home must have freedom, peace, and safety. But above all, a home is filled with love." She tilted her head slightly. "It is not a place on a map but a feeling."

His mind turned inward, remembering his mother laughing here when he was a boy. They'd dashed together around the bailey while Beck followed and Callum and Drostan toddled after them. Gylin had felt like a home then, even with the dead willow in the middle.

The doors of the keep flew open, and Rabbie rushed out, arms pumping. "Ye need to get her off Ulva," he blurted out, his eyes wild. "The curse will keep growing with a bastard on it, especially one with a tainted past."

The anger Adam had managed to stomp down rushed up within him again. He clenched his fists to keep from grabbing the man by the throat. "Neither of which is any fault of Lark's."

"Does not matter," Rabbie threw back. Behind him, his three other brothers and Liam seemed to tumble out in a pack.

Bloody Liam must have told them all of what was said in the village. Old friend or not, the man was in jeopardy. He should have rowed back with Lowder.

Adam stepped around his brothers to stride toward the castle to reassure Lark if she overheard them inside. Drostan's hand landed on his shoulder, making him turn. Adam's lethal gaze focused on him and then his brothers. The unsure stares from all of them stopped him from shoving Drostan away.

"Nothing about Lark's past is her fault. She came to our wedding a virgin, and even if she had not, it would mean nothing except that Roylin Montgomerie would soon be losing his life in a very painful manner."

"She is a bastard," Rabbie said.

Ava clasped her hands before her. "Some of the kindest and highest people in the land are bastards. Even royalty."

"Pardon, Lady Maclean, but our father made us swear not to bring a bastard on the isle," Drostan said.

"Da expanded the words of the curse to include all bastards," Adam said. "Even Ida told Lark that the family Bible only mentions us not fathering any bastards like Wilyam Macquarie."

"I brought it back with me," Beck said. "'Tis in the keep."

Rabbie came closer. "No bastards on the isle! 'Tis always been the rule. And Lark is a bastard, and Roylin Montgomerie touch—"

"Adam," Ava cut in, her voice carrying, making Adam stop from grabbing Rabbie and shaking him. But Ava did not look to him, she looked at the doorway, and Adam whipped around.

Lark stood there, her face ashen. Adam shoved Rabbie back and walked to her, but Lark held out a hand to stop him from touching her. "Your brothers…are concerned," she said, pain in her face. "I need to think."

Elspeth stood beside her with a sharp look of disdain for each of them. "We are going for a stroll while ye realize what arses ye are." She linked her arm with Lark's, and the two of them walked across the bailey to the open gate.

"I will meet up with you," Ava called. "I need to find Meg and fetch my shawl inside."

Adam watched the rigid set of Lark's shoulders. How would Gylin ever be her home with his brothers or Rabbie making her feel like her past was her fault?

• • •

Lark and Elspeth walked down the pebbled path. *Meow.* The white cat from the village trotted up, rubbing against the pregnant woman's skirt. She awkwardly bent when the cat raised up on hind legs.

"She likes you?" Lark asked.

"Saint Joan is particular, but we understand one another," she said, rubbing the purring cat against her face. "We are both bastards."

Lark's gaze met Elspeth's. "You have been living with Grissell."

The woman looked back toward the castle, her mouth twisted in a wry frown. "Nearly six months now," she whispered. She lowered the cat and rested her hand on her belly. "Once I found out I was with child. Mistress Grissell takes in girls that have no family to help them. I had heard about her at a festival I attended and made my way to Mull."

"Are there others living with her?" Lark kept her tone casual.

"Two right now."

"Did you help hang that...poppet?"

Elspeth gave a little laugh. "The other girls did the heavy lifting, but I helped make it. Grissell was worried the Macquaries would run her off the isle, so we thought we would scare them away."

The mist was growing thicker, making the boulders along the shore resemble hunched goblins. "Elspeth," Lark said, catching her arm to make her meet her gaze. "The child you carry...it is not Adam's, is it?"

The woman pursed her lips, glancing once more behind her. She met Lark's gaze, shaking her head the smallest amount.

Lark expected to feel relieved, but...she had known Adam told the truth. "Thank you for telling me," she whispered.

Elspeth gave her arm a squeeze as they continued

walking. "We tainted women must stick together. If ye decide to leave that rough group of lads, I am certain Grissell would take ye in so ye do not need to return to that devil ye lived with. I know about monsters." Her hand floated to rest on her bulbous stomach, making Lark's heart clench for her. *I could be her.*

With the mist rolling in, unease prickled across Lark's shoulder blades, and she scanned the thick fog. "We should turn back. 'Tis slippery with the seaweed."

"We could keep walking to Mistress Grissell's cottage. It is comfortable there." The girl sounded like she missed the old woman.

"I need to tell Adam that it was Grissell who asked you to lie."

"It wasn't her," Elspeth said, making Lark stop, peering at her as tendrils of fog seemed to reach out for them.

"Who told you to lie?"

Elspeth leaned closer. "The Maclean who comes across to Ulva all the time. He was here today."

Maclean? "Liam Maclean paid you to say your babe belongs to Adam?"

"Aye. I told him I did not want to lie, but he paid me ten shillings I can use toward the bairn." She squeezed Lark's arm. "Do not tell him I told ye," she whispered. "A man with a lying heart can turn to violence. I have seen it before."

"What is your real name?" Lark supported the woman as they walked slightly up an incline to stop at the top of the ridge that marked the shore.

She smiled. "Muriel. I hail from the Gunn family to the east but came this way when I was able."

"'Tis nice to meet you, Muriel," she said, her mind churning through details. She needed to tell Adam about Liam. He'd said his friend didn't support them returning to the isle, but paying a girl to lie was more than that. And why wouldn't he support Adam and his brothers in building up their clan and isle once more?

Halting them to return, Lark helped Muriel turn around on the slippery rocks. A movement in the mist stopped her. "Ava? Meg?" There was no answer, but the figure continued to approach like a shadow growing into something real. It was a man, closing in with powerful strides across the sand and stones. "Adam?" A shiver slid up her nape at his silence.

Muriel held tightly to her arm. "Lord help us," she whispered.

"Who is it? Answer me." Lark held the woman's arm. She could not run, abandoning Muriel. Glancing back the way they had been walking, Lark's chest squeezed, and her heart raced.

Two more figures approached. Muriel gasped, clinging to Lark. The two men came close enough for Lark to see two blackened eyes on one of them. *Iain MacLeod?*

"Lark," Muriel whispered, her breath coming fast.

She whipped around, and her inhale caught, her throat tight, as she recognized the deep-set, ever-watchful eyes that had condemned her mere hours ago. But he wasn't dressed like a priest, his long brown robes exchanged for boots, breeches, and a tunic.

"Father Lowder?" Lark asked, her voice pinched with growing panic.

Muriel gasped. "Let go of me, ye pocked son of a whore," Muriel yelled as Iain grabbed her arms, dragging her away from Lark's side despite her obvious condition.

The priest's lips turned up in a broad smile that did not reach his hard eyes. "You may call me Captain Jandeau."

The name struck like lightning through Lark. The bandits in the woods had been working for Jandeau, and they said he would have her first. The thought was like poison shooting nausea through her stomach.

Before she could reply, he yelled something in French to the man with Iain. The man ran past him, his boots splashing in the water, and Lark saw a dinghy in the mist behind Jandeau. Even though Muriel struggled, Iain was much stronger than her and forced her toward it.

Jandeau kept his gaze centered on Lark, a dark smile on his hard face. He had looked wrong as a priest, but his bulk and subtle leer clearly marked him as a pirate. Without glancing toward Muriel, Lark turned, grabbing her skirts to run. If she could get to Adam, they could gather a force to retrieve Muriel.

Dark laughter filled her ears as Jandeau leaped forward, catching her in two strides. His arms went around her waist, just under her breasts, and his mouth came to her ear. Hot breath rasped against her stretched neck. "*Mon chéri*. Do not struggle so. 'Tis futile. I sought the Macquarie chief at the Beltane Festival, but once I saw you..." He inhaled along her skin. "I knew you were a treasure worth following."

Her gaze tried to penetrate the mist before her. Where were Ava and Meg? Between the four of them, could they overpower the pirates and Iain? If only she could grab ahold of the blade secreted in the seam of her long sleeve. "What do you want with Adam?" she asked, her boots churning in the sand and pebbles as he dragged her backward toward the boat.

"I wanted his isle. With only five Macquaries, it should have been easy to kill them off."

She pushed against his arm, but it seemed made of steel. "Why Ulva?" she yelled. Could anyone hear her?

"'Tis the perfect place for France to land, *ma petite*. That heathen, Henry, will not expect French coming from the west. And," he paused as they reached the boat, "the isle is cursed."

He swept her around to face the boat where Muriel sat

held by the pirate. "I have heard ye are a bastard," Iain said, glaring at her, holding the oars. "Adam will want ye off his isle anyway."

"Help! Help! Adam!" Lark screamed as Jandeau tried to lift her into the boat. Her boot caught onto a half-submerged rock for leverage, but he was too strong. With another push, her boot came loose, sliding off her heel. Lark wiggled her toes until the boot slipped off. As Jandeau lifted her into the dinghy, she kicked the boot behind her up onto the beach.

The boat teetered as Jandeau threw her to the floor of the vessel. "Row," he ordered, and Iain began in earnest. Jandeau stared out into the mist as if fixed on a point, a point that grew into the massive bulk of a ship shrouded in fog.

Chapter Sixteen

"Meg thought she heard a woman yell," Ava said to Adam as she followed him back down the path to the beach. The fog was so thick, he could not see the water.

"Ye stay at the castle with Meg and Rabbie," he said. Ava stopped, and Adam led the small group of Maclean warriors, including Liam, and his brothers along the shore. The tide was receding, making Lark's and Elspeth's tracks easy to follow.

They could easily be lost in the fog. But surely Lark would just follow the shore or their own tracks back. *Unless she's decided to leave.* The thought threaded through his mind like poison, making his jaw ache. Did the pregnant woman have a way off the isle?

Only the crunch of pebbles answered him as they jogged along the shoreline. The men were quiet, listening. Liam came up to stride even with him. "I still think it would be a good idea to get her and Lark off—"

Adam's hand shot out to catch Liam's tunic in his fist. He looked right into his face. "No more talk about any of that. It has nothing to do with ye."

Liam sputtered. "I am only concerned for ye and the Macquarie line."

"Cease it or consider our friendship severed." Adam dropped his shirt and continued to stride forward, following the path of footprints. "Damn," he cursed as the prints faded along the rocks. He looked to his brothers who were higher up. "They might be in the woods. Their prints here are gone."

"Lark," Callum called.

"Elspeth," Eagan added, hands cupped around his mouth.

Beck was slightly ahead. "Shite, Adam. There are two sets of prints coming down from the woods." He met Adam's gaze with worry. "They are heavy and large. Two men, and it is recent."

"Two men? Bloody hell," Liam cursed behind him, making Adam turn. The man had both his hands up in his hair, raking it as if his scalp itched. He seemed to search the sand near his feet. His eyes were a bit wild, and his lips rolled inward.

"What is it?" Adam demanded.

He shook his head and dropped his arms. "Let us keep looking." Liam cupped his mouth. "Lark!"

Adam's chest tightened, and he ran forward into the mist, his gaze trained on the path before him, looking for footprints. Lark and Elspeth's names were being called every few seconds by his brothers and the Macleans, and yet there'd been no answer. Who the hell was on his isle?

He stopped at the waterline where the rocks were overturned and churned up by deep gouges. "Lark," he whispered, following them.

"Drag marks," Drostan yelled from a few steps ahead. "A rowboat came ashore and left here."

"Fok," Adam heard Liam curse behind him, but he

didn't look back. He jogged forward, his eyes trained on the evident struggle in the sand. His gaze slid along the shore and stopped.

Running forward, he scooped up the boot that lay on its side. "Lark," he whispered. *I am lucky. I lost a slipper just in time for you to find it.*

He stood, holding the leather boot. Even without the men's footprints, he knew she'd not left him. "Someone has taken her," he yelled, staring out at the water where the fog met it, willing her to appear. Pain twisted inside him, his heart pounding with the need to act.

"Both of them," Callum said.

Bloody hell. Lark! The mist seemed to close in around him when all he wanted was to swim through it to her. When she'd bared herself to him, pouring out the horrors of her past, it was all he could do not to pull his sword and rush off to slaughter her tormentor. The need to protect her had overwhelmed him then, and the thought of losing her now gripped his chest so hard he almost doubled over.

"Beck, Eagan, get the rowboat," he said, trying to keep his voice calm.

"We cannot even see in front of us," Eagan said. "We will be lost in the fog without a direction."

"I will go alone!" Adam yelled. "Straight out from here." He pointed the boot toward the gray swirling mist.

Liam growled as if tormented. "Damn it all! South, likely south." He threw his arm out to point farther down the beach.

Adam turned. "What the fok do ye know about this?" The look on his old friend's face was sheer torment. Adam charged across the beach, grabbing him by the throat. "Where is Lark?"

"I just needed ye to get off the isle," Liam said, his lips pinched. "But nay. Ye had to settle Wolf Isle right when I had nearly finished negotiating with the French."

"What the bloody hell are ye talking about?" Drostan yelled, all of his brothers and the small band of Macleans forming a circle around them.

"The French?" Callum asked. "What do they have to do with Lark?"

Adam shoved Liam, letting go of him so that he fell back onto the churned-up sand. "Lowder is French, isn't he?" Adam asked. "The accent was odd. I could not place it."

Liam pushed backward as Adam loomed over him. "Why would he take Lark?"

"I told him not to," Liam yelled back. "But when ye refused to leave the isle, he followed ye to the Beltane Festival, and he saw her." He shook his head. "Became obsessed with her. He was going to take her away from Roylin, but then she wed ye."

"Followed us?" Beck asked. "To kill us?"

Liam looked down at the sand as if shame weighed heavy on him. "I did not think he would be successful."

"Where would he take her?" Adam demanded.

Liam shook his head. "I swear, I thought I had convinced him to leave her be. He was looking for the gold crosses that the monks on Iona were said to hide on the isle to keep it from King Henry."

"The holes dug about the village," Callum said, spitting. "And I bet ye were going to take a portion."

Liam didn't deny it. "I was protecting Ulva and Mull from the English," he said.

"Ye were setting up an outpost for the French here?" Adam asked, remembering the ship that Cullen and Tor had seen.

"Ulva is apart from Mull and has been abandoned for a century. It is a perfect port for his men," Liam said quickly.

"Chief MacLean will flog the skin from your back," one of the Maclean men said.

This was taking too long. Adam grabbed Liam by the collar, lifting him to shake. "I do not give a fok about your deals with the French. Where is he taking Lark?"

Liam's eyes bulged in his face over Adam's brutal grasp. "The captain must be taking her to sail away on his ship."

."Captain?" Callum roared.

"What is his name?" Beck asked, but Adam already knew.

Liam swallowed, meeting Adam's gaze. "Jandeau. Captain Claude Jandeau."

• • •

The rough cording of the twisted rope cut into Lark's wrists where she sat on the deck of Jandeau's large ship, the fog still swirling around the sails as twilight ebbed to night. Muriel and two younger girls huddled next to her.

Iain MacLeod paced near the captain. "The rocks around this cursed isle make it dangerous to pull anchor with this fog blocking the stars," he told Jandeau.

The fraudulent priest looked much more at ease in sea clothes, a brimmed felt hat on his head and a long seaman's coat over his broad shoulders. How could they have possibly mistaken him for a humble servant of God? His face was hard, his eyes sharp, and scars ran around his neck as if he'd survived a hanging.

Jandeau's hooded gaze slid to Lark. "As soon as the fog thins, we depart."

Iain MacLeod stopped before him. "Two of my men are still out digging in that new spot outside the village. King Henry is stealing everything from the abbeys and monasteries. The old woman swore the Iona monks had buried their golden relics on Ulva."

"She lies," Jandeau said, the cruel twist of his mouth

making cold tingles run along Lark's skin. He turned to face Iain. "She has been lying all along."

"When your men took her girls after the storm, she swore on her mother's soul that the monk's golden crosses were buried farther to the west," Iain said.

Jandeau walked over to Lark, his gaze assessing them all. He caught a lock of Lark's hair between his fingers to rub. "There is no gold on Ulva, MacLeod, at least not the type of gold the French army needs to pay their troops. But fresh *mademoiselles* will fetch a high price when we head back to the southern islands. King Francis will need to find a different outpost."

Lark yanked her head away from his fingers, her teeth gritted. "Adam will hunt you down."

Jandeau's mouth relaxed into a wry smile, his hand still hovering in the air near her head. "In his little rowboat or maybe on his barge with one long pole?"

He grabbed her chin in a tight pinch, his other hand going behind her head as he leaned in to stare hard into her eyes. "I understand you are responsible for the death of one of my men when he tried to retrieve you in the woods."

Lark braced her tied hands before her, trying to relax even though Jandeau held her in a way where he could easily break her neck. He leaned in toward her ear, inhaling, his lips brushing the lobe. "You will pay dearly for that, Lark," he said, drawing out her name. "I can be a generous lover, but when one deserves punishment, your screams will mix with your moans."

Lark couldn't even breathe. Rape, her worst nightmare. She had managed to evade it with Roylin only to find herself faced with it again. *Not if I jump to my death.* The thought flickered into her mind, rooting there, giving her an escape that allowed her to inhale.

Jandeau leaned in, settling a gentle kiss on Lark's mouth,

as if they were lovers. Somehow the softness made it even more terrifying than a bruising kiss. She held still, waiting for it to pass. When he backed up, she stared him right in the eyes and spit. He chuckled softly and stood, smiling down at her while he adjusted the bulge in his pants.

Iain MacLeod's wide face was twisted in anger. "We had a deal, Jandeau."

The pirate turned on him, his teeth bared as if he were close to gutting Iain right on the deck. "The Macquaries are still alive, and Ulva Isle is not empty for my commander's troops to land. Your Isle of Skye is too populated, and your brother has said he will not let us set our camp there."

"But ye have the lass," Iain said.

"Whom I had to take myself."

"I helped," he murmured, glaring at Lark like this was her fault. He turned back to the French captain. "Liam Maclean said that Gometra Isle next to Ulva—"

"Is only one mile by two miles in size. *Non.*" Jandeau shook his head. "Too small for the French Navy." The angrier he became, the more his accent slid to French. "The agreement was Ulva Isle and any treasure we could recover in exchange for protection against the English for your Isle of Skye and perhaps Mull if that Maclean idiot actually helped us secure Ulva. But there has been no monks' treasure found and no foothold in Scotland for the French."

Iain grabbed his head as if to yank the hair from his scalp. "For a cursed clan, the foking Macquaries are hard to kill. Ye lost four of your own men to them when they followed them from the Beltane Festival at Glencoe." He dropped his hands. "Your crew could finish them off with your numbers alone."

Jandeau stared upward at the rigging where two of his men worked. "Tor Maclean made it clear that he and his warriors support the Macquaries and will come to their aid. I will not waste anymore months on this cursed isle." His eyes dropped to Lark. "I have what I want and will make a nice profit off the others."

He waved his hand toward the dark bulk of Ulva, still covered by fog. "Take a leap and swim back to shore with your life, little Scotsman." He shrugged.

The pirate that Adam had left alive in the clearing came close to Lark, squatting down before her. He yanked his sleeve to show the poorly healed wound on his arm. "We meet again," he said, his tongue snaking out to slide along his bottom lip. "Shall I tie her to a bed below, *Capitaine*?" the crewman said, his eyes raking down her. "For the men to take their turns." His lecherous gaze moved to the other girls. "All of them, although the whelping one may need to be standing."

"*Non*," Jandeau said, his gaze sliding along their line. "I want the two young ones pure for selling." He pointed at Muriel. "And I do not want *le bébé* to be harmed. It will fetch a good price on the market." He stared hard at Lark. "And *la mademoiselle* Lark is mine, at least for now."

"*Oui, Capitaine*," the crewman said, disappointment in the pinch of his frown.

Jandeau turned to walk back toward the wheel. The girls were weeping, and Muriel had her eyes squeezed shut. "Do not give up," Lark whispered.

"Ye have a way to get out of this?" Muriel asked, her voice wavering with subdued panic as her eyes blinked open. Hope warred with despair in her damp eyes.

Lark worked her hands behind her, her gaze remaining on the horrid pirates preparing lines about the deck. "I have a dagger," she said between her teeth, finally getting the blade to slide down from her sleeve, the edge leaving a trail of fire that probably swelled with blood. "Try to work it against my ropes." She turned so her back was to Muriel.

"Even so," Muriel said as she grasped it with the tips of her fingers, moving it in a saw-like jab, "how can we get past them and onto the shore? I cannot jump off the ship into the icy water with my bairn inside me."

"One step at a time," Lark said, her mind churning desperately.

The blade was sharp, and with Lark helping to push against it, her rope broke. Muriel passed it back, but Lark dropped it with the slipperiness of her blood on the handle. "Damn," she whispered, leaning back to find it with her freed hands.

"There is a patch of sky," one of the crew yelled, and Jandeau began to call orders as if they prepared to sail. "'Tis clearing, and it is not yet night."

Faster. Faster. How could they get away? Adam! Would he think that she left him? That her shame was too great to face him and his brothers again? If she jumped overboard, would he find her body upon the rocks and think she had killed herself?

She cut through Muriel's ropes and passed the blade back to her to free her friends. "Act as if your hands are still tied," Lark said to them, meeting their terrified gazes. They were barely breaching womanhood.

"Raise the anchor," Jandeau called out, shooting fear through Lark.

I can always leap overboard. But she could not kill herself and save the four souls next to her. She forced herself to breathe slowly to dispel the sparks flitting in her periphery. She scanned the edge of the ship. Where was the dinghy that Jandeau and his man had used to bring them to the ship? She spotted it tied along the far side where a crewmember worked on a tangled net.

"Kate and I can swim," one of the girls whispered.

"The sea is cold and dark," Muriel warned.

The girl named Kate turned wide eyes to her. "Nothing in the sea is worse than them." She cast eyes toward the pirates.

"I would rather be swallowed by a whale," the other girl said.

Lark looked behind at the coiled rope and then nodded toward the dark bulk to the right of the ship. "Ulva sits over there. Run for help at the castle." They nodded, and Lark slid the end of the rope to them. "Tell…" She swallowed past the pressure of tears. "Tell Adam Macquarie that I did not leave him." They nodded.

"Muriel?" Lark whispered.

"I cannot swim with this belly. I will drown, and so will my bairn."

Holy God. Lark couldn't leave her there alone. She glanced at the girls. "Climb over," she said, catching the knotted loop into an iron hook built into the deck.

"Come," Kate grabbed her friend, shifting slowly up the wall, their hands behind them as if they were still tied. Kate threw her leg over, caught her skirts in one hand, and disappeared.

"Go," Lark ordered, and the other girl scrambled over.

"*Stad!*" Iain MacLeod yelled from the other side of the deck.

"Run for the boat on the other side," Lark yelled at Muriel, snatching up the *sgian dubh*.

"There's a man there!"

"Just go!"

Blood had dried over Lark's hands from the slice down her arm, but seeing it didn't slow her down. Iain tripped on another coil, giving Lark time to aim as Muriel ran toward the side.

Instead of aiming at Iain, Lark threw her dagger at the man by the boat. The blade sliced into the side of his neck, and he doubled over, clutching it. Muriel reached him, struggling to lift the coiled rope, and Lark ran toward her.

"Ye whoring bastard," Iain yelled, grabbing Lark's hair from behind. She fell to her knees near the dead man, her fingers inching forward until she reached him. Desperate to hold onto the heavy body, drawing it closer, she grasped the dagger's handle, yanking it from his blood-soaked neck.

She rolled, slashing at Iain. "Damn you to Hell," she screamed, swiping a cut along his surprised face.

He reared back, holding his bleeding cheek. Two more crewmen ran forward, but Lark turned, helping Muriel throw the heavy rope over the side. "Get in the boat!" Lark yelled. "Lower yourself."

She turned back in time to meet the men, her arm slashing through the air with wild strokes. "Get back!" She needed to give Muriel time to save herself and her babe. "I curse you all!" But they did not back away. Either they were not superstitious, or they did not speak English.

Jandeau's French words boomed out over the chaos and the squeak of the rope in the wheel overhead.

Lark held the *sgian dubh* and used her other hand to grab onto the rope that was sliding steadily through the wheel. She lifted herself onto the rail with every bit of strength she could muster. Her skirts blew in the sea breeze, threatening to topple her over. But if she fell there, she could hit Muriel in the boat on the way down.

"You wish to die, *mademoiselle*?" Jandeau asked, striding toward her.

"'Tis better than being tied to a bed and raped over and over," she sneered. If she kept him talking and his men away from the rope, Muriel would get away. Then she could jump, although the impact might stun her unconscious. Dying, blissfully asleep in the cold ocean, was far better than anything else presenting itself.

Brandishing the *sgian dubh* at two more crew members

and Iain, she prepared to jump. The rope still creaked in the pulley as it slid through her fingers.

"Come now, *Mademoiselle*," Jandeau said, stalking closer, his men clearing a path for him. "Surely where there is life, there is hope, *non*." She held the *sgian dubh* in her bloody hand, and yet he continued forward. He didn't know that she'd practiced every evening behind her house when Roylin would saunter away to the tavern.

"You care nothing for my life," she said. Under her fingers, the rope stopped. Muriel had reached the water.

Jandeau shrugged. "I am a man with a love for a woman's body."

"You cannot be serious. You have no love for anything but your jack."

"And gold," one of the men said, making several of them laugh.

Jandeau's frown slid to them. It was the distraction Lark needed. As she drew her arm back, the man she'd hit in the clearing threw his own dagger. Searing pain shot from the point embedded in her arm to her shoulder, and she screamed, doubling forward.

Jump. She must jump or they would have her. *Adam. I am sorry.* As if in slow motion, Lark let go of the rope and turned, crumpling to meet her death in the dark, cold water below.

But instead of dark nothingness, Lark looked into…a face. "Adam," she whispered, not sure if the pain had robbed her of sense. His arms reached out to her, pulling her over the rail. Had God gifted her with an easy death? Falling into Adam's arms into the ocean? "I am sorry," she whispered, and black fog engulfed her.

Chapter Seventeen

"Dammit, nay," Adam swore as he saw the blade in Lark's arm. She whimpered, her eyes closed as she slumped into his chest over the side of the ship. "Watch the blade, but get her down," he called below him as he lowered her into Beck's arms.

Adam, Beck, and Callum held themselves, their boots caught in loops that they'd quickly fashioned along the sturdy rope that had been lowering the small boat.

"Keep them busy," Beck yelled up to him, and Adam drew his sword, slashing out at the line of ugly faces leaning over.

The crew spread out along the rail, their knives out to throw. "Ye bloody foking pirate," Adam yelled up at Jandeau as he directed a man with a musket.

"Some call me patriot," Jandeau called back, but Adam was distracted by the snarling, bloodied face of Iain MacLeod.

"Shoot him," Iain yelled. "Shoot them all, and ye can have the isle!"

Adam slashed his sword across the line of faces, catching

both Iain and Jandeau before they pulled back.

Bang! One of the pirates fired a musket, the ball splashing the water.

"Bloody hell," one of his brothers cursed.

Bang! A second gun fired. Water sprayed up.

"Get her out of here," Adam yelled as he continued to slash away with every bit of strength he had in his right arm. He glanced down when the rope slackened to see Lark in their rowboat, his brothers diving into the water as Drostan and Eagan rowed. Elspeth helped two other girls climb over the sides of the boat in which she had escaped.

With the rope caught by the end knot in the pulley above, Adam released his foothold, using one arm to pull himself over the lines while he kicked to propel himself sideways. He couldn't climb aboard and do much except die, but he could continue to slash away to give his brothers cover to get Lark farther out of range. And if he could kill Iain MacLeod, it might be worth dying.

Fingers curled around the rope lines, Adam swung the razor-sharp Macquarie sword at anything that came over the rail. Metal on metal as he hit musket barrels and daggers. French curses as he caught a face or hand.

"Ye will die tonight, Macquarie," Iain called.

"Come do it yourself, ye coward," Adam gritted out. As Iain's face disappeared, Adam slid between the side of the ship and the lines, climbing quickly so that he was under the rail several feet from where he'd been. He looked out to see the rowboat with Lark enveloped by the growing darkness and wisps of fog. *Let her be safe.*

The barrel of a musket came over the rail, pointed straight down where he had stood. Iain thought to shoot his head off. Catching his feet solidly into the netting, Adam used both hands to raise his sword and threw himself forward toward Iain MacLeod's unprotected neck. Adam's shoulder slammed against the hull, and his blade slid through, the musket leaving Iain's hands as his head toppled. Over the rail, it fell with Adam's sword, Adam following it to splash into the dark sea.

. . .

"Here," Beck said, handing Adam the sword they had taken from above the hearth in his bedchamber.

Wilyam Macquarie's sword had been sharpened and cleaned until it reflected the firelight in the great hall's hearth. "To replace the one that took Iain's head. It is yours anyway as the chief."

Without barely a glance, Adam slid it into his scabbard. "Dammit," he swore as he paced to the stairs that led above. "I need to see her."

"Let Ava and Meg tend her," Beck said. "Ye will get in their way."

"But what if she—"

"She will not die. The lass has survived too much to pass from a knife wound," Beck said.

Tor Maclean strode in through the doorway, Keir next to him. "Cullen MacDonald has two ships out of port, one headed west and one headed north to hunt Jandeau down, though it will be hard to catch sight in the dark."

"We need a ship," Beck said, his face firm. "I've been learning how to sail from Cullen for years, but we live on an isle; we need our own bloody ship."

"I want Jandeau dead," Adam said, ignoring his brother.

Behind Tor and Keir walked the priest from Mull, a pale, small man with a shaved head.

"Why did ye bring a priest?" Adam asked. Eagan had also been hit, but Ava had worked the shot out and he was sleeping. And Lark... "No one needs your last rites, Father."

The man stopped, his eyes going wide.

"He ain't here for that," Rabbie said. He pointed above. "Ye need to wed Lark."

Adam's mouth dropped open. Rabbie flapped his hands toward the door. "There is no Father Lowder, so ye two are not properly wed. Ye must marry Lark with a real priest."

Beck ran both hands down his face. "Rabbie. If ye don't shut your mouth, the priest will be giving *ye* last rites."

"The lass ain't dying," Rabbie said, his face stern. Beck exhaled in frustration, but Rabbie continued. "We would have Lark on our isle," he said. "So wed her right."

"Even if she is a bastard?" Adam asked, his voice low and lethal.

Rabbie sucked on his yellow teeth. "Well, if ye have gotten her with a bairn, then ye must." He shook his head. "And Beck read me what's written in the Bible."

Adam's fist clenched next to his legs. Beck put his hand on Adam's shoulder. "He's old and addled," he said close to his ear. But Adam looked to Drostan who stood frowning, same as Callum. Did his brothers think that Lark should not be on the isle, should not be his wife with her horrid past? Because he, bloody hell, did not care what they thought. She was his wife, and he... *I love her.* The realization stole his breath, a momentary quiver cutting through his gut before it firmed.

Aye. He loved her, every bit of her.

Tor Maclean cleared his throat. "The three lasses were returned to Grissell's cottage. We found the old woman tied to a chair with two white cats guarding her."

"Bloody devils," Keir said, wiping a hand over his claw-streaked face. "The lasses had to cut her loose."

Tor rubbed his chin. "Seems the crone has been taking in children and lasses that have no place to go."

"To bring more bastards to the isle?" Rabbie asked,

frown in place.

"I swear I am going to—" Adam started, but Beck braced his palm against his shoulder to stop him.

Keir ignored the old man. "'Tis a noble cause. Tor promised to bring her resources, and I will ask Grace to help Ava with the pregnant lass. And make sure the other ones are well."

"Liam says that the holes throughout Ormaig," Beck said, "were Jandeau's men looking for treasure from Iona Abbey. Every time they would come ashore over the last six months, Grissell would send them looking somewhere else. Liam was helping them by keeping people away. Iain was supposed to get rid of any Macquaries trying to land. Jandeau said he would alert the French government that they could land on Ulva to set up troops ready to battle England." Beck exhaled. "And they would protect Mull from Henry's reds."

"Without consulting me," Tor said, his words dark. "If the English caught wind that we were harboring French military, we would lose our rights and land."

"He seems remorseful that Lark was taken," Beck said.

"Where is he?" Adam asked, his teeth clenched.

"Gylin has a dungeon," Callum said, his arms crossed. "I thought it was a larder, but there are bars inside. He's down there until ye can talk to him without gutting him."

"He will starve before that happens," Adam said.

Tor glanced at Keir and then back to Adam. "We will see that his crimes against the Macquaries and Macleans are punished."

"What are ye thinking?" Beck asked. "Exile? Beheading? The man has been a friend."

"A friend who conspired to steal our isle and possibly see us dead," Drostan said, crossing his arms.

Adam looked to the steps, Liam already flown from his mind. "It's been too long. I am going up."

"The priest can go up with ye," Rabbie said.

Fury flared, scorching up inside Adam, and he drew the Macquarie sword that had just been given to him. Beck tried to stop him, but he held his hand up. Adam looked Beck in the eyes and raised the sword high. "Do what ye think to be right as the new chief of the Macquaries," he said. He turned the sword, point down. With both hands wrapped around the hilt, he thrust it downward. "My wife and I will not be staying in Gylin Castle."

"Brother?" Beck said, his voice hushed.

Adam released the hilt, leaving the blade quivering in the floorboards, and strode to the steps, taking them two at a time. He would always be a Macquarie, but making a home was far more important than being chief. Freedom, peace, safety, and...love. It was not possible here as the chief. Not with the frowns of his brothers and the foolish words from Rabbie.

Without hesitation, he opened the door to the chief's room. The hearth fire warmed the space, and candles glowed. Ava and Meg gasped, but he only cared for the figure in the bed.

"Adam?" Lark said, her voice soft.

In three strides, he was around the bed to her side and knelt to be level with her. She wore a clean smock. She looked pale but alert. He took her hands in his. "Lark, thank God, ye are well." He looked at Ava. "She is well?"

"Yes." Ava smiled. "Drostan kept the blade stationary and staunched the bleeding."

"And used more of his kilt to wrap Eagan's wound," Meg said.

Ava smiled down at Lark. "We have put some stitches inside and out and covered it with a salve. We will watch it, but I think she will be well. I will have Grace come check it, too."

"I thank ye." He met Lark's gaze even as he spoke to Ava. "Tor and Keir are down below for ye. I will stay the night with Lark." He climbed onto the big bed next to her as the ladies left the room. His arm curling around her.

"Muriel and the babe?"

"Back with Grissell, as well as her two other charges. They are all well, and Tor will be bringing supplies to help Grissell continue her good work to house lasses with no place to go."

"I would like to help her," Lark said.

"When ye have healed."

"Adam," she said, trying to sit up. He helped her lean against the pillows. "Iain MacLeod is helping Jandeau," she said.

"Not without his head," Adam said and stared in her startled eyes. "He is dead."

"And Jandeau?" she asked.

He slid his fingers between hers, locking their hands together. "Being hunted with Cullen MacDonald's two fast ships."

"And Liam was trying—"

"He is down in our dungeon, protected by bars until I calm down enough not to kill him. Tor Maclean will be more partial for deciding his fate."

"How did you know where to find us?" she asked.

"Liam said Jandeau liked to dock on the south side." He took her hand. "And ye lost a slipper for me to find."

Her lips turned up slightly. "You found the boot."

"Aye." Adam smoothed the curls around her hair. It seemed like a lifetime ago he'd found her slipper under the tree at the festival.

Her smile faded. "You did not think I ran away?"

He could lie and say it never entered his mind, but trust couldn't be built with lies. He leaned in to touch her forehead with his own. "Only for a moment, Lark, but it vanished quickly. I knew ye would return because ye said ye would."

"Trust," she whispered. "'Tis a start."

• • •

Rap. Rap.

"Thank the good Lord," Ava said, turning to Lark. "Even wounded I do not think I could keep you in here any longer." Lark had been awake for two hours with Ava helping her bathe and dress in a green gown, the one sleeve taken off to allow for her bandage.

Lark opened the door and frowned at Adam. "You sleep next to me all night and then leave me with a jailor whom I like too much to stab?"

Ava laughed behind her.

"To make ye rest," he answered, his eyes searching hers. "Your cheeks have color."

"I am thankful for such talented care," Lark said, smiling at Ava, who bowed her head in return.

Adam took Lark's hand. "I wish to show ye something."

He helped her down to the bottom of the stairs without a word and into the great hall, Ava following behind.

"Where are we going?" Lark asked.

"I can carry ye if ye tire," he said, leading her through the empty great hall.

"That is not an answer."

They dodged around a sword stuck, point down, into the floorboards. "Is that your sword?" she asked.

"'Tis Beck's," Adam said and continued to lead her outside.

They walked through the bailey where some of his brothers spoke with Tor, Ava walking over to them. "Thank you, to all of you," Lark called as Adam ignored them, leading her past the small group.

"Do not follow us," Adam said, his voice commanding. They walked along in silence, the breeze full of the promise of a mild day. Even the sun was cheerful.

"Was that a priest?" Lark asked as they continued slowly up the path to Ormaig. He was giving her all the time she needed, and she leaned on his arm.

"It seems we are not married since our wedding was conducted by a non-ordained pirate," he said, stopping at the top of the ridge.

"We are not married," she said, her smile fading. "And I am a bastard with a shameful past."

"The shame is not yours, Lark, not one bit of it."

Her heart squeezed, her lips parting. "Adam, I—"

He caught her cheek in his palm. "Before we talk, I want ye to see something."

He helped her down the slope into the village. They were not married, so no annulment was needed if they went their separate ways. The tightness in her stomach returned, but she kept one foot moving in front of the other.

The village was empty and quiet, but somehow not as frightening. Perhaps it was the sun or the mystery solved of the giggling and dolls. The windows merely looked like open windows instead of watchful eyes.

Adam stopped before the cottage they had shared during the rainstorm. A woven mat sat before the door, and the lintel above had been scrubbed clean to show the carved flowers. With a press of the latch, he swung the door inward and led the way inside. Lark stood in the middle of the pristine room. It had been swept from rafters to floor corners. A new bed was made up with bright quilts and plump pillows. The table had a plaid cloth on it. Wildflowers bent their heads in a clay crock in the middle, and two sets of dishes sat before sturdy chairs. A privacy screen was set up in one corner, but what caught Lark's full attention was the large soaking tub set on one side of the fire as if waiting to be filled and enjoyed.

She turned to Adam, her face open. "It is perfect in here."

"Like a home?"

A smile spread across her lips. "Exactly like a home."

"Our home," he said, taking her hand. "When we wed at Beltane—"

"We did not actually," she said.

He met her gaze. "Then wed me, Lark, knowing we can build a home together here or even off Ulva."

"You want to leave Gylin Castle?"

"Beck and my brothers can have it and the chiefdom. I want none of it if it means I cannot be with ye."

She glanced toward the door, recalling the faces in the bailey, the sword in the floor. "What have you done?" she asked.

He brought her chin back around. "If there is any question about your past, I care nothing about it. Our life is moving forward."

"But you gave up—"

"My mission has always been to find a home. What I did not know was that home is not a place." He ran his fingers lightly through her hair. She stared back into his deep, kind, gray eyes. "Home is a feeling, Lark. Home is…ye." His face moved in closer, and his thumb slid across her cheek. "I love ye, Lark."

Tears gathered in Lark's eyes as her smile grew. Joy twirled inside her stomach, making a happy sob break from her lips.

"Will ye wed with me, Lark, and live in the home of our making, wherever that may be?"

She slid her good hand up his muscled arm to steady herself as she leaned into him, her lips hovering before his. "Yes," she said with a small laugh as tears welled out of her eyes. He wiped her cheek, and she smiled. "Because I love you, too, Adam Macquarie." She felt his shoulder relax under her hand as his lips pressed against hers. A lightness grew within her, a type of happiness and peace she had never known before.

"Can ye two come up to the castle?" Beck's voice came from outside the cottage.

Lark pulled gently away from the kiss, and Adam exhaled long, their foreheads touching. He stepped back, his eyes still locked with hers. "I ordered no one to follow us," he called back.

"As I see it," Beck replied, "I am currently the chief of the Macquaries, and I command ye to come up to the castle."

Lark smiled and touched her fingers to her mouth to stop a laugh. "We will come up," she called out. The sound of Beck's retreat faded.

Lark tugged Adam's arm. "We should give the priest a reason for coming across from Mull."

She looked around the room, her gaze stopping on the tub. He leaned to her ear and whispered. "I would have let ye keep it even if ye said no to my proposal."

"Oh?"

"But ye said yes. 'Twas an oath."

"But I did not have that piece of information," she teased. They walked out into the sun and up the path toward Gylin, their hands clasped together. "I will have to let Anna and my sisters know where we settle."

"Aye," he said, his face hard. He pulled her into his side as they walked.

Sadness squeezed inside Lark, making her smile fade. "Adam...you cannot leave your brothers."

He stopped, pulling her around to meet his gaze. "My proposal was my oath, Lark. To ye. I love ye and cannot live without ye." He leaned in to brush a kiss across her lips and led her forward.

As they entered the bailey, all of Adam's brothers, Rabbie, the priest, Tor, Keir, Ava, and Meg, all stood waiting. Ava had a broad smile on her face. The brothers looked dumbstruck.

"Something has happened?" Adam asked, his hand going for his sword that was not there.

Beck shook his head, throwing his arm out toward the willow tree. "Take a look." Along the slender, waving whips of branches sat little green nubs. "There are buds on the tree."

"Holy God," Adam whispered next to her, moving forward. The knife was still lodged in the tree, but the tiny nubs gave the limbs a definite greenish hue.

Rabbie shook his head. "And ye have not yet wed before a real priest."

"Perhaps vows spoken aloud are not as powerful as those spoken with the heart," Ava said, making Rabbie look at her like she'd gone mad.

Lark walked up to stand with Adam before the Macquarie willow tree, intertwining her fingers with his.

Beck carried the Macquarie sword over. "The chiefdom is yours, brother, wherever ye live." With his words, his three other brothers thumped their chests and bowed their heads in agreement.

Lark looked out at the small gathering. It was their entire clan plus friends. It was a start, and it was perfect.

Adam pulled her into him. "Ye are my heart, my soul, and my home," he said, staring into her eyes. "I love ye, Lark."

Tears in her eyes made her blink. "And I love you, Adam. You are my heart, my soul, and my home."

He caught her face in his warm hands, his lips pressing against her own.

"But the priest has not married ye yet," Rabbie said.

"Those sounded like oaths to me," Beck said, laughter in

his voice.

"I now pronounce ye husband and wife," the priest intoned, and the small group cheered.

Lark wrapped her arms around Adam's neck, melting into the kiss. For she was truly free, protected, at peace, and most importantly—loved.

Acknowledgments

Thank you, readers, for continuing to encourage me to write my stories! Crafting exciting adventures and creating characters to love and hate is even more fun when I know there are readers like you enjoying them.

Thank you to my family for your patience. All five of us were COVID-bound together while I wrote this, and we all had to work together to find space and peace. May all of us, family and readers, stay safe!

Thank you to my fabulous agent, Kevan Lyon, for always being in my corner and to all the wonderful historical authors who are my friends and brilliant advisors. To my editor, the Alethea Spiridon at Entangled Publishing, thank you for coming back! I'm thrilled to be working with you again!

Also…

At the end of each of my books, I ask that you, my awesome readers, please remind yourselves of the whispered symptoms of ovarian cancer. I am now a nine-year survivor, one of the lucky ones. Please don't rely on luck. If you experience any of these symptoms consistently for three weeks or more, go see your GYN.

·Bloating
·Eating less and feeling full faster
·Abdominal pain
·Trouble with your bladder

Other symptoms may include: indigestion, back pain, pain with intercourse, constipation, fatigue, and menstrual irregularities.

About the Author

Heather McCollum is an award-winning historical romance writer. She is a member of Romance Writers of America and the Ruby Slippered Sisterhood of Golden Heart finalists. She has over twenty romance novels published and is a 2015 Readers' Crown Winner and Amazon Best Seller.

The ancient magic and lush beauty of Great Britain entrances Ms. McCollum's heart and imagination every time she visits. The country's history and landscape have been a backdrop for her writing ever since her first journey across the pond.

When she is not creating vibrant characters and magical adventures on the page, she is roaring her own battle cry in the war against ovarian cancer. Ms. McCollum slew the cancer beast and resides with her very own Highland hero, a rescued golden retriever, and three kids in the wilds of suburbia on the mid-Atlantic coast. For more information about Ms. McCollum, please visit www.HeatherMcCollum. com.

URL and Social Media links:
Facebook: facebook.com/HeatherMcCollumAuthor
Twitter: twitter.com/HMcCollumAuthor
Pinterest: pinterest.com/hmccollumauthor
Instagram: instagram.com/heathermccollumauthor

Also by Heather McCollum...

HIGHLAND HEART

CAPTURED HEART

TANGLED HEARTS

UNTAMED HEARTS

CRIMSON HEART

THE BEAST OF AROS CASTLE

THE ROGUE OF ISLAY ISLE

THE WOLF OF KISIMUL CASTLE

THE DEVIL OF DUNAKIN CASTLE

THE SCOTTISH ROGUE

THE SAVAGE HIGHLANDER

THE WICKED VISCOUNT

THE HIGHLAND OUTLAW

HIGHLAND CONQUEST

HIGHLAND WARRIOR

Get Scandalous with these historical reads...

HER ACCIDENTAL HIGHLANDER HUSBAND
a *Clan MacKinlay* novel by Allison B. Hanson

Marian, Duchess of Endsmere, is on the run from the English Crown after killing her abusive husband in self-defense. She has only one safe place to go—her sister's clan in Scotland. When one day a disheveled lass runs from the forest with an English bounty hunter right behind, War Chief Cameron MacKinlay feels compelled to protect her by claiming she is his wife. But he certainly didn't intend to marry her for real!

HIGHLAND RENEGADE
a *Children of the Mist* novel by Cynthia Breeding

Lady Emily has received title to MacGregor lands and she's determined to make a new start. She just has to win over the handsome Laird MacGregor whose family has lived there for centuries. Ian MacGregor aims to scare her away. But despite his best efforts to freeze her out, things between them heat up. Highlanders hate the Sassenach, so Ian must choose—his clan or the irresistible English aristocrat who's taken not only his lands, but also his heart.

A Scot to Wed
a *Scottish Hearts* novel by Callie Hutton

Katie has nowhere else to go but MacDuff Castle and she refuses to bow down to the arrogant and handsome Evan MacNeil. She's through with men controlling her. Now that Evan must spar with a beautiful lass for the rights to the lands, he will fight to the end. This battle is nothing like the ones his Highlander ancestors fought with crossbows and boiling oil. They never wanted to bed the enemy.

Highland Obligation
a *Highland Pride* novel by by Lori Ann Bailey

Due to a violent attack, Isobel MacLean will do anything to keep her family safe—except marry infuriating Grant MacDonald. She wants justice, not a damn husband. Unfortunately, we don't always get what we want… Grant MacDonald is determined to tame the hellion wife he was forced to wed. And he'll need to use every tool in his arsenal to distract his alluring wife from her quest for vengeance…before it's too late for them both.

Made in the USA
Coppell, TX
15 December 2022

89423525R00146